D1636382

THE SECRETS WITHIN ME

LIANA RAMIREZ

JUL 21 2020

Copyright © 2019 by Liana Ramirez

All rights reserved.

No part of this book may be reproduced in any form or by any electronic or mechanical means, including information storage and retrieval systems, without written permission from the author, except for the use of brief quotations in a book review.

Cover design by Jonas Jödicke, Cameron Macleod and Stephen Fritschle.

Dedicated to Gmom. You made this possible...

CONTENTS

"Pick a card! Any card!" I instructed a twelve-year-old, who bit his lip as he scanned the deck in my trembling hands. *Stop being nervous Mags! You got this. There is no reason to be scared.* He snatched one from the middle and showed it off to a small crowd that had formed around me in the middle of The Purple Dove—the magic shop where I was an employee and occasional performer.

"Remember what it is?" I asked him.

"Yes!" His eyes scanned the card over and over, making sure he knew it by heart.

I giggled. "Alright, place it back anywhere in the deck." He carefully placed it towards the end and took a step back, ready to watch. I shuffled the cards as the crowd buzzed with anticipation.

"The card's *on top* of the deck!"

I whipped around to glare at Danny, a tall, red-headed junior who was in all of my classes. Danny's goals in life?

Sabotaging my magic tricks and being an ass. Sadly, he was one of my coworkers/fellow magicians and his competitive impulse to always be the best drove him to try to make me look stupid in front of audiences. What's worse? I'm pretty sure he can sense my nerves at any given moment.

"No, it's not," I corrected him. I smiled, reassuring everyone that he had not ruined the show.

"You palmed the card and then did a false shuffle, resulting in the card being on top of the deck." He hovered over my shoulder with a smug grin.

"No, it's not." My cheeks burned. *Keep your cool, Magi. He always does this. Don't let him get under your skin.* I grinned at the little boy; he looked like he had just seen his parents kiss.

"Okay, then, *Margaret*, why not show the crowd the top card?" He shuffled his own deck of cards.

He did not just call me Margaret! That little prick knew I hate being called by my full name. He also purposely spelled it "Maggie" on my paychecks and loved to make fun of my unique spelling, "Magi."

"It's *Magi*." I glared at him.

"You're stalling, *Magi*." Danny smirked.

"And *you're* heckling," a deep voice called out.

Danny immediately straightened up, flustered, as our boss – and owner of The Purple Dove – Nesu, strolled over to us, his dark eyes narrowed on Danny.

"There is a shipment of false thumbs in the back,

Danny. Make yourself useful," Nesu directed in a kind, yet strict, tone that was not to be messed with. His Middle-Eastern accent made him sound ten times cooler when putting Danny in his place. Danny huffed and stormed off.

Nesu turned to me, smiling, as his famous dove and the store's namesake, Phoena, cooed on his shoulder. Nesu's signature magic trick was somehow turning Phoena's feathers purple. No one knew how he did it, and he would just grin when any of us begged him to tell us how.

He crossed his arms over the same outfit he wore every single day—black ripped jeans, a white button-up with rolled sleeves that showed off thick leather bracelets on both wrists, and a silver Egyptian necklace of the goddess Isis. Nesu spoke very highly of his home and loved sharing ancient legends with us about Isis and the Seven Scorpions, the Scarab Society, and the Book of the Dead. I loved hearing about those legends.

"Magi, would you please finish your trick?" He gestured back to the audience.

He is seriously the coolest. "Yes." I turned back to the crowd, feeling like I could take on the world. "And just for fun..." I picked up the card on top of the deck and showed it to the boy. "Is this your card?"

He shook his head, happy to report. "No!"

"That's what I thought, because it's actually been in your jacket pocket this entire time."

The boy hesitated, not believing that the card could possibly be there. He dug around in his pockets and, sure enough, whipped out a seven of hearts. His jaw dropped. He showed it to his friends and parents, and the crowd applauded and whistled, along with Nesu. My face grew hot. Seeing my mentor applaud and be impressed was the best feeling ever.

Nesu had taught me, and continued to teach me, everything I knew about magic, along with tons of wise life lessons. He was also a really close friend to my family, so he was practically an uncle to me. Uncle or mentor, it was awesome to see him applaud for me.

"Don't forget to grab your snake wands, wilting flowers, or three mummies-one coffin tricks on your way out!," Nesu called out over the din. "And remember, not everything is what it seems..." He snapped his finger and a cloud of purple dust consumed Phoena, turning her feathers lavender before everyone's eyes. She fluttered down to his finger, and Nesu showed her off with the biggest smile. The crowd roared with applause: *woos*, *ahhs*, and wild eyes. Meanwhile, I could only stand there, trying yet again to figure out how he'd pulled it off.

"Come back anytime!" Nesu waved to the crowd as they dispersed back into the streets of downtown Seattle or throughout the store. He turned to me, placing Phoena back on his shoulder.

"How do you do that?" I begged, once again.

He laughed. "My dear, some secrets aren't meant for sharing." He mimed zipping his lips together. I rolled my eyes.

"Your slights are getting better." Nesu crossed his arms.

"Really?" I honestly thought I could have done better, especially if Danny hadn't chimed in. I began to spring my cards, making my cards fly from one hand to the other as Nesu talked to me.

"You are becoming a fine illusionist indeed. It is very enjoyable to watch you."

"Thank you! I enjoy it, too. The look on their faces when you finish a trick... it's just... priceless!" My smiled quickly faded as I looked down at my hands. They were still shaking.

"What's wrong?" Nesu asked softly.

"I don't want to be scared." I lifted my hands to show him. "How do I get over this?" I rolled my wrists, almost like I could work the nerves out of them.

"Trust in your abilities. You've got more than what it takes. Just don't let the fear win, okay?" He squeezed my shoulder.

"Okay." I nodded.

"Also, keep practicing your forces and your flourishes. They're looking great, but I know you can do better before the summer showcase," Nesu advised.

"I don't know; it looked pretty great to me!" A familiar voice boomed.

My cards sprung out of my hands and went everywhere.

I whirled around to see a muscular man leaning against the wall at the front of the store. His wavy, dark-brown hair and facial hair showed some age, but his grey eyes were the sweetest you've ever looked into.

"DAD!"

I dashed over and leapt into my father's arms. He caught me and twirled me around the magic shop, laughing.

"What are you doing here?" I asked, breathless, when he set me down. "I thought you were flying in next week!"

"Well, I got in early, so I figured I stop by!" He gave me an innocent smile. "I told your mom not to tell you because I wanted to surprise you. I have to say, I think my little plan worked."

"Really? I don't think so!" I deadpanned. "But seriously, this is the best surprise ever!"

Seeing my dad in person nearly brought tears to my eyes. As an Egyptologist, he works months at a time in Egypt. So hugging him in person was better than Christmas.

"You're in town! You can watch me perform at the showcase in a few weeks!" I exclaimed.

"What day is it?" My father asked.

"The twenty-fourth," Nesu smiled.

My dad scratched his head. "I'm actually awarding a grant that night."

"At seven?" I prayed it wasn't at seven.

"Seven exactly..." He sighed.

"Oh..." I stared down my shoelaces.

"But at least I got to see your little show here tonight.

And it was amazing!" He gave me a high five. I giggled to myself.

"Hey, why don't you two go and catch up for a little bit?" Nesu suggested.

"Really?" Excitement filled my chest.

"Yes, but please be back in thirty minutes so you can close up."

My heart sank a little, but I shook it off. "Thanks, Nesu." I began to walk out with my dad.

"Magi?"

I spun back around on my toes.

Nesu gestured. "Your cards."

"Oh right, sorry!" As quickly as I could, I carefully picked up my deck. I wouldn't want to leave these cards on the ground. They had been a gift from my dad when I first started magic and had lasted a surprisingly long time. Usually, cards only last a month due to the constant bending and shuffling, but these have lasted almost two whole years. I only pulled out my all purple-and-gold deck on special occasions—and that cute kid had been worth it to me.

I placed my deck in its case, tucking it into my jeans pocket, and trotted over to my dad. He bear-hugged me and we waved bye to Nesu as we exited into the busy Pike Place Market.

"Okay, tell me about your trip." I honestly didn't care about hearing about the excavations, but I loved hearing my father tell stories.

"Oh, yes!" he replied, "But not here."

"What do you mean?"

"You know what I mean."

"Wait ..." I studied my dad's lively grin. "The Wheel?" I asked, hopeful.

"The Wheel!"

"Really? We are going?" I stopped in my tracks.

"Well, it is our sacred tradition."

I practically skipped down the street.

A FEW BLOCKS away was the popular tourist attraction: the Seattle Great Wheel. It's a one hundred and seventy-five foot Ferris wheel at the end of Pier 57, where you can see magnificent views of Seattle. Sounds great and all, but I can't stand Ferris wheels—slowly moving upward and overlooking deep waters is not something I call fun. But my dad and I did not go to Pier 57 for the Ferris wheel. We went because it was our spot.

All the way at the edge of the pier and to the right, we stood together, looking out over the water. This place had first become our spot when a friend of mine invited me to the pier and then ditched me to hang out with her crush when I was twelve. I had been gutted because I still thought boys were gross then and didn't understand the concept of dating (I honestly still don't). My dad had come to my rescue and we stood at the end of the pier talking about how I felt about being ditched. He taught me, in that moment, how to open up and talk about my feelings, something that was still very uncomfortable for me. It made me feel like a cat being given a bath, but I would talk about anything when my dad was in town. It was such a luxury to see him in person, and being with him at our spot was one of my favorite things in the world. I don't think he even knew how much those moments here meant to me.

"So, first day of summer vacation... having fun?" My dad was glowing. Seagulls flew over our heads, chatting up a storm.

"I think we both know the answer to that question," I replied.

"Yes?"

"Heck yes! I just finished the hardest year of high school with straight A's in all AP classes, I'm working at my favorite place in the world with my mentor, and soon, I will have a lot of money saved up for college."

"I can't believe you're going to be a senior." My dad was getting all grossly misty-eyed.

"Stop it!"

"I'm sorry!" He laughed. "You know I'm going to miss you when you go off to college."

"Harvard," I corrected.

"Harvard, sorry."

My parents knew very well that it was my dream to go to Harvard – to follow in my mom's footsteps and study law. My mom, Mariah Ann Davis, ran her very own law firm here in Seattle, and I dreamed of being the head of all local cases one day—or starting my own local firm. I stress *local* because I'm not a fan of traveling and being away from the people I love, and my mom – being an international criminal prosecuting attorney – was always flying over one ocean or another. I barely got to see her. She was either in some foreign country, or going over documents at her office. It was pretty much the same with my dad, but much worse. If he wasn't in Egypt for months at a time, he was at a random coffee shop working on his best-selling book series *Digging in Sand*.

I didn't care that my parents' jobs paid very well, or that they were both amazing at what they did—I hated that their jobs took them away from me.

But their success does drive me to become successful. It was a personal mission of mine to get into a better school than both of my parents— and an ambitious goal, considering they both went to Ivy League schools.

"Yeah, I'm going to miss you, too," I said. Part of me wanted to say, *It's okay, I'm used to it*, but that wouldn't have served any productive purpose. I changed the subject.

"So, why were you there this time?" I asked, feigning interest.

"Well, my team is searching for more remains of the homes that housed the people who worked on the pyramids themselves." My dad was all smiles.

"Wow ... so fascinating," I deadpanned, messing with him.

My father looked down at the water below the pier, and smiled. "It can be." He truly did have a passion for ancient Egypt. He knew everything about the subject. From all the theories of how they built the pyramids, to the pharaohs, to the Egyptian gods—he knew it all.

"Oh! I got you something while I was there." His eyes sparkled. He rummaged around in his jacket.

"Oh." *Here we go.* My dad's gifts from Egypt were kind of... lame. Of course, the gifts were thoughtful, and I appreciated that, but they were usually scrolls of papyrus teaching you how to read hieroglyphs, sand-filled leather camels that were basically stuffed animals, or miniature pyramid souvenirs that I now use as bookends on my shelves. All the type of stuff I used to love when I was little —but are just not me, anymore. Not that he would really know that, having not spent much time with me. Still, I didn't have the heart to tell him; he always got so excited about these gifts.

My dad pulled out a brown leather jewelry box from inside his jacket. "Your majesty." He grinned and placed the box in my hands. "Your majesty" was one of my father's nicknames for me, but he only said it in special moments.

A jewelry box... that's new! The leather box itself was smooth, and it weighed almost nothing. I bit my lip with anticipation as I gently opened it.

Inside was a golden Egyptian necklace. The pendant

was a long oval shape resting on a bar with four Egyptian hieroglyphs engraved down the middle. My cheeks ached from the giant smile on my face. The necklace was so beautiful and unique. I never wore jewelry, but this necklace made me want to start.

"I had that made for you in Giza," my father said.

"Made?" I ran a finger lightly over the engravings.

"Yes. You see the Egyptian symbols on it?" My father pointed to the necklace. "Well, those symbols are what's called a cartouche."

"I know." Simple enough words, though I knew my tone said what I really meant: *duh.*

"And the cartouche spells out the word 'Magi.'"

"Are you serious?" I gasped.

He smiled, proud. "You really like it?"

I stared at my cartouche necklace, trying to translate the Egyptian symbols that spelled out my name. "Thank you so much Dad! I love it." I hugged him tight.

"You are welcome." He laughed and gently kissed my forehead. "Would you like to put it on?" My father reached to clasp it around my neck.

"Yes, please!" I turned around and moved my hair out of the way.

He swung the necklace around my neck and clasped it. As soon as the gold touched my chest, a rush of adrenaline surged through my body. I stumbled, feeling a little faintish. *Woah, that was weird.*

"You okay, Mags?" Dad asked.

"Just felt light headed for a second." I waved a hand. "Probably just the excitement from such an awesome gift. Thanks again, Dad."

I wrapped my arms around him again. We stood there holding each other in silence for a while, listening to the waves crash against the pier and watching the colorful lights from the Ferris wheel reflect off the water.

"I *really* missed you, Dad," I managed as a lump formed in my throat.

He looked down at me and grinned. "I really missed you, too, Mags." He squeezed me tighter.

"As much as I really don't want this moment to end, I should probably get back to work." I shrugged reluctantly.

"Probably a good idea. We can hang out some more when you get home later tonight."

"Okay."

"Let me walk you back." My dad held out his arm for me to take hold. I chuckled and followed his lead back to the magic shop. *I am so glad he is home.*

Ugh, I hate closing, I thought as I locked the door to the Purple Dove. I sighed as I turned to face the dimly-lit parking garage. It was just down the street, but it felt miles away. I took a deep breath, readjusted my backpack straps as I began speed-walking through the empty Pike Place Market. The only people who hung around here this late were the kind who were up to no good – so I looked over my shoulder every couple of seconds. I gripped my backpack as I hopped down the several flights of stairs that led to the "employee parking" area. I reached level four and – paranoid me – checked over my shoulder again. I didn't see the person in front of me until I was crashing into them.

"Oh my gosh, I'm so sorry." I apologized breathily.

A guy in an oversized hoodie turned around, looked me up and down, and smiled through his yellow teeth.

"Hey there, pretty lady. Where are you going in such a hurry?" His voice was raspier than a garbage disposal.

"Uh, home." I forced a grin and began to walk away. He stepped in front of me with a snicker.

"Ah – that's nice, but I'm not sure if I can let this whole 'bumping' thing go that easily. It was pretty rude." He pointed his cigarette at me.

"What?" I shook my head, taken aback. A sick feeling pooled in my gut. *Something is wrong.*

Quick as lightning, he reached his hand out to grab me.

It was like time slowed down. Somehow, before he could touch me – I swung upwards and punched him in the nose. He staggered backwards, cursing in pain. Then, time seemed to speed back up, blurring together as I fell into the wall behind me and slid to my knees. My head pulsed, and I felt light headed. *This is not the time to pass out!* I forced myself to snap out of it as I saw blood spilling all over the ground from the man's nose.

"You broke my nose!" he yelled over and over. *How did I break his nose? I'm not that strong.*

I sprinted, trying to get to my car as fast as I could. I yanked open my backpack, searching frantically for my keys.

The man groaned loudly as he climbed to his feet. Fear spiraled through my bones as he charged towards me. My fingers found the cold metal of my keys, and I unlocked my door with trembling hands before throwing myself into the driver seat. "Come on, come on, come on!" As I backed out, he hit the side of my car with his fists. I screamed and drove off as fast as I could, chancing a glance at my rearview mirror as I careened through the empty parking garage. He threw his beanie at the car, cursing as more blood spilled from his nose. I pulled onto the street to a chorus of honking horns – I hadn't even noticed that I ran a red light.

That's it. No more night shifts. I finally started to catch my breath, but my pounding head made it difficult.

Seriously, how did I break his nose?

I EASED MY BABY—A black 1965 Mustang that I had bought with the money I'd been saving ever since I was nine—into my driveway. I was surprised I hadn't gotten in a wreck on the way home, between my head getting worse and the pouring rain.

I used my off-white and dark green letterman jacket to shield my dark brown curly hair from becoming a frizz ball as I stepped up onto my porch. I fumbled with my keys, trying to find the right one before I looked up and jumped.

Sitting perfectly still, on the opposite end of the porch, was a small black cat with a scar across its eye. Its bright yellow eyes stared into mine.

Every single morning, for as long as I could remember, the cat sat outside the second-floor balcony doors of my bedroom and stared at me. The weirdest part was that it never moved a muscle until I yelled at it to go away. I don't know how it got up there in the first place. I didn't even know who it belonged to. I have always wondered where it got that scar, though.

Strangest cat on the planet, I thought as I stared into its creepy little face. I rolled my eyes and entered my house.

I locked the door behind me and placed my thumb on a wall tablet that scanned my fingerprint. My name instantly popped up with a green check mark.

"House armed," a computerized female voice announced. My father had always insisted on having the best security system money could buy. "You can never be too careful," he always said. I always thought it was overkill, but tonight, I was grateful for it. No one could ever touch me or hurt me in our house – I was sure of that.

I dropped my backpack off at the door and headed into the living room to find my dad sitting on his recliner, reading a book and drinking tea—a habit we'd both adopted from my very British mother.

"Hey Mags." My dad's face lit up. He had obviously been waiting to hang out with me. "How was work?"

"It was great." No way was I going to mention the creepy parking lot guy. My dad would flip out. "Overprotective" is a synonym with "Dad" to me. He would literally make me stay home for a week from school if a little crime in the news happened nearby. I wasn't about to be on house arrest again. "Where's mom?" I had noticed her Mercedes wasn't in the driveway.

"She just texted to say she'll be home in an hour or two. She's wrapping up a case."

"Awesome," I said under my breath. *Oh man, I wish she was coming home sooner.* Finally, my family was all in one place, and I just wanted to hang out with them.

"Anyway, so what would you like to do? Board games, food, movies?" my father asked.

"Dad," I said reluctantly, "would you mind hanging in the morning? My head is killing me."

"You all right?" He got up and placed his hand on my forehead. "Hmmm, you do feel a bit warm." He gave me a sympathetic look. "Yeah, yeah. How about you go to bed? In the morning we can all go get coffee or something with Mom, too, and really catch up. Sound good?"

"Yeah," I agreed. "Goodnight." I hugged him.

"Goodnight." My father kissed the top of my head, and then returned to his recliner and book.

Walking up the stairs, my entire body felt like it was made of cement. I death-gripped the railing with each step and, somehow, made it to my bedroom.

Lightning illuminated my balcony and I gasped, startled. On the balcony sat the little black cat, fixing its unrelenting stare at me. The feline and the storm spooked me so badly that my knees buckled, and I collapsed onto my rug. *Weird cat...* was the last thought I had before I passed out.

BING... Bing... Bing....

I woke up shivering. I was in the corner of a square room built out of black stone. A massive, round stone table stood proudly in the middle of the room. Everything was fuzzy, but I made out a floating sphere – a glowing hologram of Earth – hovering over the table. Another sphere was hovering beside it, but I didn't recognize the landmarks. Goosebumps rose on my arms. *Where am I?*

I jumped at the sound of a faint beeping noise that rang through the room. A little blip on the Earth's sphere flashed gold. I climbed up off the dirty floor and crept closer to get a better look. *Huh... it's flashing near Seattle.*

Just then, a bald man wearing dark eyeliner and puffy pants stuffed into brown leather boots sprinted into the room. He wore a thick golden belt engraved with hieroglyphics, and a leather chest protector strapped around his buff pecks. He reminded me of an ancient Egyptian. He examined the flashing dot, and his breathing intensified. His demeanor scared me, so I stayed hidden in the shadows.

"That can't be..." he said, shaking his head. He pulled out a bronze dagger from his belt as a look of curiosity and determination settled over his face. He darted for the back wall, which turned out not to be a wall at all – but a cloud of mist. He walked through the mist without hesitation, as if he had stepped through a portal. A loud boom echoed throughout the room, causing me to cover my ears in pain.

THUNDER SHOOK me back to consciousness. I rubbed my head as I sat up from the only nap I had ever taken on my rug. The clock on my nightstand read 2:43 AM. I had passed out for about two hours. Still feeling dizzy, I moved towards my bed. As I stood up, my breath caught in my throat.

I fixed my eyes to my glass balcony doors. The full moon was breaking through the storm clouds, illuminating a figure standing on my balcony.

My breathing intensified. I forced myself to see if my mind was just playing tricks on me. "Who's there?"

Slowly, I reached for the curtains then yanked them open. No one was there.

I opened the doors to my balcony and walked out into the pouring rain. My balcony was L-shaped, so I checked the longer side first – the one that looked over part of our yard and the woods behind our house. There was nothing. I tiptoed back around and gasped.

A man stood on my balcony—the man from my dream.

The bald man gawked at me, clutching the same bronze dagger in his hand. He fixed his eyes on my necklace as if he were reading the hieroglyphs.

"You're alive?" the man said as if I were a ghost.

Huh?

Then, something snapped inside him, and he lunged at me, grabbing me by the arms. As I tried to scream for my parents, he covered my mouth with a piece of black cloth. The cloth stuck to my face like duct tape and when I tried to pull it off, it felt like my whole face would rip off with it. I continued trying to scream, but I could not produce any noise – it was like I had lost the ability to produce sound. *What is happening to me?!*

I struggled to get free, but the man was so incredibly strong. He brought me to the edge of the balcony that hovered over my pool below, and tossed me over the railing.

Air caught in my throat as I fell with the pouring rain right into the pool, splashing into the deep end. I frantically swam in the freezing water, my super skinny jeans restricting my movement. The cloth over my mouth made it difficult breathe as I crawled out of the pool.

The man leapt off my balcony and landed swiftly onto the grass in front of the water. *No one can land on their feet like that. That was a twenty-foot drop, at least!*

The man marched towards me, his dagger ready. Next to me was a small pool skimmer. I snatched it, scrambling to stand up in my soggy converse, and held it out front of me. The man lunged forward. I swatted at the blade as I inched along the edge of the pool. His blade clinked against the cheap metal as he sliced right through the sleeve on my shirt. I hissed, bending over my arm. The cut stung, and it was only getting worse with the rain sloshing into the seeping blood.

The man stopped in his tracks, laughing. "You don't know how to *fight*?"

A look of fascination washed over his face as he kicked me in the stomach, causing me to stumble back onto first steps of the pool and lose my grip of the pool skimmer. He repositioned his blade to stab.

"You don't know who you are, do you?" he asked, amused.

I watched his every move, more confused than ever.

"They kept you hidden all these years ..."

What the heck is he saying? I struggled against the strip covering my mouth.

"All that work for nothing...I still have to kill you."

WHAT?!

I was about to make a break for it when an unnerving, animalistic growl came from behind me. I slowly turned my head to see the little black cat arching its back, growling threateningly at the man. The man looked as though he was staring death in the face when he saw the cat, but continued to advance me.

The cat leapt past me, landing on the man's bald head. It began to viciously claw it, ripping the skin off, causing the man to fall into the pool. I climbed out of the pool, shaking. The man desperately yanked the cat off of him and threw it out of the pool with so much force that the cat smashed through my parents' bedroom window.

The broken window set off the alarm: sirens blared, and red lights flashed in every room of the house. The feline meowed loudly and jumped out of the broken window, ready to attack again as the man trudged out of the water, still clinging to his dagger.

BANG! BANG! BANG!

Blood erupted from the man's shoulder. Blood spewed into the pool as he yelled in pain. I snapped my head to see my mom and dad running out of the back doors in their pajamas, both firing handguns. I sprinted and hid behind them. My mom saw the cloth over my mouth and tore it off. My cheeks stung like crazy.

"You guys have guns?" I yelled in shock.

"Stay down!" my dad replied, still firing. I couldn't believe they had guns! There were the most chill people I had ever met, so this was completely unexpected. We all watched the man take off running into the woods behind our house.

"Magi!" My mom lowered her gun and knelt down beside me with worry in her eyes. "Are you all right?" Her voice was shaky, but the sound of it was still like a warm blanket wrapping around my shoulders.

"Yeah, I'm fine," I said automatically. Was I? I wasn't sure. Everything had happened so fast I didn't have any time to process.

"Magi!" My dad gripped one hand on my shoulder while keeping his gun pointed at the ground with the other. His body was shaking worse than mine. "God, you're soaked. Get her inside. I'm gonna go after him." He stood up suddenly.

"WHAT?" I exclaimed.

"It's okay. I'll be fine." He winked at me, showing me his gun, and then ran off.

"Dad!" I screamed. My tears mingled with the rain on my face.

"It's alright, darlin'. He'll be alright. Let's go inside." I started balling as my mom escorted me inside, her gun in front of both of us.

As we walked inside, we heard police sirens getting closer and closer.

CHAPTER 2

I could have sworn there was a police officer in every room of my house. All of them gave me looks of either reassurance or "don't talk at me, I'm busy trying to catch the guy who did this to you". I didn't know why there were so many police. Trust me, I was happy they were there; it just seemed like an excessive amount.

My mom and I walked out of my parents' bedroom after she helped me change into sweatpants and a warm sweater. My long hair soaked the back of my neck, sending shivers through me.

A muscular police officer with blonde hair approached me. The look in his dark brown eyes was sharp enough to chop a tree down, but every few seconds he rubbed them as if he had allergies.

"Magi Davis, correct?" He asked me with a small, encouraging smile.

"Yes," I answered, feeling uneasy.

"My name is Lieutenant Doyle. Are you okay to answer some questions for me?"

I shrugged. "I guess."

"Would you mind taking me to where you first saw your attacker? Your parents said that it was in your room?"

I looked over to my parents. My mom was conversing with some officers and my dad was talking on the phone. "Yeah, it was. And sure, it's upstairs."

I turned on my heels and walked upstairs, and Lieutenant Doyle marched up behind me. I opened the door to my room. The one place that had felt the safest in the world to me had betrayed me like a cheating boyfriend

The floors were drenched with rainwater, since my balcony doors had been left open. I hurried over to close them, panic rising in my chest. What if the intruder came back?

"Don't!" Lieutenant Doyle ordered. "You can NOT touch the crime scene." He glared at me intensely, and then rubbed his eyes again.

"But my floors...," I tried to explain.

"I'm sure your parents will replace them if they are ruined... you seem to get everything else you want." He gestured to my computer on my desk and my closet.

I looked away from him as I backed away from my balcony doors, almost slipping in the water puddling my floor before slumping down on my bed. Jerk.

"Okay let's start with some simple things." The officer

pulled out a notepad and pen. "State your full name, please."

I rolled my eyes to myself. "Margaret Ann Davis."

"How old are you?"

"Seventeen."

"Birth date?"

"Halloween"

"October 31st?" He clenched his jaw.

"Yeah..."

"Hmmm, my least favorite day of the year...," he said under his breath, rubbing his eyes.

"That's a nice necklace you got there. Is it gold?"

I looked down at my cartouche. "Oh, I think so. It was a gift from my dad."

"Your dad?"

I nodded.

"Not your mother?"

"Um no. She doesn't work in Egypt, so, no..."

"I see..." He paused.

I tugged the sleeves of my sweater, covering my hands with the fabric.

"So, you saw the man from outside..." He crossed his arms.

"Yes."

There was an awkward silence between us. "Keep going." Lieutenant Doyle tilted his head impatiently.

"Um, well I saw him outside and went out there to see

if I was imagining things, and I wasn't. That's when he grabbed me and threw me into the pool."

"Did he have a weapon?"

"A dagger."

"Did he say anything to you? Why he would want to kill you?"

"He said, 'you're alive?' Then he said he had to kill me."

"Hmm, that's strange... anything else?"

"Umm, he was extremely fascinated by the fact that I couldn't defend myself."

"You can't?" There was a hint of amused judgment in his voice.

"No," I said, my cheeks burning. Was this how the police in this town spoke to people who had just been attacked? *Why is he being like this?* "I guess I just...never learned that kind of stuff."

"Well, maybe you should have." Lieutenant Doyle cleared his throat "It sounds to me like we are dealing with a deranged psychopath."

"Woah..." I raised my voice. "Can you please be a little bit more sensitive? I almost died," I snapped.

"Yeah, you did almost die, kid. But you *didn't*," Doyle hissed at me as he stomped out of my room.

I sat on my bed, stewing in confused anger. For the life of me, I could not understand why he was treating me like a criminal. What an ass. After a moment, I shot up off my bed and followed him down the stairs.

He walked into my living room and approached my parents. "Mr. and Mrs. Davis, I am very sorry for how rough your night has been, but I have a very bad feeling that whoever tried to kill your daughter will be back to finish his mission. Someone that psychotic doesn't just give up."

My parents both squirmed uncomfortably.

"We will keep a police detail around your house tonight, but I suggest making arrangements to take her as far away from here possible. The safest place you know."

My parents nodded in agreement with the officer.

"I'm sure you will do the right thing." Lieutenant Doyle forced a grin and then marched out of my house, following the other officers.

"Would you like any breakfast, darling?" my mom asked sweetly as I walked into the kitchen. We had finally all gone to bed around 5 A.M. and slept in our guest bedroom, since I didn't want to be alone and all the windows were shattered in my parents' room. The only thing that was positive was that it actually wasn't raining, for once. The sun was shining through the kitchen window, blocked only by the little black cat – who was perched in its usual staring position on the window sill. I didn't roll my eyes at it for once. *That weirdo of a cat saved my life...*

"No, I'm okay," I finally responded to my mom.

"Chocolate milk?"

"No, thanks."

"It really is a bad day if you turn down chocolate milk." My dad frowned as he stood by the coffeemaker.

"Well, if you change your mind, I've made blueberry pancakes and bacon." My mom showed off her pan of fluffy pancakes, dancing around in her pink and white polka-dotted robe with matching slippers. I felt a grin crack on my face. My dad wrapped his arms around me tightly and kissed my head.

"How are you doing? Would you like to talk about it?" My dad asked slowly, testing the waters.

I immediately shook my head, "No." I wanted that event to be zapped out of my memories.

"That's totally fine. Just know we are here if you want to talk." He squeezed me tighter.

"Oh!" My mom burst out laughing, clearly changing the subject. "I had the weirdest dream last night."

"Oh no," I sighed.

"Here we go." My dad sipped his coffee.

My mom was notorious for thinking her dreams were absolutely crazy when they were, in fact, very average. But her laughing about them was the cutest thing to witness. She almost made herself pee from laughing.

"Oh hush! This one's funny!" She dropped her jaw defensively. "I think it was all that coffee I drank trying to stay up to talk to those officers. I had a lot of caffeine, Anyway, it was about—"

Her phone buzzed obnoxiously on the kitchen countertop.

"Oh, hold on, hold on!" Mom put the pan of pancakes down, sighing.

"Mariah Davis speaking... Hmmm... Hmmm..." She put her phone to the side and spoke to my dad and I. "This is work; it might take a bit. Why don't you two get started on breakfast." She hurried off into the other room.

My dad nudged me in the shoulder. "Hey, while we wait for her, I know something that might cheer you up. Come here." He motioned for me to follow him into the living room.

On the floor were dozens of board games and cards scattered across the fuzzy carpet. A smile cracked on my face. Playing board games with my dad was one of my favorite things to do, and he knew it.

"Come on. Let's get our mind off things." He patted me on the back.

I shrugged, sitting down as I began to shuffle the cards.

After a few rounds, my mood improved dramatically. I smirked at my dad, knowing I was about to win our latest game.

"I think it's Mrs. Peacock, with the knife, in the kitchen," I guessed confidently.

My father eyeballed me warily. "There is no way you got that right!"

"I guess we will see!"

"You seem very confident."

"Very confident."

"All right, let's make this interesting, Ms. Confident. If you're right, I'll give you twenty bucks. If you are wrong, you have to take a big ol' gulp of mustard."

"Eww!" I yelled. "You are evil!" My dad was well aware that my least favorite taste in the entire world was mustard.

"Do we have a bet?" He smiled deviously.

"Bet!"

We shook hands. The pressure was now on. He unfolded the envelope from the middle of the board game that held all the clues.

"You're right," my dad said in awe.

"No mustard!" I raised my arms victoriously.

"How do you do that? That was your first guess and you got it right the first time."

"Well, you have to know what you're looking at. It's kind of like a magic trick – you have to get past the trick to figure out where the truth lies. Once you do that, you can solve the mystery."

"Is that right?" my father said. "All right, one more game." He pulled out his phone and opened his stopwatch app.

"Dad, no." I knew exactly what he was doing. About four times a week, my dad presented me with riddles to solve – either in person or over the phone. I am scary good at them, and they never seemed to fool me. I think, to my dad, trying to stump me was more entertaining than television.

"Come on... twenty more dollars?"

"Done," I said with confidence.

"I have keys but no locks. I have space but no room. You can enter but you can't go inside. What am I?"

"Oooo, Mr. Davis, you don't disappoint." I leaned back against the couch, pondering the riddle.

"Thirty seconds."

I closed my eyes to think and with three seconds left I said, "A keyboard."

My father stared at me in awe once again. "You haven't gotten a riddle incorrect all year."

I smiled innocently. It was true, I hadn't missed one all year. I was proud of my weird little talent.

He nodded. "Well, your majesty, I guess I lost today. And, now I am out forty dollars."

As my dad and I headed to the kitchen to get his wallet, my mom, dressed in a blazer and pencil skirt, wheeled out a suitcase with her purse on top. She walked towards us, looking stressed. She pulled me in for a tight hug, choking me with her Chanel perfume.

She let go of me. "All right, you two, there is no easy way to say this. Um, I love you both but I've got a case and I'm – sadly – off to the airport."

"What? Right now?!" The expected betrayal went through me like a knife. *A knife*. A stranger had come after me last night with an actual knife. Even the jackass policeman had told my parents that I needed to be protected now more than ever. And yet here she was, cloaked in Chanel and indifference, running towards the part of her life that would always take precedence over me: her work. I wondered, cruelly, if things would be different had that psycho actually finished the job, last night. She'd probably still be on her way to the airport.

"I am so sorry, Mags. It's an emergency."

"Last night was an emergency! Last night was the most traumatic experience of my life! And you're just leaving? Do you not think I need you here? I almost died!"

My mom's eye shone with unshed tears. "Magi, I want to be here for you more than anything. But this is really important."

"More important than me?" I yelled.

"Magi, even if I were to stay, you wouldn't be here."

"Huh?"

My mom shook her head, confused. She looked at my father. "Have you not told her?"

"I was going to tell her after breakfast," he said.

"Tell me what?"

"We are leaving tomorrow morning... for Egypt," My father announced.

"WHAT?" My stomach dropped. "You can't be serious."

"I am very serious. We need to get you out of here as soon as possible. Plus, I have to be back Cairo in a week anyway for work, and it's the safest place I know."

"Are you completely forgetting that I have a job and summer courses?" I threw my arms up in the air.

My father's voice never wavered, but it also didn't rise.

"Didn't you just say yourself that you almost died last night? Those things aren't even close to being important right now."

"He's right, darling. The most important thing in your life right now is to get on that plane tomorrow. And – good news – the police have also agreed to stay and watch the house one more night. So, it's working out perfectly in your favor." My mother rubbed my arm.

I backed away. "In my favor? Really? If everything were working out in my favor, I would be going to work today to save up for college. I would be applying for a second job. I would be studying magic with Nesu. Last night wouldn't have happened, and my parents would actually be home in the same house for once. How exactly is anything working in my favor?"

Just then, a black SUV pulled into our driveway and honked the horn.

"Is that your ride?" I asked.

My mom's silence was louder than any yes that she could have said.

"I'm so sorry..." A tear fell from my mom's eyes.

"You know what? It's fine. Go," I spat. "This just shows me how big of a priority I am to you."

"Magi—" Mom choked.

"Just go!"

"Don't be like that." My dad raised his voice as he helped my mom out with her bags, soothing her tears. "Please be safe. Call me when you land." He hugged her.

My mom took one last look at me. I turned away from her as my dad closed the door.

He turned to me. "She didn't deserve that."

"Really? Let me repeat myself: I almost died! And my mother is choosing to go on a business trip rather than staying to care for and comfort her daughter. And my dad? He's ten times worse. He chooses to spend months at a time away from home, and from me. You love a foreign country more than your actual daughter."

My father looked as if I'd slapped him.

"And there it is..." I sighed, tears swelling in my eyes.

"Magi...that is not true," he whispered.

"Dad, do the math! I only get to spend five months out of the year with you. One-hundred and fifty-one days out of three-hundred and sixty-five. I cry myself to sleep every time you go, and count the days until you get back. You spend more time in a foreign country than you do with me." I bit the inside of my cheek, trying hard to stave off the tears.

"I had no idea you felt this way," he whispered, his own tears forming.

I looked straight into his eyes. "How would you? You're never around."

I stormed towards the front hallway, snatched up my keys, and ran outside.

"Magi! Wait!" my dad yelled after me.

As I unlocked my car, two police officers – the ones

who had been ordered to guard the house overnight – took
notice of me.

"Hey, should you be leaving?" one of them yelled out.

I ignored him as I backed out of the driveway and
floored it.

I DROVE A FEW BLOCKS AWAY, to the beach I used to go to as
a child. Sitting on the hood of my car, I gazed out over Lake
Washington. I wished I could go back in time with my
parents and play knights and dragons with plastic swords
as we stomped on our sand castles. Those memories were
the ones I cherished the most. Even though I was seventeen, I would give anything to run across the sand just one
more time with my mom and dad.

Clouds had rolled in and everything in sight was
gloomy: the sky, the water, and my feelings. I breathed in
the misty, cold air to try to relax, but it didn't work, and it
always does.

"Magi?"

My body tensed up at the sound of my name. I turned
over my shoulder and saw Nesu, wearing all black workout
clothes, running towards me with Phoena desperately
trying to grip onto his jacket. At the sight of him, I broke
down and starting crying. I crawled off the hood of my car
and ran into his arms.

"What are you doing here?" I asked, my question muffled in his shirt.

"I was out for a run and saw your car. I ran over as fast as I could, since your father called me this morning and told me what happened. Are you all right? Are you hurt?"

"Just a few bruises and scratches. I'm really lucky, actually."

"Can we sit?" Nesu gestured to my car hood as if he were seating us at a five-star restaurant.

"Yeah," I laughed and wiped tears and snot off my face. We slowly climbed on.

"Here." Nesu handed me Phoena, and I held her in my hands. I smiled. Nesu knew that I loved holding her, especially when I was down. We sat there in silence, listening to Phoena hum along with the waves.

"I'm going to Egypt tomorrow," I finally said.

He raised his eyebrows. "Your father told me. You don't sound very pleased."

"I'm not." I stared at the sand.

"What's wrong?"

"I don't understand why this happened. Why did I have to be attacked? And then there's my parents – this whole thing has made them crazy. I don't want to be running for my life or going to that desert wasteland. I just feel like they are letting fear control them. That's my thing, not theirs."

"Well, for starters– that wasteland is my home." Nesu smiled.

"Ugh, I'm sorry. I didn't mean to—"

"No, no it's not for everyone. But here is what I will say. Life is constantly changing – it's full of unexpected twists and turns. How you react during the good times doesn't determine how you grow as a person. It's how you react in the bad times. The only question I have for you is, how are you going to react right now?"

I groaned. "I want to crawl into a hole and never come out." I flopped my head onto Nesu's shoulder as I whined.

He chuckled. "I know you may not like it," Nesu started as I raised my head to look at him, "but go to Egypt. You're safest with your dad. Do you really want to stay here? With everything that's happened?"

I sighed, staring at the sand. He was right. The idea of that man coming after me again made my stomach churn. The thought would haunt me and make me paranoid. *Maybe I should go?*

"Do not to worry about everything here," Nesu continued. "Leave the past behind you. Try to look at this like a new beginning. A fresh start! And as soon as you get back, you will have a job. But you must promise me something."

"What's that?"

"Genuinely try to enjoy my home for me. Be open to the adventures it brings. And if you need any food and sightseeing suggestions, you can always ask me." He smiled.

I let out a long and uneasy sigh, but finally agreed to his conditions. "I promise." Nesu grinned at me, and then snapped his fingers. A slight *poof* puffed up from my lap, and I looked down. Pheona had turned purple right before my eyes.

"Seriously? How do you do that? You weren't even holding her this time!"

"Magic." Nesu shrugged.

"Right, magic." I rolled my eyes, laughing.

"HEY MAGI?" My dad knocked on my door later that evening, "Look, sweetie, I know you are not happy about this whole Egypt thing, but please let me know if I can help you pack, run a few errands to get anything you may need, help you find your passport – whatever. Just let me know."

"No need!" I opened my door.

"You're packed?" My dad gazed at my two large white suitcases and carry-on, all neatly packed.

"You're right. I really don't want to stay here." I glanced at my balcony door. "And maybe I'm in need of a new adventure."

My dad didn't say anything. He just wrapped his arms around me as if he were saying thank you. "What changed your mind?"

"I don't know... I guess I just don't want to think about the attack, and I'm trying to look at this trip like a new beginning – a way to heal from this."

My dad grinned proudly at me but his smile faltered. "Magi, I'm really sorry that you feel the way you do about our jobs. Please know that we love you— more than anything. Even if we're not around."

"I know." I squeezed him tighter. "I love you too."

He let go of me, and I let out very exaggerated sigh. "Let's go to Egypt!"

"Alright, listen to me very carefully." My dad leaned in close to me after parking our car in the extended-stay garage at the Seattle-Tacoma International Airport early the next morning. "You are going to stick right beside me, and will not leave my side. If anyone – and I mean anyone – tries anything, you scream as loud as you can to attract attention to yourself. We still don't know who's after you, and so we don't know if they are crazy enough to try to attack in broad daylight or a busy place. Got it?"

"Yeah, got it." I swallowed. *Thanks for freaking me out even more.*

"Here, put this on." My dad handed me an old hat from his alma mater, Brown University, and a pair of cheap gas-station sunglasses.

"Um, I'm not sure this is my kind of style," I joked.

"That's the point."

I shrugged and put them both on. Walking through the airport was nerve-wracking. I had never seen my father so laser focused on everyone near us. He eyed everyone like a threat as he tugged me through the crowds. Thankfully, there were a lot of security people everywhere, and they were really nice to us. Since my dad travels so much, he had become friends with some of the TSA agents, and they let us cut in line to get to our gate faster.

Several hours later, we had landed in New York to jump onto our connecting flight to Cairo. So far, there had not been a single speed bump, and my dad was beginning to relax a little bit. So was I.

We boarded our flight, and my dad pointed out our seats.

"Wait, this is first class," I said, trying to pull my carry-on towards economy.

"Is it?" My dad smiled as he sat down on a seat that reclined into a bed.

"Are these our seats?" I stared at the bottled water, fancy TV screens, and the extra, *extra* leg room.

"Check your boarding pass if you don't believe me!" My dad laughed as he began to get his belongings situated.

I flipped my boarding pass around and sure enough, *First Class* was printed on it in official bold lettering. I covered my mouth, laughing in shock.

"How is this possible?" I asked as I sat down in my very comfortable seat across the aisle.

"The company pays for it." My dad shrugged. "Now you get why I'm gone so much," he added.

I rolled my eyes at his joke as I stood up to put my

carryon in the overhead compartment. It didn't take me long to figure out how the reclining chair or TV worked, and shortly after the plane took off, my dad and I had the same idea: eat dinner then go to sleep. He put a sleeping mask over his eyes and pretty much zonked out in the matter of minutes. I looked out the window, staring at pitch-black darkness, save a couple stars here and there.

It's pretty freakin' great we are in first class, but still, this is going to be a long flight...

CHAPTER 3

Our suitcases came down onto the baggage carousel. We had officially landed in the Sphinx's litter box.

It took forever for my father and I to pull our four suitcases off and drag our luggage around the Cairo airport to the rental car counter.

My father approached the lady behind the desk with a smile and struck up a conversation with her. As he talked, I felt a little chilly, so I decided to go outside through the automatic doors to the drop-off and pick-up area. The hot Egyptian sun warmed my skin, which felt really nice after such a long flight. I looked around, taking in the chaotic scene. People were greeting family members in languages I didn't recognize, cars were honking, and it smelled like dust – lots of dust.

I faced my back to the road and pulled my giant suitcases up in front of me. Many people were entering and exiting through the automatic doors I had just walked out of. Each time the doors opened, I had a clear view of my father still paying for a rental car.

Out of nowhere, I heard a loud screech. I thought it came from the right of me, but when I turned to look, I didn't see anything unusual. I turned back to face my father. The automatic doors opened, once again, to let people in – and my dad turned to look at me and smiled.

All of a sudden, his loving smile vanished. He leaned his body backwards to get a better look at something. His eyes widened as mine narrowed. My father's face then went white, and a terrifying intensity filled his eyes. I had never seen my father like that. His mouth opened wide as he screamed, "MAGI!"

He threw his wallet and the rental car pamphlet to the ground and started running full speed towards me.

A strong and firm hand covered my mouth. I tried to scream, but the hand captured the sound. Another set of hands grabbed my right arm and yanked it behind my back. I let out a painful cry. As I was kicking my legs, the two sets of hands pulled me backwards and into a vehicle —a black van.

Then, I couldn't see a thing. One of the hands had shoved a black cloth over my head. The doors to the van opened, and my body was hoisted in the air and thrown. Gravity took over—I crashed into the van, yelling out in pain.

Then, something slammed against my skull and everything went black.

MY EYES SNAPPED OPEN. I was lying flat on my back on a
black stone floor, and I shivered as goosebumps rose all
over my arms. I dusted gray sand off my jeans and stood
up. All around me were carved, black stone walls with
glowing symbols. Everything was fuzzy, but they looked
similar to hieroglyphics, and they were glowing an eerie
green.

Where am I?

I was breathing heavily, and tried to force myself to
calm down. I needed to not panic. I needed to figure out a
way out.

Behind me, over a stone railing, was a massive three-
story room. I cautiously peered out from the second level,
where there was a horrifying bronze statue of cobra striking. Its mouth was massive and its giant tongue reached
the floor next to two fire pits that held burning green
flames. The air was musty and smelled like sulfur. The
floors were covered with sand, and the only light being
emitted was from the glowing walls and fire pits.

"You told me she was dead!" a voice boomed. Wait. I
knew that voice.

Marching into the room below me was...Lieutenant

Doyle? He ripped off the badge and tore his shirt to expose his toned abs. Then he yanked off a blonde wig and tossed it into a fire pit. As he marched, enraged, his skin began to slowly shed and fall to the ground. I clasped my hands over my mouth to keep from crying out. With each stomp, he crunched something dry beneath his feet – and I realized with growing horror that he was *shedding*. The old skin was replaced with tan scales – like a dried-up reptile. It shimmered against the dancing light of the green flames. He pulled more shedding skin from his eyeballs to expose all-white eyes with a black strip down the middle like a snake. He climbed up the three stairs as sweat trickled down his rough face, and then sat down on the cobra's tongue.

Another figure hobbled into the throne room, and my throat seized as recognition washed over me: it was the man who had tried to kill me. He had bandages wrapped around his chest seeping with blood stains – the marks of where my parents had shot him. He winced as knelt before Doyle.

When he bowed, the ground around him began to crumble, like someone went nuts with a jackhammer. Piles of rubble slowly moved, like an invisible wind slow dancing with the stone. It swirled upward, and the pieces hardened and compacted together. Then, just as quickly as it had begun, it stopped.

My attacker shook with fear. I held my breath, not knowing what I was seeing.

The piles of stone had transformed into masculine,

life-size stone figures. The stone men stomped and stirred, coming to life. Then they began to march around the room, exiting and reentering with grapes, bread, and wine. Some knelt before Doyle, offering him strange little gold statues and jewels. Others placed a broad bronze collar on the officer's chest – one with a green diamond the size of a baseball in the middle of it. They draped a bronze and dark green cape over his shoulders.

"Leave us," Lieutenant Doyle ordered.

All the stone figures quickly left.

"Your majesty," spoke the servant.

"Silence!" boomed Doyle.

The servant's face turned red; sweat dripped down his face. His Master fixed him with an unrelenting stare.

"How? How is she not dead?" asked the Master, attempting to control his anger.

"My lord, I believed," answered the servant.

"You—"

"The baby's room was on fire! The whole section of the palace was in flames. There was no way that baby could have survived!"

"*I* survived!" the Master stood up from his chair and glared down at his servant. "I was almost burned alive in that palace trying to kill that child, and now it was all for nothing?" He pointed an accusing, scaly finger at his servant. "And when you pulled your little stunt, you almost got captured. Do you know what would have happened if you had been? They would have linked you back to me.

Now, thanks to you, my undercover work has *also* all been for nothing."

The Master took a deep, slow breath, withdrawing his finger. "You were right, though. She has no idea who she is."

"Yes, Yes!" the servant spoke up desperately. "You have already persuaded the family to bring her here, and it will be much easier to kill her if she does not know anything. We can use it to our advantage."

"Oh, I intend to."

The Master pulled a dagger out from his belt and, in a flash, slashed it across the servant's throat.

The servant immediately fell to the ground, a shower of blood spewing everywhere.

I covered my mouth and stepped back. *Oh, my God. Oh my God!*

"You have failed me," The Master told the unhearing servant. He yelled in a foreign language, and servants entered the room to remove the body. "Tarek!"

A large, brawny man wearing some kind of ancient battle armor entered, carrying two swords. There were scars all over his body, and his face was slashed. He stomped toward the Master and knelt down before him. The Master placed his hand on the green diamond on his necklace. It began to glow. The eyes of the man kneeling before him began to glow the same dark, smoky green.

"Kill her," the Master spoke. "Use whatever means you have to."

"Yes, my lord," the menacing man answered, as if hypnotized.

"This time, bring me her body. Make sure no one knows *I* gave the order to kill her, especially the Queen of Illusions. I cannot put my plan into action until the girl is dead. 'Cut off the head and the rest will follow'... It's time to start cutting off heads."

"Yes, Master."

Okay, this guy is insane! I wasn't exactly sure what I was witnessing, but what I did know was that I had to get out.

I scurried down a long hallway. Out of nowhere, two men dressed in battle armor appeared, pointing swords at me.

"Hey!" one of them yelled at me. I tried to make a break for it, but their strong arms snatched me. They dragged me down a set of stairs. I looked down as I thrashed against them, and realized that the stone was crawling with snakes and overgrown plants. I struggled, but it was no use—they were too strong.

To my horror, they brought me before the Master, kicking my legs in, forcing me to kneel. The Master and the assassin both stared at me in complete awe.

"Impossible," whispered the Master. He moved back up the three steps, eyeing me with confusion and fear.

Something inside him snapped.

"Kill her! Kill her, now!" the Master yelled frantically.

I looked down and screamed. Snakes that had once adorned the patterns carved into the ground broke through the black stone floor. The stones had come to life, and were now climbing up my legs! I tried to escape from their grasp, but one of them hissed at me, biting my hand. I yelled out in pain as they squeezed tighter and tighter. They felt like solid cold rock against my skin.

"Now, you die," said the Master.

The assassin approached and raised his swords. I screamed for my life as he drove his swords into my chest.

I GASPED FOR AIR. I tried to stand up, but I was restrained by my seatbelt. I looked around wildly—I was still on the airplane.

It was all a dream?

We had never landed in Egypt! No one kidnapped me, and no had tried to kill me!

It was all a dream!

The panic left me when I laid eyes on my dad, who was sleeping peacefully. I lay back in my seat and watched the morning sun seep into the window next to me as I tried not to hyperventilate. That was by far the worst nightmare I had ever had. *It all seemed so real...*

"Ow," I whispered to myself. The airplane was experiencing some slight turbulence, which was giving me a headache. I touched my head. *Where did this bump come from?* As I lowered my hand, I noticed it was bleeding. *How am I bleeding?*

I thought back to my dream, when I had been bitten by the stone snake. My eyes widened in terror as I examined my hand even closer.

There was blood slowly seeping out of two tiny puncture wounds.

CHAPTER 4

"Everyone, please fasten your seat belts. We are beginning our descent. We will be landing in Cairo in twenty-five minutes. Thank you for flying with us, and we hope you enjoy the rest of your day."

I quickly fastened my seat belt and stuffed all of my belongings – in record time – into my bags. I sat as straight as possible in my seat. My knee bounced up and down. My hand tapped against my leg, and I looked down the aisle. Only a few people were packing up their possessions.

My armpits started to sweat. I was burning up. I tried to fan my face with my hand to cool myself down, but that didn't help at all. *Am I having an anxiety attack?* Then I realized I was wearing my hoodie. *Stupid.* I yanked my black hoodie off my body. I felt temporary relief, but after a little bit my body temperature rose again. Waves of heat washed over me. My face start to flush.

Okay, something is very wrong. This is not good. I was

freaked out, impatient, and super-hot—I couldn't stay still. I wished with all my heart and soul for this plane to land. *I might need to go to a hospital. How much longer?* I closed my eyes and tried to relax and focus on breathing; I didn't even notice when the plane actually landed.

"You ready?"

I jolted and my eyes flew open.

"You okay?" My father stood over my seat, looking concerned.

"Yeah, yeah, I'm good."

I bolted for the exit. I shoved people out of the way to get to the front, and while I am pretty sure I heard some words my mother wouldn't approve of—I didn't care. I was too focused on keeping myself from either fainting or throwing up.

"Magi? Magi!" my father yelled at me, confused. I charged through the tunnel to get to the terminal. The cold air was like paradise on my skin. I took in my surroundings, and saw that the airport was swarmed – filled with a bunch of local Egyptians and many tourists.

"Mags." My father jogged up, finally catching me. "What's going on?"

"Sorry, I was feeling like I was going to throw up." *So please don't punish me for running away from you in a foreign airport.*

"Oh, you okay?"

"Yeah, I feel a lot better," I lied.

"Good, well let's go get our luggage."

He'd slipped into this comfortable, methodical routine: get the bags, and pick his way through the crowd towards the exit. I stopped in my tracks and watched him. His shoulders were relaxed, and an easy smile had spread across his face. It struck me that this place, which was so strange to me, was his real home. An unexpected jolt of jealousy shot through me. *I* wanted to be his home.

AFTER WE WENT THROUGH CUSTOMS, we arrived at the rental-car counter and my mind flashed back to the dream I'd had on the plane. *This was where I was kidnapped!* Adrenaline rushed through my body. The rental counter, the pickup area, even the automatic doors were exactly the same as they'd been in my dream.

I faced the automatic doors. Outside, people were picking up family members, hugging and welcoming them; they were all smiling and cheerful. As I watched the tourists bump around like bees in a bottle, something caught my eye—a black van, slowly driving by. The passenger window was down, and I saw a man dressed in all black with a black cloth wrapped around his entire head that left only his eyes and forehead exposed. Everything around me seemed to slow down as we made eye contact. His glare was strong and firm, shaking me to the core. I swallowed hard. I couldn't breathe or move. The van slowly drove off.

"Let's go."

The sound of my father's voice made me jump.

"Whoa, are you sure you are all right?" He stopped what he was doing and faced me with a comically concerned look on his face.

"Yeah. I think I just got a little airsick." I managed a grin.

He grinned back at me. "Okay, well, the car's ready, so let's get out of here, shall we?"

Yes! Let's go! I nodded. My father walked outside the automatic doors, and I stayed glued to his hip as we headed straight to the Jeep waiting for us outside. To my surprise, the Jeep had the doors, roof and windows removed. The only window in the whole car was the windshield. My father began loading his luggage into the backseat.

"Wait, this is our rental?" I asked.

Well, technically it's a company car." my father corrected.

"It doesn't have any windows or doors."

"Your point?"

"Is it safe? I mean, you are all about safety when it comes to driving, and everything."

"We aren't in America anymore, Mags. And, besides, we'll be driving this thing in the desert. There's no traffic in the desert."

"All right." I nodded. *I can work with this.*

Because our luggage was the size of an elephant, my

father had to tie it down with two strands of thick rope. I was certain that the suitcases were going to fall out. When we climbed into the Jeep, I removed my backpack and held onto it for dear life. My father turned on the car and put the vehicle in drive. A few minutes later we were on a highway. *Only driving in the desert, huh?*

"Here. Put this on," my father said.

I raised my eyebrows. My father held a solid black, cheap-looking tie in his hands.

"I'm a girl, we don't wear ties."

"Over your eyes."

"Why?"

"Because, there has been something I've wanted to show you for a very long time, and I want it to be a surprise." My father had the same sparkle in his eyes he gets when he is really excited.

I stared at the black tie. "Do I really have to put that over my face?"

"Not over your face, your eyes."

"Smartass." I reluctantly snatched up the tie.

My father laughed as I blindfolded myself. *This had better be a good.*

He drove for what seemed to be twenty minutes. During those twenty minutes, I asked repeatedly if we were there yet, or, if I could take the thing off my face. Of course, he said no. *He already kidnapped me and took me to Egypt—now blindfolds. What's next, jail?* But I couldn't exactly explain to him that, after my dream, I hated having something over my eyes. That it made me feel like I had been kidnapped again, even though I knew I was safe.

"Where did you bring me?" I asked, as my dad was finally helping me out of the Jeep.

"You'll see." There was a playful smile in his tone.

I stepped down onto a surface I wasn't used to – sand. *Eww, NO!* Sand in my shoes was one of my biggest pet peeves in life. I searched the air with my hands, looking for the Jeep so I could get back in.

"What are you doing?" My dad chuckled. He grabbed my hands, helping me walk a few steps forward.

"If you run me into something, I will slap you," I warned.

"I'm not going to," my father laughed. He removed my blindfold and pointed behind me. "Welcome to Giza."

The sun was so bright, my eyes narrowed involuntarily. I turned to see where he was pointing.

Oh WOW. My jaw fell. Directly in front of me were three enormous, geometrically perfect structures. The Great Pyramids of Giza were standing proudly before me, their tips so high they were practically worshipping the sky. Mounds of soft sand that stretched for miles and miles surrounded the monuments stirred in the hot desert wind. Camels groaned loudly, dragging tourists in front of the great Sphinx who guarded the pyramids – and all the ruins inside the dusty complex.

"They're big," I managed to spit out. I had never in my entire life seen anything more beautiful and impressive.

My dad laughed at me. "Now you see why I like working here?" His gray eyes were shining in the Sahara sun.

I had to admit: the pyramids were stunning in a very strange way. As I studied them more closely, a weird feeling washed over me. *This place seems so familiar to me.* But that didn't make any sense; I'd never been there.

My dad put his hands on my shoulders and pointed to the horizon. "See those green tents over there?"

Whoa. There was a sea of hundreds of green, military-style tents. They were not anything fancy, just fabric draped over four support poles with a ridged roof, tall enough that a man could stand up inside them.

"That's where we are staying. We call it Camp Cheops or, simply: camp!"

"Cheops?" I laughed.

"Sounds funny, I know, but it's another name for the Pharaoh Khufu. And you see the biggest pyramid to the right?" He pointed. "That's his pyramid. The great pyramid of Khufu."

My reaction to staying in those green tents next to the pyramids surprised even me. It wasn't my typical roll of the eyes or storm away from the bad news messenger—I was actually a little excited. Something about the breeze cooling your skin in the hot Saharan air – something about just being surrounded by so many ancient ruins – made this whole place feel adventurous.

"You'll be safe here." He nodded, as if answering an un-asked question. *Why does he seem so confident?*

"Still far from home, though."

"It's closer than you think." He patted my back. "Let's go to camp."

We climbed back into our Jeep and navigated down the hill towards the campgrounds.

I had never seen so many tents before in my life. The closer we got, the more they seemed to multiply. *And this is all for digging up old pieces of pottery, treasure, and dead people?* It was crazy, but in a good way. I couldn't believe that this was what my father did for a living.

Many people in the camp stopped what they were doing and looked at us. There were tons of workers and archeologists like my father, most of them Egyptian men; I only saw a few women.

Some of the Egyptians wore clothes similar to what you would see in the United States, but many wore what looked like long-sleeve dresses past their knees, with pants underneath.

My dad slowed the Jeep down. Everyone was waving and smiling at him, and he returned the greetings. He was like a celebrity here. We parked, and Dad hefted the suitcases out of the back. "We'll have to drag these through the sand, but the good news is we won't have to drag them too far."

He led the way as we entered camp. I struggled to pull the suitcases through the sand—they kept twisting in every direction and getting stuck. The workers began to take notice of me and started laughing. *Seriously? And none of you can help? Those people you're looking for have been dead a long time. They can wait while longer as you assist me in getting a hundred pounds of luggage into my tent.* I hated it when people looked down on me and laughed. I sighed loudly and tugged even harder. After a few minutes of dragging our luggage, my father stopped in front of a tent.

"Well, Mags, this is your new home from this day forward. Or, at least for the next couple months."

"Yay." After that arm and leg exercise in the heat, the adventurous spirit that I had just gained had been stifled.

"Ah, you'll get used to it, and I am right here." My father pointed to a tent that was directly across from mine. "If you need anything, I will be in there unpacking. You should do the same so you can get some of it done by dinner."

"All right."

He grinned and dragged his suitcases to his tent. I unlatched the door – the flap, really – and pulled my suitcases inside.

To my surprise, my tent was very roomy. The floor of the room was covered with a blue tarp that blocked out the sand. Over the tarp was a series of Egyptian rugs with strange, colorful patterns. To the right of me was a little roll-away bed with two little pillows and a blanket folded neatly on top. There was a note on top the blankets with little pyramids on it that read, "Welcome to Camp Cheops!" I wondered who had put it there.

Next to the bed was a wooden night stand, and to the left of that was a medium-sized dresser with a square mirror placed on top. In front of the mirror was a giant bowl and a pitcher filled with water. *I guess that is my sink?*

Behind me were small wooden drawers for extra storage. I was really pleased with the nicer wooden items and rugs; I guess when you are working in the desert for a long time, these things are very useful. I was pleasantly surprised to find that I actually really liked it, despite the fact that it didn't have AC. It wasn't luxurious, but it was better than sleeping on the sand.

I plopped down on my floor and unzipped one of my suitcases. Folded neatly on top of my clothes was a note written on vintage notebook paper with pale pink roses on the edges. My stomach turned because I knew, right away, the note was from my mom. My mom is notorious for randomly placing sweet, loving notes in my backpacks, school lunches, and around my room to brighten my day. It was one of her ways she expressed her love for me when she was in a hurry or not around. Despite everything, I appreciated the effort, and holding her signature rose vintage paper made me feel warm inside.

I unfolded the note and read.

Dear Magi,

I gave this note to your father to give to you. By the time you read it, you'll be in Egypt.

Darling, I cannot begin to express how deeply sorry I am about leaving you. It's destroying me that I have to go. All I want is to wrap you in my arms and tell you it's going to be okay. One day, you will understand why I had to go – but right now, you promise me that you will stay safe in Egypt – and maybe try to learn a thing or two while you are there. After this all blows over, I promise the first thing I am doing is jumping on a plane to Cairo to give you the biggest hug in the world. I love you, Magi. I truly do. XOXO

I blinked back tears and held the note against my chest, wishing it could turn into the hug she promised. *I want my mom.* I rubbed away any water in my eyes, attempting to pull myself to together as I ignored the guilt in my heart the size of an Egyptian pyramid.

Then, I picked up some t-shirts and began to unpack.

"Well, here goes nothing."

I SIGHED LOUDLY, wishing I could be a wizard for a least a second. I had been unpacking for the entire afternoon, and I still had half of my belongings in my suitcases because, well, procrastination. I was in the middle of refolding a pair of jeans, wishing my clothes would magically organize themselves, when—

"Hey, Mags?" Dad called from outside my tent.

"Yeah?" I yelled back.

"Come out here real fast."

"All right, one sec!"

I set my jeans down and walked outside to find my dad

waiting for me. He put both of his hands on my shoulders and turned me around to face a tall, handsomely groomed African American man who looked like he was in his early forties.

"Magi, there's someone I want you to meet—well, again. You were so little I don't think you remember. This is R.J. Hicks."

"Wait, R.J.? As in the R.J. Hicks in your books?" I asked my father.

R.J. and my dad laughed.

"Yep! That's me!" R.J. smiled.

"I kind of remember meeting you. I was little, and remember you falling off our sailboat while trying to get on the dock at one of my dad's birthdays."

R.J. burst out laughing, clearly remembering that day.

In my father's books, he wrote the funniest stories about his best friend R.J., who liked to pull off dumb pranks, do stupid dares, and make hilarious commentaries. Reading about R.J. was honestly my favorite part about my dad's books. And the stories my dad would tell me about R.J. – the ones that didn't make it in the final drafts – made me feel like I already knew him. I guess I had just kind of forgotten that I had actually already met him.

R.J. had a super sweet smile and looked like he loved life, but his muscular body made him slightly intimating.

"Man, she is all grown up. Is she really your daughter? She looks just like her mother!" R.J. grinned at my dad. I blushed from R.J.'s compliment, even though I personally thought I looked more like my dad than my mom. "I just can't believe it." R.J. shook his head.

"What do you mean?" I looked back at my dad, and then turned my curious gaze to R.J. once more.

"Well, in order to have a kid – you have to attract a woman first." R.J. laughs, making eye contact with me. "And your dad was the biggest nerd."

"Hey." Dad laughed defensively.

"What? Please tell me more." I giggled.

"Yep. In college."

"All right, all right." My dad laughed.

"Even had the glasses and plaid shorts up to here." R.J. pointed above his hips.

"R.J.," my father interjected.

"Walking girl repellent."

I laughed loudly.

"I take full credit for your parents' marriage, you know," R.J. finished proudly.

"What?"

"Yeah, yeah, we can talk about that some *other* time!" My father cleared his throat.

I covered my mouth, I was laughing so hard. I had never heard this before. My dad was shaking his head as R.J. winked at me, and then laughed himself.

"Hey! Where's Carter?" my dad asked, changing the subject.

"I don't know. Carter?" yelled R.J.

Who's Carter?

From behind a tent, a cute teenaged boy – who looked slightly younger than me – emerged. He had short, curly blonde hair and light skin. He wore a casual blue button shirt with a tan vest over it, jeans, and sneakers. He also wore oval black-rimmed glasses that made him look really dorky. He was also kind of skinny—not super skinny, but skinnier than some of the guys that I knew from my school.

Oh wait, I know who that is. Over the years, my dad had told me stories and showed me pictures of R.J.'s adopted son Carter, who always wore these oval glasses that I thought were hilarious. My father always spoke very highly of him, saying Carter was very intelligent and went out of his way to learn and help others on the expedition digs. I never thought I would actually be meeting him.

"Carter!" said my dad, smiling as he hugged the kid.

"Hi, Mr. Davis," he replied with a smile.

"I want you to meet my daughter, Magi," my dad said.

"Carter." He stuck out his hand. *How... formal.*

"Magi." I shook it, awkwardly.

I almost gasped as we shook hands. Carter had deep, ocean-blue eyes that shined through his glasses. They were completely mesmerizing, glistening in the Egyptian sunset. I had never seen someone with more beautiful eyes.

"Well, R.J. and I have some things to discuss. Why don't

you two get to know each other?" Dad said. He and R.J. walked off and went inside a tent near us.

Carter and I awkwardly stood next to each other. We made uncomfortable eye contact that made things weirder – so we both looked away quickly. Before things got worse, I decided to ask him a question I have always wanted to know the answer to.

"So, why those glasses?"

"What?" Carter was completely caught off guard, but he seemed amused.

"Why those? They are not round. They are not square. Why oval?" I continued.

Carter shifted his stance and stared at me. "That was by far the weirdest conversation opener I have ever experienced."

I laughed. "Hey, at least I tried something. You were staring at me awkwardly."

"So were you." He laughed. "How about you try again."

"Try again?" I chuckled. "Um... okay. Where are you from?"

"Wow, you're bad at this. I am originally from Michigan."

"Ahh, cold place."

"Oh, you've been?"

"No, I just know it's cold."

Carter laughed a little. "Yeah, it is...I do miss it, but now I live in Brooklyn with R.J."

"Oh yeah! My father told me that. So, why do you live

with R.J. again? I feel like my dad has told me the story, but I completely forgot."

"Well...um...when I was seven, my parents were killed in a car accident. My dad and R.J. were best friends, so when my dad was in the hospital before he died, he asked R.J. to take care of me." Carter grinned, though he still avoided eye contact.

"Oh, I am so sorry." I couldn't imagine losing my parents—especially in such a violent way. "Now I remember."

"I'm not surprised you've heard about it. My parents and yours used to be really close, and R.J. and your dad are best friends."

Used to be close? "Have we ever met before?"

"No, I don't think so. I mean, we did grow up far away from each other."

"True. Seattle and Brooklyn are opposite ends of the country." I nodded. "So, how's life in New York? How's living with R.J?"

"Actually, pretty awesome. R.J. is my dad as far as I'm concerned, and we have a lot of fun there together. He works a lot at the Metropolitan Museum's Egyptology department, so I get free tickets I can use with friends. I really like my school, and I get to come out here every summer. I love it."

"That is really awesome."

Out of nowhere, a loud bell rang out, echoing throughout the camp.

"What's that?" I asked Carter.

"Oh, the bell?" Carter grinned. "That lets everyone know it's time for dinner, or lunch, or breakfast – but in our case, dinner."

"I could use some food right now," I complained.

"Well, let's go eat," Carter said. "Follow me, I will show you where the mess hall is."

Carter and I began to weave through the sea of tents when he blurted out, "Because of my dad."

"What?" I asked, confused.

"To answer your question about why I wear oval glasses. Because my dad's were oval."

That's really sweet. I smiled to myself as we kept walking. *He's pretty cool.*

CHAPTER 5

The mess hall was a large white, open tent with several long tables inside. People were already lining up to go down the last three tables, which were set up like a buffet.

"Let's get in line before more people arrive," Carter said, gesturing for me to go first.

Carter was extremely polite—a true gentleman; I didn't know a lot of guys my age that acted like him. It took some getting used to, but it was refreshing.

There were plastic plates at the beginning of the long catering table. As we went down the line, the caterers placed what looked like Sloppy Joe on our plates – the meat falling out of the tiny buns – along with rolls of bread, green beans, and thick fudge brownies. I was surprised to see American food being served, though there was also Egyptian food I didn't recognize being served.

At the end of the line was an area where you could

serve yourself fruit. There were pineapples, grapes, straw-berries, pomegranates and plums. Using a large spoon, I scooped up some grapes and a plum. In a large basket were chips: Doritos, Lays, and Cheetos. *Cheetos!* I took a couple of bags, and so did Carter. At the very end of the table was a cooler filled with water, Coca Cola, Sprite, and root beer. Carter and I made the healthy decision to grab Coca Colas. I was so pleased with the food and drink selection.

A lot of money was being put into this expedition— I could tell based on the nice equipment and the tasty beverages. This whole place actually felt like a summer camp. Although there was still no excuse for not having air conditioning.

Carter and I sat down and began eating. A plate dropped down in front of me, causing me to jump and bump into Carter. My father and R.J. sat down across from us.

"Wow, someone's a little jumpy," R.J. observed.

"I'm only jumpy because you guys popped out of nowhere," I said.

"She's known to spaz out." My father grinned. I glared at my dad, but I couldn't deny it—I was a spaz. Carter took a long sip of his soda.

R.J. eyeballed his son. "You better guard that soda with your life," he warned.

"Oh, no, you are not doing that again." Carter shielded it away from R.J.

"Doing what again?" I asked.

R.J. laughed. "Let me tell you—"

"No!" Carter laughed, looking embarrassed.

"Once upon a time, Carter, your father, and I were eating dinner here last summer. Carter stood up to get seconds. While he was standing in line, I poured salt, pepper, and sugar into his soda—you know, to accentuate the flavors. When he came back, he took a huge sip and spit it back out – the soda went everywhere."

"And by 'everywhere', he means all over me," my father monotoned.

"Sorry about that, Mr. Davis," Carter apologized.

"Don't worry, we were both victims." My father and Carter exchanged looks while R.J. chortled. I laughed to myself, too. My father and Carter shook their heads and turned their attention back to their food.

"Well Magi, how does it feel to *finally* be in Egypt?" R.J. asked.

"Finally?"

"Yeah, you had to wait all this time."

"I wasn't really waiting...um, I mean it is actually kinda cool here. The pyramids are amazing."

"I told you." Dad's face lit up. I just rolled my eyes.

"So, your father says you are quite the illusionist," R.J. said.

"Illusionist?" Carter shifted in his seat, interested.

"Yeah, I dabble in magic." I shrugged. "You know, card tricks and stuff."

"That's so cool!" Carter's blue eyes sparkled. "Can you show us something?"

"Yeah, of course. I always carry my deck of cards with me." I instantly pulled out my purple-and-gold deck from my jeans pocket.

For the first time in a few days, my cheeks hurt from smiling. Performing magic gave me a high that always made every situation better. I shuffled the deck a couple different ways, showing off a bit to impress the boys. Their fascinated expressions made me warm inside, and – for once – I wasn't nervous.

"Okay, R.J. Pick a card, any card." I grinned as I fanned the deck in front of him.

He chuckled, pulling one from the side.

"Carter, do you have a pen?" I asked.

"Yes." He dug around in his pockets and pulled one out just as fast as I pulled out my cards.

"Perfect, now I want you to sign your name on R.J.'s card."

Carter quickly did as I said. He handed me the card, and I laughed out loud. "Dude, your handwriting sucks!" "Carter" was barely legible.

"Yeah, I know." He scratched his head a little. "I want to be a doctor one day, so I already got one thing going for me."

Everyone at the table hunched over laughing. "I think you will be very successful." I messed with him. "Anyway, place the card back in the deck."

Carter shoved it back in the middle, and I began to shuffle. "Okay now, R.J., I want you to take my cards and shuffle them yourself – just to prove I'm not doing anything special."

R.J. took my cards and shuffled them like an amateur. He then proceeded to drop a few cards into his lap.

"Okay, butterfingers, don't lose my cards!" I reached over the table to get my cards back.

"Hey! Butterfingers over here's got it! Have some faith," R.J. reassured me. And in that same moment, he dropped a bunch more on the table.

"We have complete and utter faith in you." Carter shook his head, smiling.

"Well, it might not have looked as glamourous as when Ms. Davis did it, but I got the job done." R.J. showed off a neatly shuffled deck, indeed finishing his job.

"Okay," I said. "If you can manage to do this without dropping it, place the deck over on the furthest table away from ours."

Everyone looked at each other, intrigued.

"Okay..." R.J. stood up slowly and stared at me like a hawk as he traveled away to the farthest table. He pretended to almost drop the cards.

"Stop!" I yelled at him.

He laughed hysterically as he set the cards down and returned to his seat.

"All right, for this last part, I need complete silence so I can communicate with the spirits."

The boys all exchanged weird looks.

"What?" Carter blurted out.

"Shh!" I closed my eyes. *Ahhh, I love doing this!*

After about ten seconds of muttering gibberish to myself, I opened my eyes with a big smile. The boys all looked at me strangely.

"Your card is in the roll of bread." I pointed confidently to Carter's plate.

"There's no way!" My father shook his head.

"Someone rip it open." I leaned back in my seat.

"Open it, Carter!" R.J. motioned for him to hurry up.

Carter pulled apart the moist bread and, sure enough, R.J.'s card with Carter's horrible writing on it was inside the roll. There was a huge uproar at the table. The boys could not believe their eyes.

My dad's jaw dropped. "Mags! That was amazing!"

"Oh my god! How did you do that? That's impossible!" Carter stared at the roll.

"How did you learn how to do that?" R.J. examined the card, looking impressed.

"I don't know, I just kind of got into it after my dad gave me this deck. Then, I started working at a magic shop and my mentor is *amazing!* So, I guess just practice, because it's not like magic runs in the family."

R.J. burst out laughing and then cleared his throat, looking at his shoes. "Yeah, I guess it doesn't."

I stared at him for a second, confused. But my dad changed the subject, and we all continued eating. Dinner went on for a long time. We probably sat talking with each other for an hour or more. I hadn't had this much fun since Junior prom. I really liked them, especially Carter. We were constantly cracking each other up, and I found myself wishing we could talk all night. But my father insisted on taking showers and getting some rest for the next day.

It was pitch black outside when we finally threw away our plates and said our goodnights. My father walked with me back to our tents.

I entered my tent and grabbed pajama shorts, a black t-shirt, flip-flops, a towel, a comb, shampoo and conditioner. I juggled my belongings as I walked out my tent.

I found my father standing outside, talking with a few workers. I approached him and, after a few awkward introductions, he showed me to the shower. He escorted me over to a small camper that was near a bunch of port-a-potties and knocked on the door to make sure no one was in there.

I walked in to find the tiniest shower I had ever seen in my life. *You have got to be kidding me.* My father laughed at the look on my face and gave my shoulder a pat.

After he walked back to his tent, I stood in front of the shower for a couple of minutes debating if I should get in or not. I finally talked myself into getting inside the super claustrophobic space—better get it over with. I turned on the water, and then braced myself for the coldest and most uncomfortable shower of my life.

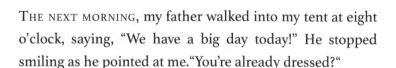

THE NEXT MORNING, my father walked into my tent at eight o'clock, saying, "We have a big day today!" He stopped smiling as he pointed at me. "You're already dressed?"

I sat on my bed, already in shorts, a tank top with a tan, button-down shirt over it, some lace-up boots, and a white bandana around my head.

"I couldn't sleep. Still paranoid." I scratched my arm. All night, images of the dagger and my attacker's blood-thirsty face circulated in my mind. I didn't know what haunted me more: him coming for me in real life, or him dying in my dream at the hands of his terrifying Master. *That dream felt so real...could it have been real?* I continued to suppress my thoughts as I stared at the ground.

"I'm so sorry, Mags. Did you get any sleep?" He sat down next to me on my bed and rubbed my back.

"Maybe an hour or two."

"Would you like to get some sleep now? What do you want to do?"

"Honestly, I just want to get my mind off things. So whatever you got planned for today, let's do it." I smiled and yawned widely.

My dad chuckled, "All right, sounds good – but it looks like you need coffee. Or an energy drink. Or both."

We walked out of my tent, and I was immediately

blinded by the shining Egyptian sun. Squinting, I raised my hands to block the light from my eyes as we walked around Cheops. Many workers were already up and at it. The sound of shovels and hammers clanking limestone echoed through the tents, and people hurried around with reed baskets full of sand. I figured that they filled the reed baskets with sand to transport it away from wherever they were digging.

It didn't take us long to reach the Mess Hall. I stepped in line, and there were biscuits, poached eggs, baked beans, oatmeal, and some Egyptian food items that seemed questionable. At the end of the line was some toast with strawberry and grape jam. I snatched up four pieces and also grabbed some strawberries, grapes, and freshly picked plums. At the very end of the line were water bottles in a cooler; I stuck my hand into the freezing ice.

"That's not pleasant first thing in the morning," I growled to myself, shaking the water off my hands.

I followed my father to the second table, where R.J. and Carter were already eating. I yawned as I sat down.

R.J. waved at me, full of energy. "Good morning, Ms. Davis!"

"Good morning," I replied, taken back. Had he had a Monster or a Red Bull or something?

"Good morning, Magi," Carter said with a smile.

"Wow! You guys are super energetic in the mornings," I said.

R.J. shoved some eggs into his mouth. "Well, there is no reason not to be."

"Except when you're tired? That seems like a reasonable time not to be energetic," I joked.

"Even then, you should try to live life to fullest," R.J. said.

"It's the best way to live," Carter added.

I nodded. *Well, if archaeology doesn't work out, R.J., you can be a motivational speaker. You already have one follower.*

"Speaking of living life, you guys ready for an exciting day in the Sahara?" R.J. asked, rubbing his hands to together as if he were pumping himself up to run a marathon.

"Define 'exciting,'" I said. The way R.J. was acting made me question if this was really going to be a fun day.

"We are going to be digging right in front of the Great Pyramid of Khufu today," my father announced. "The team has recently discovered more homes and burial chambers of Egyptian workers."

"Yay, dead people," I said.

"Are you always this sarcastic?" Carter questioned me.

"Worse." I smiled. Carter shook his head, but seemed humored.

"Oh, and hey – I know one of the pyramid tour guides and mentioned that we had a newbie in town that has never seen the inside of Khufu before." R.J. pointed to me. "He offered to give us a tour, if you all are down."

To be honest, I was kind of interested in what was inside those incredible structures.

"I would like to see it again." Carter smiled.

"Always love going in there," my father spoke up. "What do you think, Mags?"

"Sure, why not?"

"Perfect." My father beamed.

"We will meet at Khufu at six o'clock, then." R.J. showed off his contagious smile.

"Well, sounds like we will be tourists tonight. Oh, and you two." My father pointed to Carter and me. "Before we go tonight, pack a bag for tomorrow. We got a call that our team at the Valley of the Kings have discovered a possible tomb, so we're driving there first thing in the morning."

"A tomb?! No way! That is so cool!" Carter's smile was so big I thought it was going to wrap around his head.

A possible tomb? Okay, that was pretty intriguing.

"Exciting, right?" My dad was all smiles. "How about you guys go pack, and we will meet you at our first dig site."

"Okay, sounds good." Carter jumped out of his seat. I giggled, watching Carter practically skip from excitement as we headed back to our tents to gather our things for the next morning.

MEN WITH SHOVELS SURROUNDED ME. Everywhere I looked,

someone was either digging, dumping, or moving sand. What sand the men weren't moving got tossed about by the wind, the breeze blowing it every direction possible. It was very overwhelming. It was also not uncommon to blow your nose and get a tissue full of snotty sand.

I plopped down on a boulder. The Sahara sun was making me exhausted. My limbs usually felt this tired after a full day of school and a shift at the Purple Dove, but I'd only been out here for two hours. I swore I was already getting a sunburn – and new freckles – even though my dad had helped me apply nearly a whole bottle of sunscreen to any exposed skin.

It was actually fascinating to watch the workers do their jobs. Everyone had something specific to do. Some men with tiny brushes examine faded hieroglyphs on boulders. Others studied the remains of old structures and measured their dimensions, while others collected dirt samples to be studied and dated. I felt like I was in the middle of an Indiana Jones movie.

"Ahh!" I screamed, as I was pushed off the boulder I was sitting on. I fell a good five feet until I crashed into the sand, face-planting. People began to gather around to make sure I was okay.

"Sand," I growled, gritting my teeth as I spit it out of my mouth.

"Mags, are you okay?" My father rushed over to make sure I wasn't hurt.

"Fantastic," I groused. I climbed up, ignoring my

father's help, and dusted myself off. I looked up to see that two workers with huge reed baskets had accidentally pushed me off the boulder. They apologized over and over.

My father waved at them, saying it was all right. Then, went back to his work. He stepped through an entrance that led inside a small stone chamber, which I'd landed directly in front of. I followed in behind him. My father and R.J. were trying to translate the faded hieroglyphics on the walls. Carter was holding a translation book, doing his best to decipher them as I continued to dust off the sand.

"Hey, Magi, check this out." Carter motioned for me to come over to him.

"I do believe this says that crocodiles were gifts given to the Egyptians by the gods as rewards," he said, seeming proud of his translation.

I examined the hieroglyph myself, confused. I was looking at two Egyptian men with spears in their hands, pointing them at three huge crocodiles with giant open mouths that were chasing after them.

"I am pretty darn sure that crocodiles were *not* gifts. Let me see that." I motioned for Carter to hand me the translation book. I navigated through the book, looking from the pages to the crocodiles on the wall, searching for clues to help me truly translate what was painted in front of me. A rush of excitement stirred in my stomach. I felt like I was solving a jigsaw puzzle, and those were an obsession of mine.

"Here," I pointed to a few symbols in the book, feeling

confident about my research."It says, 'If thou do not obey, Ra will cast out the creatures of the Nile.'"

"You did that in like, ten seconds." Carter stared at me like I had just done a back flip.

"Really?" I said, just as stunned and very impressed with myself.

My father and R.J. turned around at the sound of my declaration. My father scooted over to me and took hold of the translation book. He examined the hieroglyphs on the wall and in the book. "That's actually correct, Magi," he said.

"How did you do that? You barely looked at the translation book." Carter gazed at me, dumbfounded.

I just shrugged. I was kind of taken back, myself, about how easy it was for me to read.

My father gave me an impressed look. He only gave me that look when I came home with straight A's on my report card, or when I mastered a new magic trick. I didn't really understand why it was such a big deal to him, but I loved making him smile like that.

Carter took the translation book back and tried to figure out what he had done wrong. All I did was grin.

"ALL RIGHT, EVERYBODY LOAD UP," my father said.

R.J. grinned, and Carter and I looked at each other, deflated. We had spent the entire day walking around in the wretched sand and had just finished an early dinner after dumping an entire litter box out of our shoes.

"Umm ... I was thinking maybe a bubble bath and some light reading," I joked.

"You don't read." My father eyeballed me funny.

"That's why I said *light* ..."

My dad shook his head, smiling. He led our group around the corner to the camp's transportation center, which everyone had nicknamed the "DMV." There were horses, camels, Jeeps, and other SUVs to choose from. I was voting for some sort of a vehicle, because I didn't feel like climbing on an animal's back.

Yes. We were getting in a Jeep. *I really like this whole no roof, doors thing.*

R.J. got in the driver's seat and started the car. "Whoo! Here we go!"

Carter leaned over to me. "I'd hang on if I were you," he warned.

"What?"

The jeep went from five to crazy fast in the matter of seconds, and it felt like we were flying. The air pressed me against my seat and stole the breath out of my lungs. Even though I was stuck in a foreign country, hiding from a psychopath, this moment felt amazing. The cool wind flowed through my messy, curly hair, and it made me feel like I was at a spa.

Then, R.J. turned on the radio and blasted rock music. I grinned. *It can't get better than this.*

I noticed my father nodding his head to the music. I was surprised to see Mr. Safety so calm. R.J.'s haphazard driving over the wavy dunes was overkill—but it didn't even make Dad flinch. He looked free.

Maybe this can *get even better.*

I unbuckled my seatbelt and stood up in the roofless Jeep.

"What are you doing?" Carter scrambled to grab hold of my legs to make sure I wouldn't fall.

"Just try it!" I reached down to help him up.

After a slight hesitation, Carter unbuckled, grabbed my hand, and stood up. I smiled as I raised my hands up in the air—and, to my surprise – Carter followed my lead. We took turns screaming and yelling into the wind. We looked at each other and started laughing.

Carter and I jammed out to the music as our hair tangled in the wind. He had no idea what the lead singer was saying, clearly, as evidenced by the fact he was yelling gibberish to the beat, causing the both of us to hunch over with even more laughter.

I put my hand out in the cool breeze, and it felt very clean on my skin. *Maybe I could do wind baths instead of cold claustrophobic showers... no one would know.*

As I looked away from our jam session, I almost gasped. The sun was beginning to set behind the Great Pyramids. The rays of sunlight shined on the ancient boulders, making them sparkle like gold, accenting the orange

"What do you think this chamber was built for?" I picked Carter's brain as we climbed over the boulders.

"My theory is that this was the place where they brought their unwanted citizens to die." Carter began manically laughing like a cheesy movie villain and then managed to get tangled in an extension cord, crashing into – and breaking – a nearby light. The obnoxious sound echoed throughout the chamber. My father, R.J., and Nandi turned to the both of us.

"Carter!" R.J. scolded.

Carter pointed his finger at me. "It wasn't me!"

"What?" I yelled defensively.

"I'm just kidding." Carter joked as he untangled himself. "I'm so sorry."

"Clearly, it wasn't you." R.J. shook his head, laughing. He turned to Nandi. "Don't worry, we will replace the light."

While everyone left and headed back up the Descending Passage, I wandered back into the Subterranean Chamber. *I actually really like this place ...*

MEOW.

I whipped around. *OH MY GOD...* Ten feet in front of me, sitting next to the bottomless pit railing, was a little black cat. It stared at me sternly, not moving a muscle.

There is no way... it's the same cat! Sitting before me was the same exact cat that sat on my balcony in Seattle! The same cat that had saved my life! It had the same look in its eyes that it always did, and the same scar down its eye.

"Magi? The tour is over. Let's go!" Carter yelled as he tried to find me.

The little black cat's eyes began to glow a hypnotizing bright yellow, shining like light bulbs. The dimly light chamber illuminated yellow, and I had to squint my eyes. My breath caught in my throat, and my heartbeat thumped in my ears—I couldn't look away. *I'm no animal expert, but this isn't normal!*

"Magi, where are you?"

The cat's eyes ceased glowing and returned to their normal color.

"Magi? Magi?!" Carter's voice grew louder as he searched harder for me.

As I turned away to see where Carter was, a bright flash of light filled the room. I looked back to where the cat was sitting—but it was gone. In its place was a piece of paper. I inched towards it, and carefully picked it up. The note was old – very old. It was super flimsy – half of it was missing, and most of the color was faded. It was vintage notebook paper with pale pink roses around the edges – the same notebook paper my mom used.

I carefully unfolded it, and sure enough, it was my mom's handwriting.

Dear R.J.,

Today is a big day, and I am rooting for you, darling. I'm sure you will pass the test with a perfect score. Let's see if you can beat my record! I will meet you in Giza, and then we can go to that restaurant we like with the colorful lanterns. I love you so much, and the day where we can be together forever is coming soon. There is so much love in the air right now. I can't believe Steven is about to—

The note stopped there. I turned it over several times, desperate to read the rest, but the other half had been ripped off. I stood rooted to the spot, utterly flabbergasted.

"Hey, Mags!" Carter jogged into the chamber. I quickly shoved the note in my jeans pocket. "The tour's over. Let's go."

As soon as we arrived back at camp, I jumped out of the jeep. My mind was swarming with questions... Did my mom and R.J. used to date? Was the 'Steven' in the note referring to my father Steven? If so, what was he about to do? And how did the note even get here?

I desperately wanted to know how a cat from Seattle had gotten inside one of the Seven Wonders of the World on the other side of the planet—and why it had a note from my mom that was addressed to R.J. of all people. And, of course, why it vanished into thin air and had glowing eyes.

I dashed into my tent. I opened up my computer and began a video call with my mom. The ringing seemed to go on forever until she finally answered.

"Hi, darling! How are you doing?" She was sitting at a

desk in a hotel room that had brilliant view of Big Ben, and she was holding a cup of tea.

"I'm doing alright." I sat crisscrossed on my bed. "Hey, before we start saying anything else, um, I want to apologize for being so mean to you when you left. I shouldn't have been like that. Your note was really sweet." I picked at my nail after showing her the note.

"And I apologize, too, for leaving," she said. "I really shouldn't have. Sometimes... sometimes I hate my job." She looked out her window.

"Is it at least going well? The case, I mean?" I tried not to act liked I hated it, too.

"Slow, but good so far. We are making progress, but I really don't want to bore you with the details. Please tell me about your day."

"Um, well, we woke up, had breakfast, translated some really old hieroglyphs, and explored the great Pyramid with a friend."

"Oh, who is that?"

"This kid named Carter?"

"Carter! Was R.J. there?" She sat up straighter in her chair.

"Um, yeah. How did you know?" I fumbled with the note in my pocket.

"Oh, I've known R.J. for years. Longtime family friend. And he's Carter's guardian."

"Right..." I wasn't sure if it was the best strategy, but I

went for it anyway. "Hey, uh, random question: did you and R.J. ever date?"

My mom choked a little on her tea. She cleaned up the tea that had spilled onto her robe, and finally responded, "Yes, we did, but it was *way* before I knew your father. Why are asking me this?" she asked.

"R.J. told me. So I was just curious."

"What?" Mom blurted out. "What, exactly, did he tell you?" She calmed down a bit.

"Um, the same thing has you, pretty much," I said as casually as I could. *That was weird.*

My mom shifted uncomfortably in her chair as she laughed. "Oh, good. Good."

There was an awkward pause between us, and then I finally said, "Well, I'm going to get ready for bed. Talk to you later?"

"Yeah, sounds good." My mom smiled.

"Great. All right—goodnight." I hovered the cursor over the *end call* button.

"Goodnight, darling."

CHAPTER 6

I couldn't sleep. No matter what I did, or what position I laid in, it didn't help. All I could think about was that note, what my mom had said, and that little black cat.

I gazed over at my clock on the nightstand. 12:37 A.M.?! That's it? I wanted answers! *I'm finding that cat!*

I yanked off my covers and sprung out of my bed. I dressed rapidly and swiped my silver flashlight. As quietly as I could, I stuck my head out of the tent flap to see if the coast was clear. A couple campfires were still burning and a few tent lights were on, but I crept out of my tent and discreetly closed it back up, trying not to wake my father in the process. I silently tiptoed through the sea of green tents.

Wait. I stopped. *Do I really want to go inside the Great Pyramid by myself...at night?*

I tapped my finger against my leg repeatedly, almost

paralyzed at the thought. *But have to go! I have to get answers. This is not a time to be scared. Now, who would be stupid enough to join me?*

After a couple of minutes of sneaking through camp, I finally made it to Carter's tent. I stealthily unlatched the tent flap and stepped inside.

Oh, god. Carter was sprawled on his cot, snoring. Except for the sheets bunched at his feet, all of his covers had slid off his body – exposing his sinewy, gangly limbs. He was only wearing underwear. *Ewww!*

"Carter," I whispered, "Carter?"

He twitched a little.

"Carter," I whispered a little louder. "Carter!"

"All right. Dream's over, buddy." I raised my flashlight and shined the light in his face.

"Caaarrrtttteeeerrrr," I whispered again, a bit more sweetly.

"Wha!? What?! What?!" Twig-like arms and legs went flying as he flailed around, trying to hit his assailant. I sprang onto him and covered his mouth. I moved the flash-light out of his eyes, so he could see that it was only me. I watched as the fear on his face turned to confusion, and then to disbelief. He slapped my hand away from his mouth.

"Magi?!"

"Shh!" I gave him a sharp look, willing him to keep his voice down.

"What are you doing here?" Carter changed his voice to a harsh whisper.

"Get up. I need your help."

"Get up?"

"Yes, get up."

"Well, I would, but it seems you're ... sitting on me ... in my ... bed ..." A deep flush burned on his face.

I looked down and realized that I was straddling him. *AHHHHH! No! God, no!* "I need your help." I rolled off his bed, onto the floor, changing the subject as quickly as I could.

"With what?" Carter covered himself with his sheets, his voice cracking.

"I'm looking for something."

"Looking for what?"

"That's not important. Let's go!"

"Where are we going?"

I paused before answering. "The Great Pyramid."

"Magi, are you crazy? We can't go in there!" Carter gestured towards the monument.

"Yes, we can. If we sneak in—"

"No! We can't. If someone caught us, we would get in so much trouble."

"Ah! I have an idea...how 'bout we sneak in there and we don't get caught. And then, if we don't get caught, we don't get in trouble? Okay, problem solved." I showed off a big smile.

"Problem not solved." Carter frowned. "There is a camp rule that no one is allowed to leave their tent at night. It's not safe. I'm *not* going."

"Why not?" I crossed my arms.

"I'm not about to walk into trouble."

"What about living life to the fullest? *It's the best way to live.*"

Catching the reference, Carter rolled his eyes. "Not going." He gathered his blankets up off the floor, laid them over himself, crossed his arms, and settled into his pillow. I glared at him.

"Yeah, you are."

I glided over to the opposite side of Carter's bed. With some strength, I lifted the bed up and Carter fell to the floor, buried under all of his pillows and covers. After he ripped the blankets off himself, he gawked at me.

I smiled innocently and batted my eyes. "Well, now that you're up, get dressed and follow me. We're going on an adventure." I smiled determinedly and ducked out of his tent.

CARTER WAS TAKING FOREVER. *All right, Carter. It's not like you have to apply mascara.*

"Couldn't stop looking in the mirror, huh?" I sassed as he finally walked out.

Carter scowled at me. "I couldn't find my glasses."

I tugged on his wrist.

"Wait!" he hissed as he yanked his hand away. "*Why* are we going? At least tell me that."

I hesitated. "Well, when we took the tour earlier today, I saw something."

"What did you see?" He crossed his arms and waited for me to continue.

I hesitated some more. *Ughh he's going to think I'm crazy.* He started to huff back towards his tent.

"Okay, fine!"

He stopped, raising his eyebrows.

I sighed. "Earlier, I saw a *cat*."

"A cat?" Carter said. "You got me up for a *cat*?" His jaw dropped then clinched in frustration.

"It's not just a cat, Carter!" I waved my arms passionately.

Carter settled down. "I'm listening."

"Okay, I know this is going to sound nuts. But go with me for a second. I have been seeing this same cat for as long as I can remember. Sitting on my balcony, in windows around my house, on my car, or around my neighborhood in *Seattle*. It sits perfectly still with these bright yellow eyes that stare into your soul like a human and has this deep scar over one of its eyes. And earlier, I saw it in the great pyramid. The same cat, with the same scar." I sighed. Here went nothing. "I haven't told you this, but I was almost murdered a few days ago."

"Oh my god," Carter breathed. "Are you okay?"

I shrugged. "Anyway, this cat attacked my assailant, allowing to get me away. I don't know if I would be here now if it weren't for that little black cat. But seeing it in the pyramid wasn't even the weirdest part."

"Go on."

"I don't know how to explain it, but its eyes started glowing—"

"Glowing?"

"Yes, and then it just disappeared. But it left this." I pulled out the old notebook paper and unfolded it. "It's a note, from my mom to *R.J.*"

Carter shook his head.

"Read it. I think they dated."

When he finished reading, he let out a flabbergasted sigh. "I don't know anything about this. Are you sure this is your mom?"

"One hundred percent." I pulled out the note that she had given me only a few days ago. "Same paper. Same handwriting. Just a lot newer. And she always refers to the people that she loves as darling," I explained to Carter.

"I also called her tonight and asked if they dated, and she said yes – but she also said it was way before she knew my father. But that's just the thing. She mentions my father, 'Steven,' in the note." I pointed to my father's name.

"That could be any Steven," Carter said.

"Sure it could, but I'm telling you, she is hiding something."

"Maybe finding the rest of the note will give us all the answers."

"Exactly."

"I can't believe I'm saying this…" A grin of determination cracked on Carter's face. "Then let's find it."

"Really?"

"Yeah, let's go find your little savior and the rest of that note."

"You've never been cooler than in this moment."

CARTER and I weaved in and out of the sea of tents, making it all the way to the giant stone paws of the ancient Sphinx. We crouched down to remain hidden as guards in white and khaki uniforms patrolled the bases of the pyramids.

"Well, this could be tricky." Carter narrowed his eyes.

We trotted behind a small trailer. Through the windows, we could see two guards sitting in front of security monitors, talking about politics and how great their lunch was, completely oblivious to what was appearing on the screens. Carter and I nodded at each other. This was our chance.

We made a break for it. We sprinted as fast as we could through the thick sand, almost making it to the base of Khufu, when—

"Stop right there!"

We stumbled to a halt. Slowly, we turned around to

face a slightly overweight patrol guard, blinding us with his flashlight.

"Carter?" he said, confused.

"Hey, Ziggy." Carter shrugged innocently.

"What are you doing out and about? You, of all people, know the rules. No one is allowed to wander Cheops at night."

"I know, I know. I'm sorry... it's just...I—"

"I dropped my wallet," I blurted out. Carter narrowed his eyes. Ziggy titled his head.

"Yeah, we toured the pyramid earlier today, and that's when I lost it." I slouched my back, whining, and attempted to channel any Oscar-winning actor.

"She's really clumsy." Carter played along.

"Hmmhmm." I smiled as innocently as I could.

"Guys, I want to help you, but I can't let you inside until morning." Ziggy shook his head.

"Oh, come on, Ziggy." I pleaded with him.

"Magi can't help the fact that she's clumsy. Plus, we don't want her dad getting involved." Carter added.

"Yeah, my dad can be pretty scary when he's upset, and I don't want to let him down. He's already stressed out enough running this whole expedition."

"Wait, what's your name?" Ziggy asked, pointing at me.

"Magi. Magi *Davis*."

"Davis!" Ziggy exclaimed. "You're Magi..." He began to break out in a sweat as he stared at me. "Yeah, I'm sure he can get scary, and we don't want to make the boss mad, now do we?" He stepped out of our way. "Make it quick. Find your wallet M-Ms. Davis."

"Thank you." I smiled. Ziggy practically bowed down to me as I walked by. Carter and I awkwardly scooted along.

"That was really weird," I whispered to Carter.

"That *was* really weird. Normally he's cool." He shook his head.

"WE ARE ALMOST at the Subterranean Chamber." Carter finally broke the silence as I led the way down the Descending Passage. "Are you sure the cat was in here?"

"Yeah, I saw it by the huge hole in the ground," I said as I hurried into the familiar, ancient room. I dashed over to the back wall where the cat had stood earlier, but it was nowhere to be found. "It was right here."

I let out a sigh and researched the entire chamber. No cat, no note. Nothing.

"Magi, there's nothing here. Let's go." Carter walked up beside to me.

Dang it! He was right. I shook my head, discouraged.

"Hey, we tried," Carter said, taking pity on me.

I huffed and followed Carter to the exit.

MEOW.

Carter and I gasped. We snapped our heads around.

There, sitting in another passageway inside the chamber, was the little black cat! I fixed my flashlight on it.

"Do you see that?" I asked Carter, continuously slapping his shoulder to make sure he was paying attention.

Carter's eyes were wider than an owl's. The black cat didn't move a muscle. It stalked me with its eyes, like it usually did. But its ears titled back, like it was high-strung about being seen. In a split second, it darted up the passageway.

"Carter! Come on!" I yelled.

We charged after the feline. It bolted through the passages like a bullet, but Carter and I were right on its tail. We chased it into a large, rectangular chamber—way more impressive than any of the others we had seen before. The stone ceilings were very high, and on each side of the room stood five square columns that stretched the width of the chamber.

"Where'd it go?" The cat was gone, but there was nothing on the floor for it to hide behind. The only objects there were large wooden crates in the corners, like someone from the expedition was moving artifacts in a museum. I heard Carter mumble to himself.

"What did you say?" I asked.

"I have been inside this pyramid countless times, and I have never seen this chamber before." Carter's eyes were huge as he inspected the room, still gasping for air.

I marched over to a wooden crate and looked inside. The crate contained pristine Egyptian swords and spears –

almost like they had never been touched before. The weird thing about them was that they weren't covered in dust or cobwebs. They were as clean and shiny as can be.

"Whoa," Carter said as he saw the weapons, and instantaneously became occupied with them. I shifted my focus back to finding the cat. I noticed two burning torches hanging on either side of the entrance of the chamber—they looked freshly lit.

"That's weird..." I whispered.

I turned back around and glanced at the back wall of the chamber. The hieroglyphics on the wall appeared to be beautifully preserved, as if they had been carved and painted yesterday. Nowhere else in the pyramid had walls that even compared to this one—it was a vibrant masterpiece.

There were ten Egyptian warriors chiseled into the stone. All of them gripped weapons in their hands, and appeared to be running into battle. My eyes were drawn to one of the warriors, in particular – and the hieroglyphics next to him. As I studied it, I felt frozen, like in a trance.

My brain began to somehow translate the hieroglyphic, in the same way that I can catch glimpses and phrases of what is being said when I stop on the Spanish channel on TV. When I realized what it said, the memory of my dream with the Master came to the front of my mind.

The hieroglyphics translated into the exact same words the Master had spoken to me in my dream: "Now, you die."

"Carter, we have to go." I backed away from the wall, trembling, trying to shake myself out of the trance I was in. Something about what I had just seen sent my body into panic mode. We were in danger. "Carter, we have to go!" I raised my voice.

"Hold on." He waved his hand, shooing me away, still wanting to study the weapons.

As I stepped back, one of the stones underneath my foot began to give way. A sudden crash shook the ground, and one of the torches blew out. Carter and I ran towards the entrance, but there was one problem: our way out was blocked by a massive boulder. I had stepped on a pressure point, releasing the giant rock from the ceiling. There was no escape.

"Help!" we screamed, pounding against the boulder.

"It's no use. We're too deep inside. No one will hear us!" Carter said, helplessly.

"This is all my fault." I had convinced Carter to help me, and now I'd gotten us trapped. *Where had that boulder come from?*

A bloodcurdling screeching sound reverberated through the chamber, jarring my nerves. Carter and I exchanged horrified looks as we turned around to see that the back wall was moving. The ten Egyptian warrior hieroglyph paintings were gradually coming out of the wall, like objects in a 3D movie. All of a sudden, the warriors collapsed into ten piles of tiny, crumbled pieces of stone on the ground—and then the piles began to move.

I've seen this before...

The piles of stone swirled into the air, and compacted together. Then, everything stopped. There was dead silence. All you could hear was our petrified breathing.

My dream! I've seen this in my dream! Standing before us were the same stone warriors I had seen in my dream with the Master. They were stomping their legs and swinging their arms. They readied their stone swords, khopeshes, and their bows and arrows. The weapons flashed like light bulbs and changed into very real – and very deadly – weapons.

The hieroglyphs had come alive!

One warrior, who stood in the middle of the group, raised his arrow and aimed it at my head. He grinned like a devil and said, "Now, you die!"

He released the arrow.

"NOOO!" I panicked, closing my eyes and raising my hands in front of my face in hopes of somehow defending myself. After a few seconds passed, I opened my eyes. *Why am I not in pain?*

The arrow was directly in front of me— floating towards my face in slow motion. Without thinking, I commanded the arrow to veer left with the wave of my hand. It shot into the wall with great speed—completely avoiding me.

"I just did that." My eyes widened. "HOW DID I JUST DO THAT?"

Carter stood there with his mouth hanging open, and

even the stone warriors shifted uncomfortably. Another warrior shot an arrow at Carter. "No, no, no!" I barreled into Carter, shoving him out of the line of fire. We both fell to our knees, recovered, and then scrambled back to our feet before sprinting towards the pillars. The warriors positioned themselves—arrows flew everywhere. Carter and I took cover, pressing our backs against two square pillars. I screamed in terror as an arrow flew within inches of my face.

"What do we do?" I cried.

"Something! Anything!" Carter yelled, holding his head, hopelessly protecting himself.

Out of the corner of my eye, I caught sight of the wooden crate of weapons—I made eye contact with Carter and pointed. "Carter! The weapons!"

He rapidly glanced at the crate, and back to me. He got the message. I looked past my shoulder to see that the warriors were advancing towards us.

"Carter, now!" I yelled.

He dove and rolled, crashing against the crate. Three of the warriors were charging in between the pillars!

"Magi!" Carter yelled as he threw me a sword.

I caught it. My arms sank towards the ground with the unexpected weight of it. I whirled my sword in front me, even though my muscles were shaking worse than an earthquake.

One of the warriors thrust his sword at me.

"NO!" Again, somehow, I controlled the speed of the

sword coming towards me with my mind. Everything and everyone around me moved in slow motion, except for me —I was moving full speed. Like I was standing in the middle of a Matrix movie.

Using my sword, I knocked his weapon out of his hand. I screamed as I used every muscle in my body to slice at the warrior's head, which fell to the ground with thump.

Somehow, I released my control – and everything went back to normal speed. Bile rushed into my mouth as I watched the warrior's head roll around near my toes. The rest of his body collapsed into tiny, cracked pieces of stone —I nearly fainted at the sight.

I retreated back to Carter. In his sweaty, nervous hands was a shiny, silver sword. He gazed at me in awe while my body shook like crazy.

The two more warriors pursued us. With my mind, I attempted to delay the faster one, and just barely prevented him from reaching us. I lunged forward and drove my sword into his stomach—and he fell to the ground in pieces. The third warrior swung at my feet, but I jumped and launched myself into the air towards the wall next to me. Instincts kicked in, and I managed to push my legs off, back-flipping directly over the warrior. Before the warrior could figure out where I was, I stabbed him in the back. The warrior fell to pieces, and I released my control. Everything went back to utter chaos.

"How did you just do that?" Carter yelled, backing away from me.

"I don't know!" I panicked, feeling dizzy and disoriented after the flip.

"Magi! Behind you!" Carter pointed.

I dropped to my knees. A warrior swung his sword at my head from behind. I dove and rolled away from him into the middle of the chamber, slamming my back on the rough ground in the process.

I was surrounded. Sweat popped out on my forehead, gluing strands of hair to my face. I tried to wipe the droplets out of my eyes, but the next warrior charged. I ducked as the fourth warrior swung his heavy sword. Missing me, his weapon clanked into the stone, and the sound made my body jolt. *It's not working.* I tried to slow him down, but it didn't work – I was too panicked. Then, he kicked me in my chest, and I crashed to the ground. Before he could stab me in the back, I twisted around and stabbed him in the stomach. He crumpled on impact.

The fifth warrior shot arrows at me like a machine gun. I dropped my sword in panic and raised my hands defensively. My instincts kicked in again, and I decelerated all the arrows. I struggled to keep them from shooting me, because my head hurt from intense throbbing, a side effect, I guessed, from focusing with such great concentration. I forced all of them to turn around one-hundred and eighty degrees.

Suddenly, I felt this strange – yet exciting – sensation stirring in the pit of my stomach. It felt better than ten shots of espresso. An enormous amount of energy was building inside me. The energy surged into my hands, making them scalding hot. I focused it on the arrows, and aimed them at the warrior. It became too intense for me to hold it in. The energy shot out of my hands, and the arrows pierced him in the chest. He crumpled to a pile of stone.

I looked down at my hands and screamed louder than I ever have, straining my throat. They were glowing a beautiful, misty gold.

"What is happening to me?!" I screamed.

Carter cursed loudly. He stared at me like I was an alien while I screamed at my glowing hands. Warrior Six rushed at me, waving his blade in figure eights. As fast as lightning, I picked up my sword and managed to block a couple of cuts before he slashed me across the face. I felt blood drip down my cheek.

"Ahh!" I cried, hunching over. *God, that stings!*

Not wanting to get cut open again, I felt the same sensation that had caused my hands to glow. But this time, it was more powerful. The golden energy shot out of my hand, causing me to stumble as it smashed directly into the warrior's chest. He flew backwards, crashing into the seventh warrior. They flew into a pillar, and were crushed to pieces.

I made a weak effort to control my breathing as I surveyed the chamber. I didn't see any more warriors, but I could hear them.

"Carter!" I screamed.

In the back corner were the last two stone warriors – along with their leader. Warriors eight and nine were pinning Carter against the wall by his throat! The warrior leader prepared to stab him in the heart. Carter's feet were dangling, and he was gasping for air.

MAGI, DO SOMETHING!

I harnessed my energy, feeling my mind go thick and slow, and the last warriors' movements slowed as well. This was my chance. I yanked Warrior Eight and Warrior Nine away from Carter with my mind, slamming them against the wall. They crumbled instantly, and I sprinted to the warrior leader. With all of my strength, I pried his sword out of his hand and sliced clean through the warrior's neck. The only reason I didn't cut off Carter's head in the process was because the corner of the wall stopped the blade. The leader fell as I released my grip on it all – time, space, motion – and tripped over the pile of stone, causing me to fall into Carter.

Our faces were inches apart, and the only thing separating us was the sword at our necks. We held unbreakable eye contact. For a second, everything melted away... I heard waves crashing and seagulls crying when I looked into Carter's ocean eyes. They were so beautiful.

Magi, stop it! I yanked the sword out of the wall abruptly, and Carter hunched down, coughing.

"Are you okay?" I bent down over Carter. Carter nodded his head, though he was wheezing uncontrollably.

I dropped my sword out of shock. Carter and I

panicked as the piles of stone began to stir again—the warriors were trying to resurrect! *NO, NO, NO!*

Using the energy inside of me, I lifted all the piles of stone into the air with my mind. I pulled all the pieces together to the center of the room, and forced them to compact together. I formed them into what looked like a giant floating ball of stone. More power surged out of me, and I smashed the stone into the boulder that blocked the exit – the boulder collapsed.

I felt very light-headed after releasing that much energy, and I was seeing stars as I stumbled over into Carter. He helped me up as I said, "Let's go!"

Carter nodded, and we sprinted as fast as we could out of the chamber. We ran for our lives down the long passages in the pyramid. We booked it out of the entrance and down the boulders.

"Hey, did you find your wallet?" Ziggy yelled out at us from the security trailer.

"Yeah, yeah we found it!" Carter yelled back as we continued to sprint towards camp.

Once inside the campgrounds, we scampered into Carter's tent. I bent over, trying to get air into my lungs. My heart was racing, and my brain was going a hundred miles per hour. Carter was pacing back and forth, trying to calm himself down.

"Did that really just happen?" He clasped his hands behind his head.

"Insane..." I whispered to myself.

"This isn't possible."

"I'm going insane."

"Magi."

"Or – I'm dreaming."

"Magi."

"Am I in your dream or are you in mine?"

"Magi."

"WHAT JUST HAPP—"

Carter clasped his hands over my mouth, knocking me into his bed as he tried to prevent me from waking the entire camp. My breathing became intense. I clenched my fists. Carter loosened his grip as a terrified look washed over his face, causing him to turn pale. I saw the reflection of my eyes in his—my eyes were glowing.

I slapped his hands away from my mouth and ran over to his mirror. My brown eyes were glowing a vivid gold.

I exhaled sharply and rubbed my eyes to try to get them to stop. My legs gave out, and I fell to the ground. Carter assisted me up onto his bed and tried to calm me down as tears escaped my eyes. He nudged me to look up at him.

"Magi, you aren't going insane. I saw everything you saw. How did those things come out of that wall?"

"I don't know," I whispered, thinking about how I had seen them in my dream with the Master. "It's not humanly possible. It makes no sense!"

"Shh! Keep your voice down!" Carter whispered. He

placed his hand on my shoulder. The touch was comforting. "How did you do all that?"

"I think we both know I don't have the answer to that question."

"And, you smashed that boulder. You cut their heads off...your hands...your *eyes*..."

"Carter ... I ..." But it was no use; I couldn't answer. I had never been so scared and confused in my life. A long pause stretched out between us.

"Let's just go to bed and try to forget whatever just happened." I tried my best to speak with a sore throat.

Carter nodded. When his eyes left mine, I stood up to exit, my entire body shaking with every step. I couldn't do it.

"Can I stay here?" I asked, tears running down my face.

"Yeah, yeah. Of course. Please. Uh, here, take my bed." Carter began to fix his blankets.

"No, no – it's fine." I sniffled.

Before I could refuse, Carter was helping me into bed. He made sure I was comfortable before making a spot on the ground for himself with a pillow and blanket. He reached over to his lamp.

"Can I?" He asked in mousy voice.

"Please." I exhaled.

Carter quickly lit the lamp, and the flame illuminated the tent. We both didn't know what to say as we stared at the tarp overhead. My mind was still reeling.

Why were my hands glowing? How did those stone

things come to life? How did I know how to use a sword? How did I kill all of them? How did I do any of that?

"Goodnight." Carter whispered.

"Goodnight."

Am I really safe anywhere?

CHAPTER 7

I woke up lying flat on my back. I propped myself up on my elbows and saw that I was in a completely enclosed room – there were no windows or doors on the white stone walls covered in hieroglyphs. Two burning torches hung beside the only object in the room: a golden-framed mirror.

Slowly, I stood up and approached the mirror. Upon gazing at my reflection, I discovered I was wearing a beautiful, flowy light gray, black, and white two-piece dress. I looked like I was about to perform a contemporary dance.

I touched the surface of the mirror and gasped. The surface rippled like a pond. I touched it again; the ripples grew larger. The mirror itself wasn't glass or water. It felt like cool smoke between my fingertips. Near my fingers, swirls of color began to appear. Before I knew it, the whole mirror formed a picture—a moving picture.

The mirror displayed a room of white stone walls with

colorful hieroglyphs and beautiful rugs that covered the floor. Shimmering golden blankets and pillows spread across a small bed with a child's mobile dangling over it. A sun, a falcon, a cat, a dog, and a pair of wings dangled over the baby's bed.

Suddenly, a young man rushed into the room, carrying a wailing infant. In his other hand was a sword dripping with blood. The man was out of breath as he snuck behind the baby's crib, out of sight.

The man holding the baby looked like he was in his early twenties, and he was wearing a tight white button-up like he had just gone out to a fancy dinner – but it was ripped and slashed. Dad! *What was he doing holding a baby? And why does he look so young? Why does he look like he has been attacked?*

A few seconds later, a bronze-skinned woman in a long white dress dashed into the room and locked the door behind her. She turned to face my father, sweat dripping down her face.

Wow... The woman was stunning. I had never seen a woman that beautiful, ever. She was an eleven or an easy twelve. But her beauty isn't what grabbed my attention. Her eyes looked so similar to mine, they were almost identical.

Her pitch-black hair blew behind her as she hurried over to my father.

"Who is after her? Why would someone want to kill

our baby?" my father asked in a hushed tone as he tried to calm the baby down.

"I don't know! Everyone on the Council agreed to her birth, and all of my enemies have been banished. I don't have the slightest idea of who would want her dead!" the woman said frantically.

BOOM! Toys fell off the shelves, and the curtain rods clanked loudly.

"And to blatantly attack my palace! The nerve!" She clenched her fists. Then, the woman quieted her voice as she gazed up at my father with tears in her eyes. "She's not safe here."

"What do you mean?" My father's lips trembled.

"Steven, this world – my palace – is supposed to be the safest place for our daughter...and now look what's happened! She will die if we don't do something—we can't keep her here."

"We can fight back, right? You and I, together, can protect our child. We can fight this!"

"My love, I'm not about to let *you* stay here, where you could so easily be killed, when you are no match by blood. You have to leave!"

The woman waved her hand and, like magic, a passageway opened up in the middle of the nursery leading underground.

BOOM!

"Here, take this!" The woman lifted the necklace from her neck. I looked closer—it was the necklace my father had given to me when he'd first returned home! "This will protect her."

"A necklace? How is this supposed to protect her?"

"Give it to her when she is old enough." Tears streamed down the woman's cheeks.

My father placed his sword in his hostler and wiped the tears from her eyes nervously.

"Old enough...what are you saying?" My father caressed the woman's face as she tried to keep herself together.

"She is too vulnerable here. You know how to defend yourself. But–" she looked at the baby, her mouth twisting in anguish, "she doesn't."

"I'm saying that she has to leave this place until she is old enough to protect herself. And she *cannot* die. She's too important." With the back of her hand, the woman smoothed the baby's cheek. "You have to take her out of this world and keep her hidden in yours. Promise me that you will not tell her who she is, or what she can do. You can never mention me – not until she is ready to take her place."

"I—"

"Steven, promise me!"

"I promise," my father said, choking on his tears. "What about us?"

BOOM! Savage yells and battle cries echoed from the other side of the door.

"You need to leave now!" she yelled hysterically. Tears

flowed down my father's face as he pulled the woman close and kissed her passionately. My heart crumbled into pieces as I watched, feeling inexplicably betrayed. They looked down at their swaddled bundle, tears streaming, while the baby cried.

"I love you," my father barely managed.

"And I love you, too. But this is the only way to keep her safe."

"HELP!" Multiple voices cried out. They banged violently against the nursery door.

"My friends!" My father looked back and forth between the woman and door.

"Here! Give her to me, and let them in! They have to escape, too!"

Gently, he handed the baby over then sprinted to the door.

The woman rested her face close to the baby's as tears streamed down her cheeks. She looked into the child's eyes. "I'm so sorry, *Magi*."

All the blood drained from my face. I didn't want to believe what I was seeing.

The woman propped the child – *me* – on her chest. She pulled away the cloth covering the baby's back and set her hand on the newborn's left shoulder. The woman's hand began to glow gold. The baby cried, as if the glow were burning her back.

Out of nowhere, I felt an excruciating pain in my left

shoulder. I hunched over, screaming. The woman pulled her hand away, and the pain in my back subsided.

Appearing on the child's shoulder was a strange, solid black Egyptian symbol – one I did not recognize. The symbol was a weird looking "U" shape with an ankh in the middle, along with a straight line at the very bottom. The woman waved her hand in front of the symbol. As she did so, the symbol vanished.

BOOM!

The woman panicked. "Steven!" she cried.

My father returned with a man with curly blonde hair and blue eyes, holding hands with a beautiful strawberry blonde who was in early stages of pregnancy and... *R.J.?* R.J. gripped a sword in each hand as he stood close to the others.

"It's time for you all to go!" the woman ordered. She handed the baby back to my father then crouched down to the floor.

A little black cat with a scar down its eye was sitting before her, as if it were bowing to her.

"You have been given your orders, now. Do not fail," the woman said sternly but warmly to the cat.

"Your majesty, is this really a good idea, after all she has done?" the pregnant woman asked incredulously.

The black cat lowered its head in shame.

"If she fails, her father will take care of her... permanently," the dark-haired woman said, "But she is being given a second chance. Even the worst of us deserves a second chance."

The cat lifted its head, determined.

BOOM! Battle cries intensified in the hallway.

"Now, go!" the woman yelled.

The black cat darted into the passageway, followed by the blonde man and pregnant woman. As he held the baby, my father exchanged a long, heartbreaking glance with the stunning woman before R.J. pushed him along.

The woman sobbed uncontrollably as she waved her hand over the passageway, making it vanish. All of a sudden, the terrible pain returned to my shoulder. The woman cried and cried, while the pain progressed, like a million sharp needles stabbing at once – the pain and confusion was unbearable.

I JUMPED, waking up too fast. *Ow.* I felt light-headed as I sat up in Carter's bed. I looked down where he had been sleeping, but he was gone. *Where did he go?* As I was rubbing my eyes to wake myself up, I felt a terrible, aching pain in my shoulder. I massaged it through my shirt, groaning when I touched it. *That's really weird. My shoulder was hurting like crazy in my dream, and now in real life?*

The sun was rising, and I knew I had to get back to my tent before my father and R.J. found me in here. That was an awkward conversation I was not about to have.

I crawled out of his bed and hobbled over to his dresser. I patted my face to wake myself up. *Ow.* My right cheek stung. I studied the deep cut on my cheek in the mirror.

My heart pounded. I forced myself not to think about the events from last night – the lack of an explanation terrified me. I groaned as a sharp pain shot through my shoulder, and I turned to look at it in the mirror.

I gasped and stumbled backwards onto the ground. My body temperature was rising rapidly – just like it had on the plane. I clasped my mouth shut with my hand to prevent myself from screaming and waking up the whole camp. On the back of my left shoulder was the same Egyptian symbol that had been on the baby's back in my dream! I started hearing workers outside say 'good morning', and I knew I had to move. I popped my head out Carter's tent, making sure the coast was clear, then sprinted back to my tent.

Once inside, I threw off my shirt, frantically grabbed a damp washcloth, and scrubbed at the mark with wild desperation. It wouldn't budge. I yelped in pain as I scraped the symbol so hard my skin started bleeding.

"Hey, Mags?" my dad yelled from outside my tent.

I screamed and immediately covered my mouth. *What if he sees the symbol? What if he found out what happened in the pyramid? What do I do?*

My father started unzipping my tent. As fast as I could,

I dove into my bed and wildly covered myself in my blankets right as he walked in.

"Hey, what was that?" He looked at me, concerned.

"What was what?" I asked innocently.

"You just screamed."

AHH! I did just scream! "Oh yeah, I, uh, saw a spider."

"You should get used to that." My dad rolled his eyes. "It *is* the desert." He smiled. "Well, anyway, it's time to get up. We have a big day today!"

"Uh, Dad, I don't feel good," I said.

"What's wrong, Magi?" He sounded sympathetic.

"Umm, my throat hurts." I rubbed my neck. My father strolled over to my bed and sat down near my legs. He placed his hand on my head.

"You do feel a little warm." He narrowed his eyes. "Where did you get that cut?"

The cut! "Uh, oh, yeah, I fell into my nightstand as I was getting in bed last night." I acted tired.

"That's a pretty deep cut."

"Really? I hadn't even noticed." I continued my innocent act. *Please don't be mad that I am totally lying to you right now.*

He examined it some more. "Good job, Mags," he said sarcastically. "Well, I might have something in my tent that will help with your throat. Be right back."

"Thanks." I pretended to laugh, then acted like the laugh hurt. My dad narrowed his eyes in concern. *I can't believe he's buying this. Someone give me an Oscar.*

Once he left, I let out the biggest sigh then leapt up out of my bed. I raced over to my dresser to cover up my cut with makeup as best as I could. I stared at my reflection, grateful that the only thing he'd noticed was the cut. *That was too close.*

"Magi?" someone whispered. Carter barged into my room.

"Ah! Hey, I'm not dressed!" I covered my chest. I was only in a bra and jeans. Carter and I didn't make eye contact, and I am pretty sure his pale cheeks were pinker than mine.

"I'm sorry." He covered his eyes.

"Turn around," I ordered, so I could get a shirt on. He did immediately.

I searched around my tent for a shirt. I threw on a white tank top only to realize that it didn't cover the symbol on my shoulder. *Why did I only pack tank tops?!* I snagged my black school hoodie and crawled into it.

I faced Carter. "Okay."

"Hey." He exhaled loudly.

"Hi."

"R.J.'s on to me."

"What?"

"R.J. can tell something is off about me and won't stop asking me why I'm stressed."

"Shh, keep your voice down! My father is right across the way!" I whispered harshly. "Have you said anything?"

"No, of course not! He wouldn't believe me, anyway.

But I don't know what to do. I suck at lying." *Oh, great. Why did that not surprise me?*

Just then, my father re-entered with medicine.

"Oh, hey, Carter."

"Hi, Mr.—Sir Davis."

"You feeling sick, too?" My father said, clearly noticing Carter's obvious weirdness.

"Just terrific. Couldn't be any better!"

I eyeballed Carter. *Knock it off!*

"You two are acting funny. Everything okay?" My dad raised an eyebrow.

"Yeah, we're great."

He handed me a pill and a water bottle. "Hey, make sure you guys are all packed up. We are leaving in an hour."

"Leaving?" I asked.

"We're going to the Valley of the Kings remember? Possible tomb discovery?"

That was today? That was today! Why did it have to be today?

My father headed out of my tent. I smacked Carter hard in the chest.

"Ow!" he blurted out.

"What was that?" I whispered harshly.

"I told you I'm not good at lying."

"Well, you are gonna have to get good at it fast, for both of our sakes."

"I know, I know! BUT. I think I may have an explanation."

"For what?"

"For last night." Carter rubbed his arm. "It's pretty far-fetched, but it's all I've got."

"I will listen to anything at this point... what do you have?"

"Follow me."

I followed Carter through many rows of tents and people before reaching an impressive enclosed marquee full of desks, bookshelves, maps, work stations, chalkboards, and globes. It was empty, and most of the desks were packed up.

"This is where all the main archeologists work," Carter explained. "This is R.J.'s station – and your dad's over there." He pointed to a desk that was separate from the others.

"I really couldn't sleep, so I got up early and went through everything I could find. And I found this." Carter held up a brown book that was falling apart. I pulled a chair up next to his, and we sat down at R.J.'s desk.

"This book shares an old Egyptian legend about the most despicable god in Egyptian mythology: Apophis, the god of serpents. The legends states that Apophis became insanely jealous of his brother Ra – the sun god and king of all the gods, one of Egyptian people's most cherished gods. In the legend, it says that Apophis wanted Ra's position so badly, he attempted to murder Ra by bringing the walls and floors of Ra's palace to life to surround him and kill him in his sleep. He was unsuccessful..." Carter trailed off, pointing to a painting in the book depicting rough-looking human figures attacking the mighty warrior, Ra.

"We did see a wall come to life as human-like figures. Maybe Apophis did this?" He shrugged, shaking his head – not truly buying his own theory. I shook my head too. Every inch of my body hated this theory, and I felt nauseous thinking about it... because it felt like it could be true.

"Like I said, it's far-fetched." Carter closed the book, uneasy.

I rubbed my eyes, not knowing what to believe. I wanted to believe logic and reason, but nothing was logical about seeing walls come to life in a dream and then again in real life. I stood up and paced.

"Okay, I don't know if that is the answer, but maybe what we can find an answer to is when my mom and R.J. dated. I have a really weird feeling that that information is somehow tied to this. And it is the reason why we went in the pyramid in the first place..."

Carter scratched his head skeptically. "All right, let's look. I will start with R.J.'s desk."

Carter began sifting through R.J.'s notebooks and papers while I journeyed over to my father's desk. I found a bunch of notebooks, maps, and more documents recording previous findings and their locations. I opened up a few drawers and found an old picture of my father and me. I sighed as I picked it up.

It was my seventh birthday, and we were both dressed up as cheesy pirates. I had just blown out my candles on a bright orange jack-o-lantern cake when the picture was snapped. My dad was leaning over my shoulder, licking the icing off my finger as I laughed. I felt slightly sick to my stomach, like something was off about the picture. I put it back where I had found it.

I continued searching, and opened a drawer filled with drawings. I knelt to the ground as I pulled a few of them out. The drawings were all of the same beautiful Egyptian goddess – there must have been hundreds of pictures, drawing, and hieroglyphs of her. It was like my dad was obsessed with her. I narrowed my eyes. She looked oddly similar to the woman from my dream. *Why does my father have all these drawings of her? Does he really know this woman?*

I frantically shoved the drawings back in the drawer. As I did, I bumped my fist into the drawer above, knocking the bottom plank out of place. I tried to put it back in place, not wanting my dad to know I had been snooping around in his things. As I tried, I heard rustling coming from where the plank had fell out. I scooted closer. There was something in between the wooden plank and the bottom of the drawer – a hidden compartment. I tugged on the loose plank, reached my hand inside, and pulled out a dusty papyrus scroll. I clenched my jaw as I unfolded it, trying desperately not to rip it.

Across the whole scroll were bold hieroglyphs depicting gods, birds, babies, snakes, cats and thrones. I huffed, wishing I had a translation book. I sat the scroll down to look for one, but froze instead. There was a symbol on the back of the scroll. I turned it over, dropped the scroll on the ground, and gasped.

"You okay?" Carter asked.

"Yeah, just saw another spider," I lied.

I made sure Carter wasn't looking and picked the papyrus up again. On the back of the scroll was the same Egyptian symbol that had appeared on my back this morning.

"Oh my god!" Carter exclaimed. "Magi, you've got to see this!" His voice was shaky.

"Coming!" I quickly rolled up the scroll, stuffed it in my hoodie sleeve, and then shoved the wooden plank back into place before closing all the other drawers in my father's desk.

I hurried over to Carter, and saw that he had a Polaroid in his hands. He stared, open-mouthed, at the picture – and then at me.

"Is this your mom?"

I took the picture, and my stomach did an intense backflip. It was my mom, in a white dress, being kissed on the check by R.J. in front of the Statue of Liberty. There was no mistaking that is was him. But the picture wasn't old; it was dated only a few months back.

"Yep, that's her." I handed the picture back to Carter forcefully.

He snatched it and shook his head. "Why wouldn't he tell me he was in a relationship?"

"Because! My mom is cheating on my dad. Of course he wouldn't say anything! My dad is his best friend!" I whispered, holding back tears. I had never felt more betrayed in my life.

"Magi! Carter!" R.J. yelled our names from outside.

"Hurry! Hide it!" I ordered Carter. He shoved the photo inside the notebook where he had found it. We quickly dropped to the ground next to some bookshelves and pretended to read as R.J. walked in. I couldn't even look at him.

"Hey kids! Doing some reading, huh?"

"That's right!" Carter blurted out.

I gritted my teeth.

"Well, if you guys are all packed, let's load up. We might leave a little bit earlier, if that's all right."

All I did was nod. We sat our books down and headed for the exit. I must not have been hiding my anger very well, because R.J. asked, "Are you okay, Magi?"

"Great." I stormed off right past him.

CHAPTER 8

I swear the drive to the Valley of the Kings took years. I was in the back seat with Carter, as always, but we barely talked. R.J. and my father would not stop commenting about my black hoodie.

"Aren't you hot?" Dad asked. "It's the desert, not Antarctica."

I lied, telling them that it was comfortable. In reality, I was burning up. I didn't have time to change before we left, and I couldn't take it off now and risk one of them seeing the symbol.

We got to the campsite around mid-afternoon. To me, the Valley of the Kings didn't look any different than the rest of the desert – just add some hills here and there, and that was it. The campgrounds didn't seem different from the camp at Giza, either – green tents everywhere.

My father and R.J. unloaded the Jeep, and Carter and I removed our oversized backpacks from the vehicle. I needed to figure out how to hide the scroll. I still had it in my hoodie, which was not, by any means, the best hiding place. I wanted to put it in my backpack somehow, but everyone started walking towards the new campgrounds.

As we walked, two fairly well-dressed archaeologists approached us. One had white hair and looked about fifty with a slight beer belly. He wore a white button up with a khaki tie. The other had dark brown hair, and seemed to be in his early forties. He barely made eye contact, and his brown shirt was neatly tucked into his pants. He had a nice watch.

"Mr. Davis," the older man said with a British accent similar to my mom's.

"Professor Wilson. Professor Gaynor. Wonderful to see you both again." My father shook their hands.

"Thank you, again, for traveling here," Professor Gaynor said in his distinguished accent. "We do believe we have found something extraordinary, and we wanted the best man in the field here."

"Best man in the field? Wow," I said, under my breath.

R.J., having overheard me, leaned in. "You do realize your dad is the world's leading Egyptologist?" he whispered.

"You do realize the sky is blue?" I deadpanned, not making eye contact. *Of course* I knew. I'd just forgotten.

R.J. leaned away awkwardly, his perma-smile finally fading. "It's part of the reason why he is gone all the time.

He is a very important man in this line of work," R.J. continued.

I was so used to resenting his work, I guess I hadn't really thought much about it. But seeing everyone treat him with such respect and hearing about how well-regarded he was actually made me really proud.

"Ahhh, this must be Magi," Professor Gaynor said, snapping me back into the group conversation.

"How'd you know?" My dad smiled.

"She looks just like you – minus the gray hairs and the wrinkles," Professor Gaynor teased him.

My dad laughed, and I forced a giggle. I personally didn't think that my dad and I looked exactly alike, but – despite how awful I felt – I was giddy inside when I was compared to him. I quickly silenced my giggle when I began comparing myself to my mom. I looked nothing like her.

"Well, shall we show you what we have found?" Dr. Wilson – the one with the boring American accent – spoke up shyly, snapping me out of my thoughts.

"Yes, please." My father grinned.

Everyone made their way towards a large open tent with desks, tools, and papers scattered everywhere. I slumped into the closest chair I could find and whipped droplets of sweat off my face. I was dehydrated and on the verge of heat exhaustion from wearing this hoodie. I placed my backpack underneath the table next to me and quietly unzipped it so I could put the scroll inside. I began to pull the scroll out of my sleeve when my father stepped up next to me.

"You are really not looking too good," he said, patting me on the back.

I carefully pushed the scroll back up my sleeve and replied, "I told you I wasn't feeling well this morning." I avoided eye contact as I zipped my backpack back up.

"Maybe you should take off that hoodie?"

Air caught in my throat. "No, no – I'm good."

"Mags, you are sweating like crazy. Take it off."

"Dad, I'm fine." Being short with him quickly backfired.

"What's the big deal? It's going to make you feel better." He gestured towards the hoodie.

"I don't want to, okay!"

The others around us started noticing our conversation, and my temperature was rising from embarrassment.

My father narrowed his eyes. "Are you hiding something?"

I froze. My hesitation to respond answered my father's question.

"Take if off, Mags."

"Dad, no—"

"Take it off!" he said sternly.

Furious, and on the verge of tears, I grabbed the bottom of the hoodie, ready for the scroll to topple to the ground, and was about to pull it off when a there was a chaotic shouting across the way.

"IT'S OPEN! IT'S OPEN!" Dozens of the workers were yelling; it seems that they had discovered the entrance to whatever they had found. The other archeologists sprinted towards the possible tomb. My father looked back at me, concerned, but then rushed off to see it all for himself.

That was way too close. I moaned as I placed my head on the desk next to me. I needed to find a translation book... the scroll could have some more answers. I stood up, made sure the scroll was still tucked inside my hoodie, and began to look around the tent, picking up every book I could find. Several minutes went by with no luck when Carter jogged up to me.

"Dude, you are missing everything!" he said.

"Missing what?" I acted like I wasn't up to anything.

"They *did* find a tomb! R.J. and your dad are in the tomb right now!"

"No way!"

"Don't just stand there – let's go!"

Carter and I dashed up to the dig site. A colossal stone wall was uncovered, and it had a sizable hole in it. I guessed that the workers accidentally dug into the wall and created the hole. *Nice subtle entrance, guys.* Dr. Wilson stood in front of us.

"Hey, Dr. Wilson," Carter got his attention. He turned around to see us.

"Hello, Carter. Magi." He smiled timidly.

"Can I—"

I cleared my throat to get Carter's attention.

"Can *we* go inside?" Carter corrected himself.

"Yes, you may, but please be very careful as you go in," he said.

"Thanks!" Carter yelled as we ran towards the tomb opening. Despite how I was feeling, I was super anxious to see what was down there.

"Magi, let's go." Carter tugged on my arm, pulling me inside. The hole was about four feet wide, with a seven-foot drop to the chamber below. Several workers helped us down a ladder into the chamber.

Inside the stuffy chamber, Carter and I found my father and R.J. already busy examining dull hieroglyphics on the walls and organizing ancient Egyptian artifacts.

"Whoa," Carter gasped.

He was immediately drawn to the dusty, ancient pottery scattered across the floor. The dirty tomb was incredible, but it was hot, and the air was stagnant – I couldn't focus. My own personal swimming pool of sweat was growing.

"Magi, follow me." My dad grinned as he gestured me towards a three-foot hole in the back wall. He crawled through it and told me to follow him.

Oh. My. God. I had crawled into ancient treasure tomb – real treasure! The tomb had two levels. The top had several stone pillars holding up the structure, showcasing colorful, faded hieroglyphs with a ramp that led down to all the treasure. There was piles of jewelry that sat neatly on colorful tables, cobwebs dangled across gold thrones, hundreds of pieces of faded pottery, old rotting chariots that were somehow still standing, ancient weapons stacked together, and ton and tons of intricately designed furniture. "This is the most incredible find that our team has ever had. Extraordinary ..." My father scanned the treasure with pride. "Soon, all of this will be in a museum, where we can continue studying this unbelievably fascinating culture."

Egyptologists filed in with Carter close behind. Carter couldn't breathe when he saw all the treasure. Everyone laughed at how overwhelmed he was at the magical sight. Even I couldn't help cracking a grin.

I drifted around the treasure room, eyeballing everything. My attention was drawn to a golden chair with a silver plate full of precious jewels sitting on top.

I picked up a gold necklace outlined with red gems. It was stunning, despite all the dirt and cobwebs covering it. I wiped the dust off with my fingers.

A sharp pain spiked me in the stomach, and I become light-headed. The necklace had reminded me of the woman's jewelry in the dream – the one where she kissed my father. I put the necklace down, blocking out any thought of her.

"Absolutely incredible, isn't it?" My dad walked up behind me.

"Yeah, it is." I forced a smile, and then hurried over to Carter who was checking out a huge golden statue of a Pharaoh.

"Carter!" I whispered.

"Yeah?" He turned around and noticed I was uneasy. "Hey, what's up?"

"I need a translation book."

"Uhh, okay, why?"

I pulled Carter behind one of the pillars. "I found something in a secret compartment in my father's desk that I need to translate."

"Secret compartment?"

"Yeah, it was like something out of a spy movie. Now, I just need one of those books."

"All right, easy." Carter walked off and approached R.J., innocently asking for his translation book. He told him he was going to get a head start of translating the walls. Without hesitation, R.J. handed him the book.

Carter walked back and grinned. "Easy."

"Easy." I rolled my eyes. "Come here."

We both ducked behind the pillar again and sat down on the dusty stone ground. I made sure no one was around, and then pulled the papyrus scroll out of my sleeve.

"Whoa." Carter clearly didn't expect me to have this.

I was extra careful unfolding it – since my sweat had dampened scroll. I showed Carter the message, and we began working together, writing the words down in one of Carter's mini-notebooks he kept handy in his pockets.

"We're missing a couple things, but I think this is what this message reads..." Carter fixed his glasses as he read.

"Do you agree to protect and parent the child of both the Earth and the Realm—"

"What's the Realm?" I questioned.

"I don't know." Carter shook his head. "I also don't know what the rest of these symbols mean, but it sounds like some sort of contract. A contract agreeing to be the parent of 'this child.'"

I couldn't help thinking I was the child in the contract. I mean, I was the only child in my family, and this had been in my father's desk. Not to mention the dream... I blinked it away and grabbed the scroll, nervously turning it over.

"Do you know what this means?" I asked Carter, showing him the symbol on my back.

"I've *never* seen that one before." Carter buried his nose in the book. I helped him look, but after several minutes, it was clear: this hieroglyph was nowhere to be found.

"Hey, guys!"

I jumped at the sound of my dad's voice. He and R.J. popped around the corner. "What are you doing?"

We were caught red-handed with the scroll in my hands! *Crap, I wish I could hide this thing!* Intense panic shot through my body. Carter held his breath. *We're screwed.*

"Translating the pillar, huh? What does it say?" my father said with a smile.

Carter and I both looked at each other, confused, and then at the scroll.

"Uh, we don't know yet. Just started working on it," I said as casually as I could.

"All right, let us know what you come up with." My dad beamed and walked off. R.J. titled his head, looking at me like I was that kid from school who always talked about video games and death. He slowly walked away.

"How did we just get away with that? I'm holding my dad's secret scroll from his secret drawer, in plain sight."

"Magi, it wasn't there." Carter eyed me like I was a ticking bomb.

"What are you talking about?" I shook my head, confused.

"Before they walked up, the scroll was in your hands. After they walked up, it disappeared. Gone! And when they left, it reappeared in your hands!" He whispered animatedly.

I looked down at the scroll, clearly seeing it in my hands. I remembered that, when they walked up, I wished I could hide it from them. *Could I have?*

STARS FLICKERED in a perfectly black sky as I walked towards my new tent. I listened to the loud voices and festive music coming from the Mess Hall a couple hundred yards away as I traveled past multiple campfires. The entire camp was celebrating the incredible tomb discovery.

As I walked by my father's tent, I overheard heard R.J.

talking to my dad.

"Steven, I'm telling you – she knows something."

I stopped in my tracks, peering inside to hear more.

"That would be impossible. Come on, let's just go to the party and celebrate." My father brushed R.J. off.

"I am dead serious," R.J. said.

"How can you be so sure?"

"She was holding something in her hands—" R.J. started, then stopped and glanced over in my direction.

I ducked out of sight and dashed towards my tent as I heard them walking through the tent flaps. I sprinted as fast as I could into my tent and latched it shut. I paced, breathing heavily. *Come on, come on, think!* I had to come up with some kind of plan to stop them from coming inside.

I spotted my phone on my table. I heard my father's and R.J.'s voices round the corner, heading right for me. I snatched up my phone and before they unlatched the flap, I yelled, "Hello!"

I watched them freeze.

"Hey mom! Oh, it's so good to hear your voice!" I prayed my fake phone call was convincing. "How are you doing? ... oh, that's good... me? Oh, I am doing SO good!"

I heard my father persuade R.J. to leave me alone. Their shadows soon disappeared. I peeked my head out my tent and saw my father and R.J. walk up to the Mess Hall.

I dropped to the ground. A rush of homesickness came over me, and I hated the feeling so much that I began to cry. Not that I even knew what home was, anymore. But at this point, I'd settle for knowing my parents were my parents and not having anything to challenge that.

I was about to finally take off my hoodie when my phone started ringing in my hands. My body jerked when it vibrated. I looked at the caller ID; it was my mom calling me for real. I answered immediately.

"Mom?" I hesitated saying the word.

"Hey, sweetheart, how is your trip going?"

"Trip?"

"Egypt, with your father?"

"Right, it's ... going ..."

"Honey, are you all right? You seem off."

I hunched over and cried. Hearing my mom's voice after everything that had happened last night was too much.

"Yeah, yeah. I'm just not feeling too good, and this place is just..." *Mom, please help me! I don't know what's happening to me!*

"Oh, honey, I'm sorry."

"God, I wish I weren't here." *I am so scared right now.*

"Magi, please try to keep a smile on your face. It will be safe for you to come home soon. Promise me you will hang in there."

I wiped away tears. *You don't understand. I'm not safe here!*

"Magi?"

"I promise," I managed.

"Thank you, Darling. You know I love you?"

"I love you–" As I responded, my phone died.

"No no no." I cried.

I curled up in a ball on top of my covers and shut my eyes, crying. All I wanted was to talk to her, and now my stupid phone was dead. I plugged my phone in, and listened to the workers singing off-key at the party while I waited.

"Grab Margaret," a voice whispered from outside.

"Who's Margaret?" another voice asked.

"The girl inside this tent." The hairs on my arms rose.

"Why do we need the girl? I thought we only came for the treasure."

"Don't question me. Do as I say."

The voices stopped whispering. *Please tell me that my mind is just playing tricks on me and that I need sleep.*

I put my phone down and crawled under my rollaway bed. Then, a bandit dressed in all black with a knife in one hand and an AK- 47 slung around his back stepped into my tent. *Oh my god... this is not happening!* I watched his black boots as they stepped in front of my bed.

All of a sudden, my bed was flipped over, and I was completely exposed. I tried to use whatever magic I'd used before to slow him down with my mind, but I couldn't. Before I could scream, the bandit gripped my face and yanked me to my feet. He rammed me into another bandit, who wrapped a piece of cloth around my mouth and tied up my hands. I kicked and struggled to get free and –

somehow –managed to break loose from them. I fell into Carter's tent, which was directly across from mine. Carter was in bed, reading with headphones in his ears.

"Magi?" he said, confused, as he noticed the cloth tied around my mouth.

The bandits busted in to Carter's tent. Shocked, Carter ripped out his headphones and threw his book at one of the bandits, hitting him in the head. The bandit retaliated, punching Carter in the face. I screamed as I watched him fall to the ground. Carter's nose was bleeding everywhere – he struggled to remain conscious. One bandit tossed me over his shoulders. The other tied Carter up and seized him.

We were being carried out of camp towards three run-down vehicles with machine guns mounted on them. I counted ten other men, and they were loading up all the treasure from the tomb.

"Oh my god!" I screamed, slobbering into the cloth. All the tomb guards had slit throats or had been knocked out unconscious. I screamed as loud I could with the cloth in between my teeth, kicking as hard as I could. Carter did the same. The workers at the celebration – including my father and R.J. – were completely oblivious as to what was happening.

The other bandits clutched robust machine guns in their hands. A bandit with two long swords attached to his belt slowly approached us. His dark eyes glared into mine. Tears streamed down my face as he inched closer to me.

"Tie them up in the back. We are finished here," he ordered. The bandits transported us forcefully tying us to poles inside the bed of a vehicle.

"Move out!" the leader ordered.

The bandits loaded the rest of the treasure and drove away.

EVERYTHING WAS blurry as I opened my eyes. There was a large black object in my vision and I blinked, trying to focus. Panic shot through me like a thunderbolt when I realized what I was staring at: a machine gun, about three feet away from my face. The bandit holding it was so relaxed he could have been at a resort.

I slowly tried to shift my body away from the gun, but my hands were tied up. Terror- stricken, I yanked at the ropes and bumped into Carter, whose back was pressed against mine.

"Magi?" he whispered.

I faced him. His face, neck and shirt were stained with dried blood. I looked into his eyes. He looked terrified.

"Are you okay?" he managed.

Am I okay? I realized I was extremely dizzy and very nauseous. It was probably over a hundred degrees, and I was still wearing my black hoodie.

"No, I'm not," I whispered, "I have to take off my hoodie or I'm gonna overheat."

Carter was so concerned as he watched sweat drip down my cheeks. He built up the courage to talk to one of the bandits.

"Excuse me, sir?"

The bandit who was sitting behind me slowly turned around and leaned towards us.

"What?" he said.

"Uh ... um ... Sir, my friend ... she's, uh, she's feeling really sick and her hoodie is making her feel worse. Can you please untie her so she can take it off?"

"Untie her?" The bandit just laughed at us. The others with him.

"But, sir?"

The bandit stopped laughing and cocked his gun, pointing it at Carter.

"Sir, with all due respect," I said, trying my best not to get the both of us killed, "you have two options. One, you untie me so I can take off my jacket, and we won't bother you again. Two, I will regurgitate every meal I've had in the past seventy-two hours all over this vehicle."

The bandits exchanged glances.

"Fine." the bandit grumbled, repulsed. He untied the rope around my wrists and I ripped off my hoodie. Immediately, I felt a million times better.

"STOP!" the bandit yelled. The driver slammed on the brakes. My head pounded into the back-passenger seat. The other two vehicles stopped suddenly as well. The bandits, one by one, climbed out of the cars and hopped onto the sand.

"What is going on?" the leader of the bandits said, as he gripped his swords and marched towards the back of our car.

The bandit next to me was staring at me, wide-eyed—he was completely silent. Instead of using words to reply to his leader, he just pointed at me. The leader advanced towards me. I was now breathing heavy and was failing at staying calm. The bandit clasped my shoulder and turned my back towards the leader.

All of the bandits were staring at the symbol on my back! The leader rubbed his hand against it—I jerked away. His eyes grew intense when he discovered the mark was real. A look of accomplishment came across his face. Carter couldn't believe his eyes.

"Change of plans," the leader said, "We will be taking *her majesty* to the Red Pyramid."

Her majesty?

The bandits were frozen in fear. "This was not our mission!" One spoke up.

"Our mission was the treasure!" the bandit behind me spoke.

"Our lord never said anything about *her*!" Another pointed at me in fear.

"This was our mission all along, you cowards! Who are you more afraid of? This girl? Or what will happened to you if we fail our Master?"

The bandits exchanged horrified looks. *Master? What is going on? Why are they all scared of me?*

"Get back in your vehicles. And tie her back up. NOW!" the leader yelled.

The bandit reached over and yanked my hands. I squealed, panic-stricken as I felt energy surge through my body. To our horror, my hands were glowing gold—I screamed. When I did, a burst of energy shot out of my hands into the desert like a shockwave. All the bandits were thrown to the ground by the blast.

"Magi!" Carter cried.

The blast made me collapse into his lap. My whole body felt like a wet noodle. I couldn't move. The bandit rapidly retied me and cocked his gun at me. I began to hyperventilate as we sped through the desert.

"Magi? Magi?" Carter whimpered. "It's okay. You're okay. I need you to stay awake."

Carter moved closer to me. His shoulders leaned in on mine and he looked into my eyes.

"You need to calm down. You're scaring me—and yourself." I looked away from him, but he nudged again. "Hey, I'm right here, it's going to be okay. It's okay."

Carter's kindness had relaxed me instantly, and the will to stay awake grew stronger. How did he do that?

TWENTY MINUTES LATER, the vehicles were decelerating in

front of a ginormous Egyptian pyramid: The Red Pyramid. Carter and I leaned in closer to each other, both fearing what was about to happen next.

The bandits leaped out onto the sand and slammed the car doors. They swarmed around our vehicle. The leader snapped at two bandits to untie us. They reluctantly did as they were told—none of them wanted to come near me. The two bandits pulled us out by our arms. Carter and I both struggled to get free, but it was useless. The rest of the bandits raised their guns and pointed them directly at us.

"Well, your majesty, I hope we didn't cause you too much discomfort," the leader taunted me as he slowly raised his one of swords to my neck.

"Why do you keep calling me that?" I confronted him, incredibly confused.

The bandit lowered his sword. "You don't even know..."

What on earth is he talking about?

"What a pity that you won't get the chance to find out who you are." The bandit smirked. He was going to kill me.

"Hello, there!"

The bandits turned, on high alert. Off in the distance, a man dressed in a white cloak and white head piece that only exposed his eyes came riding up on a camel, with two more traveling behind him. He rode up next to the bandits' vehicles.

"I was wondering if any of you men would be interested in purchasing any of these handmade quilts. They are very fine, indeed. I made them myself." The man on the camel displayed several colorful blankets and quilts on the backs of his camels.

"Not interested. Now be on your way," the leader ordered the merchant.

The merchant on the camel noticed me and Carter. He locked eyes with me and stared. There was something very familiar about this man, but I couldn't put my finger on it.

Help us! I prayed that he could hear my thoughts. He nodded as if to say "don't worry."

"Is everything all right, here?" the merchant questioned the bandit leader. The merchant glanced at all the guns the men were pointing at him—it didn't seem to shake him.

"Everything's fine. Be on your way," the bandit leader said again, raising his volume.

"Your two children seem very displeased. Or are they even your children?" The merchant dismounted his camel.

"Get back on your camel and be on your way, or I will drive this sword through your throat!"

"Before I leave, may I make a suggestion to you?" the merchant said, barely even seeming to notice the sword near his neck.

"And what is that?" the bandit leader snarled.

"Let her majesty go."

The leader's eyes widened and he lunged with his sword. The merchant pulled out a golden khopesh and blocked the bandit's attack. Effortlessly, the merchant swung his weapon forward with so much force, it knocked the bandit to the ground.

"Attack him!" the leader yelled.

Bullets flew.

I stomped the bandit's foot as hard as I could, and he loosened his grip on my arms. I pushed him away, freeing myself, and quickly spun my arm around to punch the bandit in the nose.

Carter followed my lead and tried to free himself, too. I helped him out by kicking the bandit in the groin. "Carter, run!"

He took off as I kicked the bandit in the face, knocking him to the ground. I was about to start running away when—

"Carter, no! Stop!" I yelled after him. *Why is he running towards it? Run away from it, you idiot!*

He was sprinting straight up to the pyramid entrance! I chased after him, only catching up to him at the top. I screamed as bullets hit the ground near our feet.

"Magi!" Carter yelled, pointing to two bandits who were chasing after us. He shoved me towards the entrance.

"Wait, no!" I yelled.

"We don't have a choice!" He pushed me in.

"We did! THE DESERT!"

We shuffled down an ancient, slanted stairwell, almost tripping over ourselves.

"Hurry, hurry, hurry!" Carter repeated over and over.

"I'm trying!" I panicked.

The bandits were approaching the entrance—the gunshots booming louder and louder. Carter and I made it to the bottom of the shaft just as the bandits began to shoot down into it. We scrambled to our feet, and rushed through the aged chambers of the Red Pyramid.

We shrieked.

Somehow, a bandit had gotten into one of the deepest chambers of the pyramid! As fast as lightning, he jumped in between me and Carter and kicked us against opposite walls. My back slammed into the stone—I grunted in pain. The bandit aimed his sword at my head. As he swung, his eyes began glowing dark green.

"Magi!" Carter screamed.

I raised my arms in front of my head for protection. Everything fell silent, and I opened my eyes.

The bandit was standing right in front of me, still in mid swing, but he was in slow motion. *Am I doing this?* I looked down and, sure enough, my hands were glowing gold.

I imagined throwing the bandit across the room, and I made a throwing gesture with my hands. The bandit went flying. Everything unfroze, and Carter did a double-take.

"How did you..." Carter yelled.

The bandit crawled onto his feet and let out an animalistic scream. As he turned, his eyes glowed dark green.

"Are you seeing what I'm seeing?" Carter's voice cracked.

"Run!" I screamed.

Carter and I sprinted as the bandit chased after us. We scampered into a large, eerie chamber where there were four large statues – one in each corner – all depicting horrifying Egyptian creatures ripping humans to shreds. The carvings and the hieroglyphics on the long black stone walls looked brand new, and there were large blood stains everywhere on the ground. It didn't take us long to realize that there was no exit.

"What do we do?" I cried.

On the walls all around us were lit wooden torches. I sprinted as fast as I could towards them.

But as soon as I tried to grab one off the wall, the bandit slammed his body into mine, knocking me to the ground. He pinned one of my wrists to the ground to restrain me and, with his other hand, tried to stab me with his sword. Using my freed arm, I pushed against him. *Oh, god, he is strong!*

Out of the corner of my eye, I saw a small dagger attached to his belt. I promptly snatched it and jabbed it into the arm that was holding me down.

He cried out in pain. Now wasn't the time to get complacent. I punched his arm, knocking his sword out of his hands and rolling away from him. For a long moment, we locked eyes and I found myself staring into the green, viscous glow that emanated from his gaze. It looked exactly like the glow that had appeared in the assassin's eyes from my dream with the Master.

The bandit scrambled onto his feet and charged me

without his weapon. He hooked his fist toward my head—I ducked under. He came in with the other hand and punched me in the stomach, and I fell to the ground, gasping for the air that had been knocked out of me.

He stood, towering over me with his glowing eyes. And then, he gasped, doubling over.

Carter had grabbed his sword and stabbed him in the back! Carter yanked the sword out, and we both gasped. The sword was stained by the bandit's blood. But the blood was not red—it was dark green!

"He's not human," I whispered.

I scampered over to Carter. We watched the bandit stumble around, trying to stay upright. Slowly, he turned to us. A demonic smile was plastered on his face. He stepped towards us, and with each step he gained speed – and I swore I could hear laughter in his coarse wheezing.

I took the sword from Carter and swung with all my might, slicing him in half at the waist. The bandit fell to the ground in two pieces, forever motionless. He was dead —he had to be. *I CUT HIM IN FREAKIN' HALF!* My white tank top was stained dark green. Carter and I were both out of breath.

"Your majesty."

I whipped around to find the bandit leader standing directly behind me. He attacked instantly with his two large swords. I was starting to accept that I would die here; he was so much stronger than the other bandits— defeating him seemed impossible.

I cried out in pain as one of blades sliced into my thigh. I forced myself to power through, and somehow ripped the black cloth around his head off with my sword.

I gasped in terror. Standing before me, glaring at me with blood-thirsty, glowing green eyes, dripping in sweat, was the assassin, Tarek, from my first dream. I knew it was him without a doubt—I couldn't ever forget a face has terrifying as his.

A sharp pain ripped through my ankle. *WHAT?!* I looked down to find the halved bandit clinging to my ankle, biting it—he was still alive!

"CARTER, HELP!" I wailed as I pushed against Tarek's blades.

Carter hesitated, in shock, but dashed over and stabbed the bandit several times with the dagger I had dropped—but the bandit wouldn't let go! I finally was able to kick my leg loose from his grip, and Carter finished him off with a stab in the neck.

Tarek's sword rammed so roughly into mine that it sent my sword flying out of my hands. He kicked me to the ground with his boot. He stepped over my body, placing both of his swords around my neck.

"Only two left... now, you die."

Two left? I guess I will never know what that means. I took my final gasp.

"MAGI! NO!" Carter cried.

Before Tarek could finish me, a dove swooped in and landed on my knee.

What the–

Tarek's confused expression mirrored my own. A cloud of purple dust consumed the dove, turning its feathers lavender. I held my breath. *There's only one person I know who can do that...*

The merchant appeared behind Tarek and decapitated him with his golden khopesh.

Tarek's blades fell to the ground. Frantically, I scrambled away from the assassin's bleeding body as he collapsed next to me. The merchant examined him, making sure he was dead. I retreated to Carter, who was throwing up. I was about to join him when the merchant approached. The dove flew to his shoulder.

"Get away from us!" I threatened as I took the dagger away from Carter and held it out in front of me.

"Magi, it's alright. I'm not going to hurt you," the merchant spoke softly. He removed the white cloth wrapped around his head.

I dropped the dagger. Tears flooded my eyes.

"N-Nesu?"

"You know this man?" Carter blurted out.

"He's my boss."

I leaped into Nesu's arms, bawling, and he squeezed me so tight. "Hello, my dear." His voice shook from heartbreak. I buried my face in his chest.

"So tell me, both of you, what happened?" Nesu nudged me to answer.

Carter and I exchanged looks as I wiped tears and snot off my face.

"We were kidnapped," I started.

"Her father and my guardian are archaeologists, and they were working on a find in the Valley of the Kings. These men kidnapped us for some reason," Carter answered, staring at the dead bodies, shaking.

"I see." Nesu paused.

"What are you doing here?"

He froze, as if he didn't want to answer my question.

"And why did you call me *your majesty*?"

Nesu sighed and knelt down before me. "I want nothing more than to be honest with you, but it is not my place to answer your questions."

"What?" I shook my head, even more confused.

"But what I can do for you right now is to get you and Carter back where you belong."

"Wait, I never said my name... how do you know my name?" Carter questioned suspiciously.

Nesu didn't answer his question. He turned his back to Carter, pulled something off his shoulder, and handed it to me.

"I saw this lying in the sand. It is yours, right?" Nesu held my black hoodie.

"Yes, thank you." I collected my hoodie, dusted the sand quickly off of it, and used it to wipe the green blood off of my skin and stained shirt.

Nesu leaned in and whispered to me, "May I suggest

something that I say quite a bit?"

I narrowed my eyes.

"Some secrets *aren't* meant for sharing." He motioned his head toward the symbol on my back.

With an uneasy feeling in my heart that told me he knew exactly what the symbol meant, I realized what Nesu was saying. I immediately pulled my hoodie back over my head.

THE SETTING SUN made the sand sparkle like diamonds as we climbed out of the Red Pyramid. It was weird to see such beautiful scenery after almost dying.

A short distance away, Nesu's three large camels patiently awaited their owner's return. Nesu lead the way through the carnage – all the bandits' lifeless bodies around the vehicles and in the sand – as if nothing out of the ordinary had happened. Then, he bandaged up our wounds before climbing up on the lead camel.

"Hop on, you two. We'll be riding for a while. We must be on our way."

Carter and I hesitated. I had never ridden a camel before.

Nesu grinned. "They are harmless creatures."

Carter and I shrugged, and we both climbed on. I pet my camel's fur with shaky hands.

"Up, up!" Nesu yelled at the camels. In a hurry, the

three large animals stood.

Oh, you're tall.

Nesu gently kicked his camel. It moaned, but it got the message and it moved forward, leading ours forward, as well. We began to travel slowly through the sunset-lit Sahara.

The swaying motion of the camel soothed me as the sun slowly went down below the horizon. Before I knew it, my eyes were heavier than fifty-pound weights, and I couldn't lift them, anymore. I fell asleep.

IN THE DISTANCE, little parts of the desert sparkled in the dark. My eyes were very heavy and were having trouble adjusting. What was I seeing?

They were lights. And, as the lights came closer, I made out – they were headlights. My head slowly lowered. I couldn't hold it up anymore. I laid my head back down on the camel's neck.

Minutes later, the sound of moving vehicles got closer. I could have also sworn that I heard a helicopter, but I was too out of it to be sure. The camels came to a complete stop.

The sound of the vehicles was so loud that it sounded like they were driving right by me. I heard car doors open and close. I made out the sound of footsteps in the sand coming towards me.

"Magi?" Someone said my name. The voice sounded familiar.

"Magi? Carter?"

I felt someone's arms wrap around my waist gently.

"Magi! Oh, my god!" The person picked me up and carried me, holding me tight.

"Dad?" I spoke in a daze.

"Yes, Mags! It's me! It's me. You're safe now! I've got you. I've got you. "

"I wanna sleep," I said softly.

"Yes, Mags," my father laughed emotionally. "You can sleep now."

I opened my eyes slightly. My father was gazing at Nesu in disbelief. "Thank you. Thank you."

Nesu nodded his head towards my father, as if he were bowing down to him. "My pleasure."

My father turned and walked away from Nesu. R.J. followed, carrying Carter in his arms. My father and R.J. carried us toward what looked like six tan military vehicles filled with men. They all held machine guns and wore bulletproof vests.

My father laid Carter and me in the backseat. My head rested on Carter's shoulder, and his head rested on mine. As I began to fall back asleep, I felt something jump on my lap. I opened my eyes and saw the little black cat rubbing its head against my arms as if comforting me. It curled up on my legs. A smile cracked on my face before I drifted off again. I was finally safe.

CHAPTER 9

I woke up sitting in a cold metal chair, my vision fuzzy. A single light hung over me like I was about to be interrogated, but there was no one in the pitch blackness around me, which made me feel uneasy.

"Hello?" I heard my voice echo on for what seemed like forever.

A loud voice responded: "*Ask!*"

The voice was coarse and sent chills down my spine.

"*Ask!*" it repeated. "*It's time to ask!*"

I cringed at the sound, shaking my head, praying it would stop.

"*It's time to know your secrets... time to know the truth! It's time...*"

I clapped my hands over my ears, the voice ringing in my eardrums.

"*It's time. It's time. It's time.*" The voice was like a broken record, and it kept getting louder and louder, until my eardrums felt like they were going to explode. Then—

Everything went silent. I opened my eyes. In front of me, a mirror suddenly appeared. I saw myself in it, wearing the same disgusting, blood-stained shirt. I turned away. Seeing how awful I looked made the reality of my circumstances too real. I stood and anxiously searched all around for an exit, but I didn't see a thing. I returned to look at the mirror and screamed.

I fell backwards onto the metal chair, and then the floor. I slowly crept back up onto my feet and stared at my reflection in the mirror, gasping. My reflection was me, but it looked nothing like me.

The girl in the mirror was wearing a long, white flowy dress with a golden belt around the waist. She had long, jet-black straight hair, tan skin, and wore the same makeup as me – but with thick black eyeliner and bold red lips. She stood like royalty. Her skin glowed gold, with transparent Egyptian symbols shining through like a stained-glass window.

I slowly raised my hand and touched my face. My reflection did the same. I moved my hand away from my face and moved it up and down. My reflection mirrored me perfectly.

"Who are—"

"—you."

My eyes widened in terror. My reflection had finished my sentence for me.

"I'm you." My reflection spoke on its own.

"That's impossible!" *This is so not happening right now!* My whole body was shaking.

"It's not impossible ... I am you."

I shook my head. "I'm losing it. A mirror is talking to me, my freakin' reflection is talking to me! And you don't even look like me!"

"I–" my reflection raised its voice to drown out my nonsense, "–am your true form."

"True form?"

"Your royal self." My reflection paused. "Strange things have been happening to you recently."

I narrowed my eyes.

My reflection continued, "Strange things have been happening to you ever since your father gave you your necklace. And even stranger things have happened since you arrived in Egypt – the kinds of things that make you question who you are. The kinds of things that make you question even your blood."

"Blood?"

"You are not who you think you are, Magi Davis. You will soon learn that there are many secrets within you."

My reflection slowly began to turn, as if it was about to walk away. "It is time."

"Wait!" I yelled.

My reflection returned back to its normal state. I stared at the glass as the room around me started to spin, causing my head to ache. The room faded away.

I WOKE up so fast I almost managed to fall out of bed, but the IV needle stuck in my arm pulled painfully.

"Ow!" I contorted my face as I pulled myself back into a comfortable position. I almost screamed when I looked at my arms. My skin was glowing with the same transparent symbols that my reflection had in my dream. *What is happening to me?* The glowing subsided right before I hyperventilated.

I rubbed my forehead, which was now pounding extra hard. I looked around and saw that I was in the camp infirmary – which was a little building in the middle of the campground. There were medical beds across from me, shelves and cabinets full of medicines, rolling tables with surgical tools, and other medical machines I did not recognize. Carter was in a bed right next to me, fast asleep. He had an IV in his arm, too, and was wearing a hospital gown. I glanced down; I was wearing one too.

On my gown was a ripped note. My eyes bulged. Pale pink, vintage paper with roses around the edges. My mom's beautiful cursive handwriting was inked across the lines. I began to read what I knew was the other half of the note I found in the pyramid.

...getting married in a few days! Can you believe it? He is about to marry a goddess... I can't fathom the reality of this! I am just so happy for him. Anyway, darling, good luck today, and I will see you tonight.

I love you so much,

Mariah

I dropped the note and felt my esophagus tighten as the tears began to stream down my face. I want to go *home*. I wanted none of this to have ever happened. I wanted so badly for it all to have been one horrible, horrible nightmare. I tried so hard not to wake up Carter as I rocked back and forth, holding myself.

I felt someone's arms wrap around me and squeeze. I knew those hands better than I knew my own face. I couldn't hold it in anymore. All my barriers were down, and I cried uncontrollably, making my bed creak from my body shaking. The arms around me loosened. I rubbed the tears from my eyes, and my father sat down next to my bed. Neither of us knew what to say.

Finally, I caught my breath in my lungs and handed him the note.

He unfolded it and read it quietly to himself. He rubbed his face and then sighed loudly, looking up at me with guilt in his misty eyes.

"What is going on?" I blubbered.

My father scooted his chair closer to my bed, fighting back tears. He wrapped his rough hands around mine. "This how this conversation is going to go. You and I are going to be completely honest with each other, no matter how crazy or weird the things that come out of our mouths are. We say them, and we tell the truth. No more hiding anything. No more secrets. Deal?"

I felt the pressure on my chest—the anxiety I'd been feeling for days— increase, but I ignored it. I wanted answers more than anything. "Deal."

"Why don't you go first?" My dad leaned forward in his seat ready to listen. My heart raced as tears continued falling down my face.

"I feel like I am losing my mind. Why...why is everyone in my life lying to me? To my face? Everyone that I thought I had unconditional trust in. And I know what they —*you*-- are hiding has something to do with why I've almost been killed three times in one week."

My father swallowed hard, nodded his head like he was agreeing with me. "Keep going."

"Things are happening to me that I can't explain. Mom is cheating on you with your best friend." I paused for his reaction, but he only nodded in encouragement for me to keep on. "I'm seeing the cat from my childhood neighborhood in the great pyramid with its eyes glowing, leaving me notes from Mom. I'm having nightmares or dreams that are insanely realistic, and things just appear in real life from the dream! Like a tattoo...Dad, there is a tattoo on my back that I didn't get!"

"Can you show me?" he asked gently.

I lowered my hospital gown to show him the black markings on my shoulder.

My dad leaned back in his seat and smiled like he had flipped to a page in a photo album he was fond of. "That's *your* symbol."

"My what? You know what this is?" My voice trembled.

He bent over and pulled something out of his back-pack. *The scroll!* My father placed the scroll on his lap and unfolded it to show me the same symbol. "When did it appear?"

"A couple nights ago. You said 'that's your symbol'... Do you know what this is?"

He grabbed my hands again, squeezing my them tightly, and let out a deep sigh, as if gathering the strength to speak. "Please forgive me. I have wanted to tell you all these years, but I didn't, because I needed to keep you safe. What I'm about to tell you is going to change your life forever."

He gulped. "The symbol on your back is the mark of your identity. The ankh in the middle represents life or eternal life. The line at the very bottom connecting it all means foundation, truth, and the Divine Order. The U-shaped part surrounding it all are cow horns, symbolizing the goddess Isis' crown."

He paused to take a deep breath. "Together it means *the daughter of Isis*."

"I don't understand."

"Magi, Mariah isn't your real mother."

I couldn't breathe.

"She is one of your many protectors, but not your biological mother. Your real mother... her name is *Isis*. The Egyptian goddess, Isis."

"Please tell me you're joking." I bit my lip.

"I am not," he said calmly.

"Dad, that's not funny!" I hissed.

"It's the truth."

"The truth?! That can't be possible." I raised my voice.

"If it's not possible, then how were you able to send out a giant shockwave of energy into the desert yesterday? That was you, right?"

"How did you..."

"It's how we were able to find you. And only a god has those kinds of abilities."

"Are you telling me that I'm a god?"

"The daughter of a god," he corrected. "Thousands of years ago, the gods roamed the earth and humans were allowed, through a complicated process, to enter the *Realm*: the domain where the gods dwell. Apophis, the god of serpents, became insanely jealous of his brother, Ra, the sun god, who was by far the most loved god, other than Isis. Not only did Apophis try to murder Ra to steal his throne, but he also married a human woman—which is considered a major crime to the gods. His pursuit to steal Ra's throne became relentless, which caused a seven-year war to break out between the gods.

"Thousands and thousands of humans died during this time. When gods are at war, humanity is not looked after. Apophis refused to stand down, so Isis and Ra were forced to kill Apophis' human wife, which lead to Apophis's capture and the end of the war. Apophis was then banished to the farthest part of the Realm and banned from ever returning to Earth."

"How does this relate to me?" I was confused and still full of doubt, thinking this sounded like a completely made up fairytale.

"I'm getting to that. After the war, a group of humans believed that the gods were too dangerous to be around mortals. They couldn't defend themselves against their power. The humans demanded the exile of the gods – that they would forever return to the Realm. The gods and this group of humans – whom we know as the Scarab Society – agreed to the terms: that the gods would only return to Earth under special circumstances."

"Nesu told me all about the Scarab Society! But in his stories, they hated the gods. He didn't say anything about Scarab Society *knowing* the gods."

"Well. There is no other information to be learned about them and their knowledge of the gods, because they destroyed any record and evidence of them. The only things that remain about the gods are myths. Myths can be controlled."

"Okay...this is a great story and all, but I still don't understand what it has to do with me."

"After the gods returned to the Realm, Isis came up with an idea and presented it to Ra. Her idea was to have a child with a mortal. Her idea was that the child, being of both god and human blood, would step in and become the *peacemaker* for both worlds. Ra was hesitant, but agreed—

if Isis would wait until a time where humans stretched to every inch of the earth. She waited patiently for that time – and for the right person. Apparently, she thought that was me. And then you came along... making you the *only* one of your kind."

I sat there in silence struggling to process it all.

"*Your majesty...*"

My father and I looked over my shoulder. Carter was sitting up in his bed; he had clearly heard everything.

"That's why the bandits and Nesu called you *your majesty*." Carter turned it all over in his head, staring at me in awe.

"It also explains how you were able to read those hieroglyphics so well," he continued, "and how you were able to fight the stone warriors and the bandits. And your glowing eyes! And that golden power in your hands?" He looked at me as if in a trance. "It's crazy, but it makes sense."

I shook my head. "So that's just it? I'm the daughter of Isis?" Everyone else in the room seemed to be convinced. I was full of even more anger and confusion than I was, before.

"Yes, you are," said R.J. He stood in the doorway, and had clearly also been listening in. I shifted in my bed uncomfortably. I still felt inexplicably betrayed by him, even now that I knew the truth.

"Think about it, Mags," R.J. continued. "Just by walking into the pyramid, you unlocked secrets chambers. You saved your life – and Carter's – with your glowing hands. Right?"

I nodded my head, beginning to feel like a tea pot at the brink of whistling. So R.J. was in on it too? *Wow... everyone knew my secret—except for me.*

"Well, I guess that's your power. And I thank you for saving both your skins." R.J. grinned at Carter.

"Your life is about to change, Magi, in ways you might not understand right away." My father looked straight into my eyes. "It's not going to be easy. But the most important thing – and you will have to follow this rule for the rest of your life – is that you can *never* tell anyone who are you are. You could be killed, or put others in danger." He looked to Carter. "And that actually goes for both of you. You can't say anything to anyone about this, either, Carter."

Carter nodded his head vehemently.

"You both understand?" my father questioned.

I nodded, but I couldn't help the tears that threatened to roll down my cheeks once again.

"Dad? How does *Mom* fit into all this?"

My father sighed. "Oh, honey." He wrapped his arms around me, and R.J. sat down next to him. "Before you were born, Mariah and I were really close friends. When you were born, someone was after you, so I was forced to flee from the Realm with you. I went to her for help. The best way to ensure your safety was to raise you in a normal family with people capable – and trained – to handle someone of your kind. Mariah was by far the best fit for the job. I love her, and I always will, but I love her as a friend. Our marriage is a cover."

"Which also means I am not persuading Mariah to cheat on your father," R.J. explained. "I have too much respect for him to ever to that."

I exhaled, confused.

My dad continued, "Mariah my not be your mother by blood, but she has loved you like one. She had to give up everything. Her home, her family—"

R.J. swallowed. "She gave up everything to keep you safe."

"Why did she do that?" I stammered.

"She knew how important you were. Mariah is part of an agency that monitors and protects the human world from the Realm," said R. J. "It's her job to keep Earth safe. That's actually why she is in London right now."

"What do you mean?"

"When you were attacked," my father explained, "she was ordered back to the London base to investigate what happened, and quickly got busy with another case the involving gods."

Seriously?

My dad continued. "For Mariah, protecting you meant she was protecting your well-being, as well as anyone around you, from any unworldly danger. That alone was a good enough reason for her to do her job as an *agent*, but she fell in love with you. She loved and cared for you as her own child. She became the mother you needed."

"One hundred and ten percent true." R.J. grinned.

Tears fell down my face. *I can't believe she did that for me.*

"Wait... did you just say *agent*?" Carter asked. My father looked up at R.J., who stiffened and nervously avoided eye contact with anyone except for my dad.

"I am really sorry you had to find out this way," my father said, pressing forward. "Trust me, this is not at all how I imagined telling you."

"There is a lot that you're going need to learn." My father wiped away my tears. "I was hoping to have trained you little before I told you the truth, but that didn't exactly work out. But I think now is more than a perfect time to train you for your future responsibilities."

"Train me?"

"Yes. As a matter of fact, I think it's best if we start training you right away. R.J., let's get the doctor in here to clear them so we can go."

R.J. left the room to look for the doctor.

"Training? What training? And where are we going?" I shook my head, upset they were still being secretive with me.

"You'll see."

CHAPTER 10

We were speeding through the desert in my father's jeep. After Carter and I had been cleared by the doctor, my father told us to jump in. Now, we were sitting in silence listening to the radio, watching the desert go by. I tried my best to focus on the music, but nothing could stop my brain from going a million miles an hour. I was overthinking and, at the same time, not thinking at all. My head hurt from the whirlwind of it. I had never felt so alone.

Off in the distance, I noticed a large structure. Carter, who was sitting next to me, noticed it about the same time I did.

"How many pyramids are there out here?" I asked. It was rhetorical, but my dad answered, anyway.

"There are over one hundred known pyramids spread out for miles and miles throughout the Sahara, but only a handful have survived," my father explained. "Sand storms, earthquakes, pillagers that take the stones to use for other projects, and – simply – time, are to thank for the others not existing anymore."

"Dad, you're talking like a textbook again." I rolled my eyes.

"Sorry. "

About ten minutes later, we pulled up in front of the enormous pyramid. It was different than the others at Giza; it had many layers that grew smaller as they reached the top, like a birthday cake.

"Where are we?" I stood up on my tiptoes and tried to get a better look at the ruins.

"We are at the famous Step Pyramid," my dad said. "This pyramid was the first ever built. It was built by a pharaoh named Djoser the First. He built it about 2667 B.C. So, basically, it's very old, very old."

"So why are we here?" I asked.

"To train you," my dad answered.

"You guys keep saying that. Training for what?" I asked, irritated. Couldn't they just tell me what the heck was going on, already?

"For combat." R.J. walked up from behind our Jeep. He wore a black tank top, cargo pants, combat boots, and was holding two sharp silver swords in his hands. He looked like a total badass. I remembered my dream about when I was a baby and how, in it, R.J. had gripped two swords.

"Whoa! Where did you come from?" I asked. I looked

over at Carter and I could tell he was thinking the same thing.

"I thought everyone knew I could teleport," he joked. "I got here about thirty minutes ago." He smiled, pointing to a Jeep parked a short distance away. "I left before y'all to get set up."

"Cool story! Umm, what's with the swords?" Carter crept closer to me, uneasy, clearly having never seen R.J. like this before.

"These will be part of your training." R.J. twirled one his swords as he spoke. "Sword fighting is one of the most important skill sets to have in order for you to be prepared for the Realm."

"The Realm?" I scoffed.

"The Realm of the Gods," my father said, completely serious, like I shouldn't even joke about it. I crossed my arms as he continued, "After we train you in sword fighting, hand to hand combat, martial arts, archery, and *other* things, you both should be well prepared for the Realm and anything that decides to come out of it...which seems to be happening rather frequently, recently."

"You both?" Carter questioned. "Am I training too?"

"Yes, you will be," R.J. answered, "Not a lot of humans get the privilege of knowing what the Realm is, and you need to be extra prepared."

"Plus, you are friends with her, so that automatically puts you in danger," my father teased.

"Thanks a lot." Carter smirked at me.

R.J. rubbed his hands together and said, "So, despite all the horrible things that have happened to y'all the past few days, like almost dying—"

"Thanks for the subtle reminder," I sassed under my breath.

"We are going to have a fun time, and we are going to learn how look cooler and fight better than the Power Rangers." R.J. swiftly circled his swords in figure eights, showing off.

"Dad... who's coming after me?" Asking the question I was sure we were all wondering.

My dad and R.J. exchanged looks. "We don't know..." My father admitted. "We have all our resources trying to figure it out as we speak."

"What resources?" I pressed.

"*The Organization's,*" My dad lifted his chin in complete confidence. "But for now, we got to keep a positive mindset and stay focused on training." He smiled. "Mags, see your necklace that I gave you?"

"Ummm...yeah?" I looked down at it.

"Take it off."

I exchanged a confused glance with Carter. He shrugged. I took off my necklace and placed it in my hands.

"Okay, " said Dad, "now, I want you to think of a sword – or a spear, a dagger, a bow and arrows – anything. Once you have it, I want you to concentrate all your thoughts on that weapon."

Okay, how about a spear? A great weight filled my hand and I squealed. My necklace wasn't a necklace anymore—it had turned into a shiny, silver spear. I threw it to the ground.

"Your necklace is special," my dad said.

"Really?" I yelled sarcastically.

My dad chuckled. "Your necklace can turn into any ancient weapon you want. You think it, it will appear in your hands—just like that."

"Yeah, just like that." I frowned. "I would've liked to have had a little bit of a warning before my necklace turned into a freakin' spear!"

My dad and R.J. laughed. Meanwhile, Carter looked like he had just seen a ghost.

"Isis gave this to me before I took you into hiding," my father told me. "She thought it would be clever – since you are a girl – to disguise your weapon as a necklace,"

It actually was clever. Kinda cliché, but clever. My dad knelt down and picked up the spear. It changed right back into my necklace the second he grabbed it.

"Isis wanted you to have this when you were old enough so that you could protect yourself when you knew the truth." My dad placed the necklace back into my hands. "Let's get to work."

MY FATHER and R.J. ran the show, and we started off with

group stretches that lead into jogging around ruins in the pyramid courtyard. A summary, in brief: *Sand? Not fun! Jogging in sand... even worse!* I was thirty minutes into training and sweat was already running down my face from the blazing heat.

R.J. tossed Carter and I wooden sticks heavier than our training swords. They told us that training with something heavier than your actual weapon would allow you to maneuver your weapon more fluidly when the time came to use it. R.J. and my father showed us how to hold, swing, and spin our wooden sticks without hurting ourselves.

"So, how do you guys even know how to sword fight and all this stuff?" I asked as I wacked my funny bone with my stick.

"Yeah, since you two are just archeologists," Carter added.

R.J. and my father looked at each other awkwardly, and my dad took the initiative to answer with uneasy laugh.

"Let's just say that we've been put in some situations that have required us to learn."

"What kind of situations?" I pestered.

"Yeah? And how did you learn? Who trained you?" Carter pressed further.

"How about we stick with one thing at a time?" R.J. said. "Let's focus on training, for now."

I rolled my eyes as Carter and I went back to practicing blocks with each other.

"Is it me, or did he just completely shut down that conversation?" Carter whispered to me as he eyed R.J.

"Yeah it's just a whole lot of secrets." I gritted my teeth.

"Ugh!" I sighed.

"Don't worry, Mags, you'll get the hang of it," Dad encouraged.

I was failing miserably at learning how to shoot a bow and arrow. Every single time, my arrows would completely miss the target and pierce into the sand. The people in the movies made it look so easy.

"Just keep trying." My father patted me on the shoulder. I jerked away from him as I pulled back the arrow and aimed at the target. I took a deep breath, then released. The arrow went soaring through the air, past the target.

Carter and R.J. snickered. They were eating snacks between a target to the left of me, watching me like a sporting event. I gritted my teeth as I clutched another arrow lying on the table next to me and inserted it on the bow.

"It's okay. Let's keep going. Practice makes perfect, and we have to start somewhere, right?" my father tried to encourage. "I'm sure you understand you have to learn this stuff."

"I don't understand anything." I snapped as I released

another arrow. The arrow went soaring over the target once more. Carter and R.J. busted out laughing. I was so angry that I clenched my fists and yelled. When I did, a knife zoomed off the weapons table and struck the target that Carter and R.J. were sitting under.

"Magi!" My father was pissed, but the two cacklers zipped their lips shut.

I dropped the bow onto the table with a loud thud and stormed off.

"Magi, get back here!"

"I don't want to do this! I don't want any part of it!" I yelled.

"You have to!"

"I don't want to do anything, and I especially don't have to listen to someone who lied to me my whole life!" I sprinted away.

I LEANED against the back of the bed of my father's jeep and sniffled as I watched the sun go from a bright orange to a fading pink.

Carter strolled up. I crossed my arms, avoiding eye contact.

"I want to apologize. I shouldn't have been laughing at you. You are going through way too much to be laughed at right now, and we should have been there to support you." He sighed.

I looked up at him, tears still burning my eyes. "Thank you. That was really nice."

"I guess you're not handling this all well." Carter sat down next to me.

I snorted. "Understatement of the century. It turns out I've never even met my real mother, and apparently the mother I have known my whole life... I can't comprehend it,"

Carter leaned over and hugged me. "I'm not even going to begin to say that I understand what you're going through, because I don't. But I do understand how it feels to not comprehend a situation."

"What do you mean?" I wiped my nose.

"Little seven-year-old me didn't know how to comprehend never seeing his parents again," he said flatly.

I sighed at how horrible those words were.

"But it's not like you are never going to see Mariah again. She is still going to be around and will still be a mother to you. You've just been given a second mom! Heck, I'd give anything to have my parents back and then be told I have even more parents. Dude, you have two moms now! That's so cool. And she is a goddess. That's even cooler."

I laughed, but it got me thinking: would I ever get to meet her?

Carter's caring blue eyes were fixed on me. "Look, I know it's a lot and I'm not promising I can do much to help... but you do realize that I am here for you, right?"

I finally made eye contact with him and saw the sincerity there, deep in his irises.

"Seriously, if you ever just need to rant or need someone to get your mind off things, I'm here," he offered.

"Thank you. Same goes for you, too."

"We're set up! Let's go, you two, before we lose the light!" R.J. yelled. R.J. and my dad were waiting for us to do more sword combat drills.

I sighed loudly.

"Hey look, I know you don't like this, but it's only good for you. I think you and I owe it to ourselves to be able to defend our lives better after everything."

"Do you just always know the right thing to say?" I messed with him.

"It just comes naturally." Carter grinned. "Come on." He pushed me off the jeep and then winked at me. I knew what he was thinking.

"Three ... two ... one... GO!" Carter yelled.

Carter and I dashed across the sand, racing each other to see who could get to my father and R.J. first. We pushed and shoved each other as we laughed hysterically. In that moment, I knew Carter and I had a very special friendship.

"Is your wrist feeling any better?" R.J. asked, as he handed me an ice pack. My wrist was sore and a little twisted after all the sword drills.

"Yeah, it will be fine. Thanks," I reassured him. I gazed into the warm fire that my father had built, now that it was dark and cold in the desert. Its warmth was soothing after an entire day of training.

R.J. sat down next to me. "Hey, could you do me a favor?" he asked.

"Depends on the favor." I grinned.

"Please don't hate your father."

I was taken aback by the request. "What do you mean?"

"It's understandable that you are upset with him for keeping something as big as your mother being goddess a secret," he laughed nervously, "But please don't hate him for it. He has spent every waking moment ever since you were born trying to keep you alive and safe. I truly want you to understand that."

I exhaled as I took that in. "I guess I am learning to understand...*everything*."

"You will, but just please promise me you won't be angry with him?" R.J. wasn't fooling me. He wasn't just asking on my dad's behalf; he didn't want anyone to be angry with him, either. His knee was bouncing up and down.

"Why does this seem personal for you?"

R.J. let out a deep sigh. I could see the burden in his eyes.

"Carter. You're keeping something from Carter, aren't you?"

"He's not the son of a god, if that's what you're thinking." He laughed a little. "But, he does need some serious protection from one."

"Why?"

"Listen, you're trying to make me talk about things I am not ready for."

I decided to be honest with him. "Okay, that's fine, but after all this, trust me when I say telling the truth sooner rather later will make a big difference to him. But, I don't think he'll hate you – regardless of what you do."

R.J. smiled a little. "Thanks...I sure hope not."

"Just don't wait until he's attacked by more demon creatures, okay?" I joked.

R.J. laughed with me. "Deal."

My father and Carter joined us at the fire after finishing up their last set of sword drills for the day. Carter slumped into the sand, out of breath. My dad sat down next to me and patted me on the back.

"Hey, I'm sorry for blowing up." I apologized.

"Trust me, it's okay." He rubbed my back.

I grinned at him.

"Would you like to try something?" he asked.

"Try what?"

"Isis's greatest power is creating illusions. Mortals call it magic because they don't understand what an illusion is. It simply hides the truth from people who are evil, can't handle it, or are unworthy of the truth. Illusions can be classified as magic tricks, mysteries, visual puzzles, riddles, games—"

"Riddles? Games?" *Oh, my god.* "You've been training me this whole time!"

"I have." He smiled. "Because I wanted you to be good at solving any kind of illusion. Why do you think you are so good with magic? It runs in your family, after all."

I blushed, embarrassed, remembering how I'd claimed it didn't.

"You may be excellent at solving illusions, but now it's time for you to create them." My father raised his eyebrows.

"Okay...what do I do?" I was on the edge of my seat.

"You see how the fire is orange?"

"Yeah?"

"I want you to make everyone believe that the fire is purple."

"What?" I sunk back into my seat, completely doubtful.

"Just concentrate. Command your power to hide the truth from us."

"Do I think purple thoughts?" I shook my head. Carter chuckled.

"Just concentrate," Dad reassured me.

I took a deep breath, closed my eyes, and did exactly as my father said. *Purple. Purple. Purple...I feel stupid...*

I took another breath and tried harder. I commanded my power to show their minds that the fire was actually purple.

Carter gasped loudly. I opened my eyes to discover the campfire glowing a deep, majestic purple. Golden and purple sparkles of my power were floating all around like fireflies, enchanting us all.

I gazed at the fire. I could see the orange hue emitting from the blaze when I titled my head. I straightened back up and saw my own illusion again. That was when I realized that I had the ability to see both my illusion as well as the truth. *Ha! This is so cool!*

I looked up and saw R.J. and my father tilting their heads in the same fashion. *Can they see it too?* I wondered. Carter, on the other hand, stared straight ahead ...mesmerized by my mirage. My thoughts were interrupted when I saw my father gazing deeply at me.

"R.J. and I can see the real fire and the purple one when we tilt our heads. Kinda like you, right?" My dad grinned.

"But, I don't understand how you can see the truth. I thought I was hiding it from you." I felt discouraged.

"Spoiler alert: You can't hide anything from us. Isis had R.J., Mariah, and I do this very *interesting* procedure that allows us to always see the truth when it comes to *you*, her, other gods, and powers of the Realm."

"It was pretty messed up." R.J. shook his head. "Stupid beetle ..."

Beetle?

"No one – not even the gods – can fool us with illusions. And, as your dad, I am perfectly happy with the fact that you will never be able to fool me. The good thing is that you didn't know about your power until now, so we never had any problems. Except only with your words."

Ahhh yeah, that was true. I was a good liar. *I should not be proud of that.* "Why did R.J. do it?"

"Let's just say he is one of your many protectors and, believe it or not, has had a huge part in helping raise you. Carter, on the other hand, has clearly not had it done."

Carter was still wide-eyed as he poked the purple blaze with a stick like he was a caveman who had just discovered fire.

Knowing that I couldn't hide anything from my dad was reassuring, yet also terrifying. It made sense, though. I mean, if you were raising a kid with magical powers, you would want to know if your kid was messing with you or not.

"Mags, let's see the real fire again," my dad requested.

"And how do I do that?"

"Command your powers to show us the truth."

I did exactly that. R.J. was instantly impressed.

"Whoa, whoa, whoa. Bring it back!" Carter complained.

"We will continue to work on this while we train but, congratulations, Magi, you've just created one of your first illusions." Pride burned in my dad's eyes, and I saw his shoulders relaxed for the first time in a while. "By the looks of it, it really worked," he said as we watched Carter hit the fire with his stick, wanting the pretty purple back. We all laughed at him.

I'm going to enjoy this...

"IT'S ABOUT TO GO DOWN!" R.J. yelled out, as if he were a really bad sports announcer. Carter stood next to him, holding a notebook and marker, ready to score us. It was the next day, and the four of us stood in the middle of the Step Pyramid courtyard.

"In the right wing, we have the terrible, the awful, the weakest, most ugly middle-aged man there ever was—"

"Why are we even friends?" My dad shook his head, chuckling. R.J. gave my dad a look that said that he was not going to finish introducing him.

"AND in the left wing, we have the feisty magician, the queen of freckles, daughter of a goddess, Magi Davis!"

"My intro was better than yours," I sassed my dad, grinning.

"Rub it in, smart ass," he sassed back.

"Queen of freckles!" I posed like I was on the cover of Vogue.

R.J. continued, "There will be no stabbing, no gut slushing, no head pounding, and –Magi – no power-using."

"I don't even know what I am doing, anyway," I mumbled to myself.

"And – most importantly – NO killing," R.J. finished.

"I don't think you're ready for this, your majesty," my father taunted.

"I guess we'll see." I smirked.

"Twenty bucks you can't beat your old man."

"You're on!"

"Three, two, one ... fight!" R.J. yelled.

My father yelled as he charged me and, as hard as he could, slammed his sword into mine.

I struggled against his force. My dad was incredibly strong; I had definitely underestimated him.

"Come on, Magi! Fight!" my father yelled.

Our blades clashed, and my father pushed his sword into mine with so much force that it caused me to lose my balance and fall flat on my back into the loose sand.

"Mags, let's not get comfortable down there! Let's go!" He circled me like a shark.

He swung his sword at my chest.

Arghhh! I delayed him. I rolled away, scrambled onto my feet, and released him. I stood up before he realized what had happened. He turned sharply over his shoulder, and I was there waiting for him.

"You delayed me, didn't you?" he spoke, as our blades met.

"How'd you know?" I was shocked.

"No one is that fast. You are a delayer, Mags! Just like your mother! You can slow down your opponent's speed. But don't rely on that power. Fight me as if you are unable to use that power."

"Oh, come on! I just figured out how to use that power without freaking out!"

Our blades clashed once again. He cut at my chest several times, and finished his attack by swinging at my head. I ducked under the blade swiftly – without needing to delay him. My dad grinned.

"That's what I'm talking about, Mags!" he yelled.

I gained some confidence as I switched from defense to offense, throwing my strikes, forcing my father to block me. The same sensation I'd felt when I defended myself against the stone warriors returned. The adrenaline was overwhelming—I let my power surge. It hit my father's chest, sending him flying backwards. His back pounded into the rough, ancient stone.

"Hey, what did I say about power-using?" R.J. yelled. "You know, never mind! That was awesome! Please continue!" R.J. applauded me.

My father groaned as he slowly regained his footing.

"Sorry!" I said.

My father gaped at me and pointed at my face.

My reflection on my blade revealed that my eyes, and my hands, were glowing gold. *This is still weird.*

"Magi," he said soothingly, "don't be freaked out! Your power is a gift. You are just freaking out because you're not used to it."

"You can say that again."

"Let me help you control it. Concentrate all your

thoughts on defeating me. Focus and you can do anything!" my father instructed.

Anything, huh? All right, let's test that. I raised my hand out in front of me and let out a deep sigh. The surface of my hands rose in temperature as I commanded the sand around me to move. Manipulating the sand to move was extremely difficult, like trying to lift a heavy object, but I was doing it. The ground rumbled underneath us, the sound roaring like an approaching train as the sand whistling in the air. It started to get a little easier as I forced it to spin around my father like a tornado. My father stood inside the swirling sand, helpless.

I'm doing this. I can't believe I'm doing this. All right, let's finish this!

I sprinted towards the spinning sand storm—then dropped to my knees and slid inside. I kicked my dad's feet out from underneath him—he crashed onto his back once again. I transformed my sword into a small dagger and stabbed the edge of my father's shirt into the ground, preventing him from moving. I commanded the sand to fall back to the ground, and it immediately dropped around us. I hovered over my dad, grinning.

"I believe you owe me twenty bucks." I winked.

He eyeballed me. "I believe I do."

My father laughed. R.J. whooped and hollered as he applauded loudly. Carter held up a large scribbled "10" on his notebook.

I stared at my glowing hands. *I could get used to this.*

CHAPTER 11

Goosebumps spiked up all over my body. My back was propped up against a wall in a long, grand hallway that seemed to stretch for miles. The white stone walls were covered in vibrant hieroglyphs. The ceiling was plated in solid gold.

I realized I was not wearing my pajamas, anymore. Instead, I was in a white long-sleeve dress that stretched to my mid-thigh. Gold and blue jewels covered the chest and neck area, and parts of my arms. I was also wearing gold gladiator-style sandals with blue jewels across the toes.

A gold mirror hung on the wall in front of me. I stood up to look at myself, and was shocked when I saw my reflection. My long, naturally curly hair looked like it had just come out of the salon. It was pin straight, pitch black, and my skin looked like it had been out in the sun for a month. *Well, this is different ...*

"Your majesty."

I turned around and gasped. Nesu was standing right in front of me!

"Nesu! Where did you come from? And...what are you wearing?"

Nesu was dressed in full Egyptian battle armor, and his dark purple cape made him appear undefeatable.

"What are you wearing?" I laughed.

"I know it's a little different from what you are used to." He smiled.

"A little?" I remarked sarcastically.

"Isis would like to see you," Nesu said, smiling as if he was about to give me a present.

"Isis?"

"She awaits your presence."

"You know her?"

"I am the commander of her majesty's army," he announced proudly.

My jaw dropped. "What?"

"Isis ordered me to protect you, and to keep you safe while working alongside your parents."

"That's why you've been in Seattle all these years?"

"Yes."

"It makes sense: you're a magician, Isis is the goddess of Illusions..." I was quickly starting to realize that our meeting wasn't a coincidence. I remember when I was twelve, my dad took me into The Purple Dove for the first time, and I felt this amazing connection with Nesu. I immediately wanted to be a "super cool" magician like him.

"Only the most powerful illusionists can fight in your mother's legion. Speaking of your mother, would you please follow me, *your majesty*?"

I grimaced. "Please don't call me that." It just felt too weird, coming from him.

"As you wish." He chuckled.

Nesu lead me further down the grand hall, until we reached two stately wooden doors with an image of Isis carved into them. She was kneeling, spreading her wings, showing her strength and power. *I hope I don't get wings.*

Two guards held spears in an "X" formation in front of the wooden doors, and they bowed as I approached before quickly moving their spears to open the doors.

Inside was a stupendous throne room. Huge torches hung on the walls, pots of flames lit up the room, and there was a large statue of Isis inside a stunning water fountain against the left wall. Hued hieroglyphics covered the white stone walls, and the ones behind her throne shimmered, glowing gold. *That looks like my hands when they glow!* Streams of this golden power flowed into tiny channels incorporated into the stone floor, along the sides of the throne room. The golden liquid flowed through the channels, creating a magical atmosphere.

"Words can't describe how wonderful it is to finally see you again," said a strong, comforting voice.

An extraordinary, radiant light floated above the

throne. I shielded my eyes with my hands. But I could see enough to know: it was her. Isis and all her glory hovered gently in the air. Her golden power silhouetted her wings, just like in the image on the wooden doors. The sparkling wingspan was at least twenty feet across. She dazzled in a white flowy dress; a simple golden crown engraved with a cow horn was placed on her head. She looked exactly the same as she did in my dream where I was a baby—absolutely stunning.

She touched the ground, and her glow dissolved. She tiptoed quickly over to me, as if trying not to be overly excited. We stared at each other, not knowing what to do until she stuck out her arms for a hug. I giggled nervously, and accepted the offer. She wrapped her arms around me and squeezed tight. I didn't mind losing all the air in my chest for a moment. She let go, and I took a deep breath. She smelled like roses and vanilla.

"Look at you. You are so grown up." Isis examined me, smiling.

I felt an enormous amount of peace and comfort in her arms. "Well, I'm not completely done growing," I joked nervously, fumbling with my nails.

"Your power is also growing." She beamed.

"Yeah?"

"It will grow as you grow, and as you grow, you will discover new abilities. By the looks of your training, you are becoming very powerful."

"Training?"

"Yes, I do recall your father was training you outside of the ruins of the Step Pyramid."

"How did you kno—"

"I was watching you." Isis laughed.

"Watching me?"

"Yes, Magi, I watch you all the time," she said softly. I could tell she really missed me by how she tried to cover up her feelings with a wide grin.

"All the time?" I narrowed my eyes.

"Oh! I give you your privacy. I do not watch when you shower, don't worry," Isis laughed.

"I was about to say, 'You may be a god, but you might also be a creep.'"

We laughed together a little awkwardly.

"Your majesty."

Isis and I both turned to the voice.

"Your majesty, there is someone here to speak with you." Nesu's tone was deeper than usual, and that wasn't the only thing different about him. He looked like he had watched the scariest horror movie of all time.

"Thank you." Isis nodded her head. "Magi, I have a feeling this is an urgent matter. Go out in the hall and wait there. I will be finished shortly."

"Leave us," Isis ordered all the servants, and they began to take their leave. Isis nodded at me to do the same. I followed everyone out a small exit behind Isis' throne. Out of the corner of my eye, I spotted a hidden entrance to her throne room. I made sure all the servants and guards had passed me, and then crept to the entrance. Carefully and quietly, I opened the door enough to see Isis waiting for her guest on her throne.

Then, the large wooden doors to her throne room opened – and in walked the Master from my first dream. I covered my mouth to prevent from screaming. He walked with purpose, approaching Isis with an evil smirk.

"What do you want?" Isis immediately straightened her back. "You know you're not supposed to be here."

"Ahhh, good to see you, too, my darling." He grinned, showing his teeth.

"If you are here to beg for your position back on the Council, you can go out the same doors you entered."

The Master laughed. "Isis, why must you always assume the worst about me? I am here to ask you a simple question."

"Go on."

"Why?"

Isis was silent.

"Isis, why did you lie to all of us?"

"Excuse me?"

"You knew your child was alive this whole time, didn't you? Why didn't you ever say anything? Why did you pretend she was dead?"

"Someone was trying to kill her. I did whatever I had to in order to keep her safe. To secure her future. Even if that meant keeping the truth from the Council and everyone else."

The Master suddenly spun around and threw a small dagger, striking Isis in the stomach. I tried to scream, but the sound died in my throat. Isis fell to her knees, and the golden glow on the wall and floor began to fade. I then felt a great amount of uneasiness in the pit of my stomach. Several guards rushed the Master, but he swiftly cut them down like butter. It was now only him and Isis.

"Your little lie has cost me so much unneeded suffering and wasted time." The Master spit.

"You ..." Isis whispered, gritting her teeth.

"It was you."

"Don't act so surprised. I was the main suspect." The Master strolled up the steps towards Isis. "Yes, I tried to kill the thing you loved the most. Your symbol of hope and love for us all."

The Master knelt down, getting in Isis' face. "Why should you have yours, when you took mine away?"

"We didn't want to kill her, *Apophis*!" Isis cried, her eyes pleading.

"But you did, anyway!"

Apophis clasped his hand over Isis' mouth and yanked the dagger out of her stomach. Her cry was muffled in his hand.

"You will know my pain." The Master gritted his teeth. He wiped the blood off his dagger with Isis's dress and marched out the room. Isis' white dress was turning red all around her mid-section.

I dashed into the throne room and dropped beside Isis,

holding her body up with shaking arms. "Help!" I screamed.

Several guards came sprinting in after me. They examined the wound.

"My Queen!" Nesu fell to Isis' side. He touched her dress and when he pulled his hand away, it was covered in blood. He looked at the blood carefully—it was then I saw it was hardening and turning black.

"She's been poisoned," he announced. "We need to get her to the infirmary, now!"

"Magi, Magi," Isis tried to say.

"I'm here," I whispered.

"Magi, listen," Isis gripped my arm tightly with her bloody hand. "You have to stop him. You have to stop him ..."

She fell out of consciousness. Guards frantically picked her up and carried her away from me.

"Wait!" I yelled. So many people were rushing every which way, and I lost sight of her. The palace began to shake. Guards yelled out that it we were under attack.

Apophis's men charged the guards, running into the palace and waving swords. All this commotion was making me dizzy. The room started spinning—I felt sick to my stomach—I fell to my knees, then to my side. Everything went black.

My eyes opened suddenly, and I breathed heavily. My whole body shook, and air was getting caught in my throat. *Is the Master really Apophis? Was that just a bad dream?* I looked down and gasped. *Yep, she is definitely in trouble!*

I tore off my covers, leaped out of bed, and bolted out of the tent. I sprinted as fast as possible across the thick sand.

"Good morning, Magi!" R.J. yelled. Carter and R.J. were already up and practicing sword combat.

I didn't say a word to them. I kept running and dashed into my father's tent. He was sitting at his desk writing on some maps and a notepad. He turned around and noticed me panting.

"Running much?" my dad smiled. "What's up, Mags?"

"Dad, I think Isis is in trouble."

My dad's happy-to-see-me expression faded.

"What are you talking about?" he asked.

"I just had a dream and she was stabbed. She was poisoned, and she went unconscious, and then her palace was under attack—"

"Whoa, slow down. You had a dream?"

"Yes! And I woke up with this."

A look of complete fear washed over his face. My arm was covered in a blood-shaped handprint—Isis' hand. My father stared at the blood on my arm. An expression washed over his face that I had never seen before: utter heartbreak. The worry in his eyes was almost unbearable for me to look at.

"Is that hers?"

I nodded. "Dad, the person who stabbed her is the same person who has been trying to kill me."

My dad set his jaw. "Do you know who it is?" He waited, uneasy.

"It's Apophis."

My father didn't move. "Are you absolutely sure?"

"He admitted it."

My father exhaled as he stood up, and he then swallowed me up in his arms and held me tight.

"I'm so sorry," he said. He released me and placed his hands on my cheeks, looking into my eyes. "I am so sorry." My dad's lip quivered as tears escaped his eyes.

I had never seen my father in a state of panic. I didn't know what to do, other than feel completely helpless.

"Why are you apologizing?" I asked.

"Because I never should have brought you here." He wiped away his tears and attempted to collect his composure.

"Okay. Okay! We are going to figure this out."

My dad hurried back over to his desk and pulled a gun out from the drawer. He shoved a magazine filled with shiny red bullets into the butt of the gun, and stuck it in the back of his pants. *Red bullets?*

"Wait here," he ordered.

He rushed outside his tent.

"R.J.!" he yelled.

A few seconds later, Carter walked into my dad's tent.

"Hey, I was told to come in here. What's going on?" he asked, concerned.

"A lot." My voice shook.

"What do you mean?"

I raised my arm, showing Carter the bloody handprint.

"Whoa ... what is that?" Carter's eyes widened.

"Isis' handprint."

"How?"

"Ever since my dad gave me this necklace, I've had these strange and terrifying dreams. Each dream I've had has let me take something from my dream with me. I woke up with snake bites, huge headaches, the Egyptian symbol on my shoulder, and now..."

"Isis' bloody handprint."

"The worst part is, that I think the dreams allow me to see a glimpses of the past, present or future. And my past dream showed me who has been trying to kill me. It's Apophis...you were right."

Carter's face went slack—I could see his chest rising and falling faster. "That's not great news."

My father and R.J. rushed back into the tent. R.J. had a large machine gun strapped to his back.

"We need to go off the grid. No one needs to know where we are at." My father was debating with R.J.

"But we should bring in a team. A unit to protect and assist us to Ra's palace," R.J. argued.

"That many people would only attract a lot of

unwanted attention. The four of us going in by ourselves is not going turn a lot of heads."

"But Steven—"

"But no! I just found out my daughter is being hunted by the deadliest god in existence! I need you to trust me. Please. Let me be her father, and let me do this my way. If something were to happen, I need to know that I did everything I could."

R.J. nodded uneasily. "All right, I hear you." He tossed Carter and I sleeping bags. "This is going to sound weird, we need both of you to go back to sleep," R.J. told us.

"What?" Carter asked, confused. "Why?"

"Wait! What about Isis? We have to go save her!" I said.

"The first priority is the get you to safety. Then we will worry about Isis." R.J. responded calmly. "Look, we will explain everything later, but you two need to get your rest. Please trust us."

"I don't understand how sleeping is going to help her. " I narrowed my eyes.

"Just trust me," my father begged me. "And do *not* leave this tent."

Carter quickly began to lay out our sleeping bags, and I slumped down into mine, tearing up. Noticing I was emotional, Carter grabbed a towel, poured water out from a bottle and sat down next to me. He began to wipe the blood off my arm. I pulled my arm back, resisting his kindness –like a jerk.

"You don't have to do that." I sighed.

"Just let me."

"Look, I'm not your problem."

Carter stopped and just grinned at me. "I have this feeling that you are always going to be my problem." But he didn't say it in a mean way; he said it like he was looking forward to it.

He is literally amazing. I smiled, letting a few tears fall as he continued to wipe the blood off.

"Look, I know we are both terrified out of our minds, but maybe falling asleep might be the perfect way to stop thinking about it." Carter said.

I don't think I am going to sleep one bit.

We both crawled into our sleeping bags and stared up at the top of the tent.

"Well, good morning, Carter," I joked.

He chuckled. "Good morning, Mags."

It was now Midnight and I woke up fists clenched. My father and R.J. were loading up the Jeep outside the Step Pyramid.

"Dad, what's going on?" I tried to control by breathing. I needed to stay calm.

"Magi, there is no easy way to say this, so I am going to give it to you straight." He stopped in his tracks and faced me. "Your life is in grave danger. If the god Apophis is really set on killing you, he will succeed –

unless we get you to the safest place in both worlds – Ra's palace. "

"Ra? The sun god?" Carter asked.

"Yes. Usually I would say Isis's palace is the safest. But if she's been attacked, her palace is now compromised – and we can't take any chances. I had you two sleep for the whole day because you are going to need every ounce of energy to make it through the Realm. I have a bad feeling this won't be easy. Let's load up."

We all jumped into the Jeep.

The drive back to the great pyramid of Khufu took forever.

We parked outside of camp and began sneaking through Cheops. According to my father, it was critical that we were not spotted by any pyramid security.

"Shh!" my father hissed at Carter and I, pointing at our backpacks, which were filled with knives, daggers, flares, ropes, flares, food, and flashlights – all clanking together obnoxiously.

I winced "Sorry."

"We're trying," Carter said.

My dad nodded.

Everyone made it to the base of the pyramid without being spotted. The four of us made

it to the top.

"This way," R.J. said. His whole demeanor had changed dramatically. I honestly didn't think R.J. could be this serious—but he was scary focused.

We followed R.J. and my father down the narrow Descending Passage of the pyramid. After a few long minutes of walking like hunchbacks, we reached the Subterranean chamber. The air was hot and stuffy, and all I could think about was the little black cat again. The last time we were in here it almost lead us to our doom. *Where did that thing go?*

My dad traveled to the far wall of the chamber and studied the hieroglyphics carefully, as if he were searching for a something. He stopped on a particular one, put his hand on it, and pushed.

"Watch out," R.J. warned.

A loud rumbling echoed from the middle of the chamber. I covered my face. Carter wrapped his arms around me and pulled me away from the cloud of dust that suddenly surrounded us. Carter and I coughed wildly.

Once the dust settled, we realized all the commotion had come from inside the bottomless pit. We cautiously approached and discovered that, down inside the pit, a stone slab had moved out of place to create a new passageway!

My father climbed over the metal railing and lowered himself down into the pit.

"So, we are going into the large, creepy hole. Perfectly logical." Carter exhaled.

R.J. motioned for Carter and me to follow, and then he jumped in. Carter shook his head, but we both climbed over the railing and carefully lowered ourselves down. R.J. and my dad assisted my landing.

We walked through the strange new passageway into an oddly shaped chamber, like an awkward rectangle with crumbled pieces of stone in the corners. There were two wooden torches on the far wall, and I could tell they had been burning long before we entered.

Everyone's attention was focused on the very large hieroglyphs etched on a far wall covered with a giant ankh carving. My father pulled out an old papyrus scroll from his bag. Faded hieroglyphs had been painted onto the paper thousands of years go.

"You see the hieroglyphs on the wall?" my father asked Carter and me.

We nodded.

"These symbols right here mean *Earth*. The wall around this symbol asks visitors to recite the *God's Longing* riddle to gain entrance to the Realm. The riddle is on this papyrus. Saying the answer – then the riddle, and the answer again – out loud will lend you passage into to any Realm entrance. Here." He handed me the papyrus. "Try to see if you can pick up on a few words as I say them."

I nodded and moved to stand before the wall.

"Ready?" my father asked.

"Ready," everyone replied.

My dad began to recite:

"*Earth*... loved by all, but most take it for granted
it sprouted from a miracle therefore never planted,

a place all beings desire to be,

to see every sunset, soul, and shining sea...

Earth..."

My father stepped back as the hieroglyphics on the wall began to glow a bright, blinding white.

"Welcome to the Realm," my father announced.

The stone wall fizzled away like mist in a fan, and a warm wind rushed into the chamber through the opening. As the air hit my body, adrenaline shot through my veins.

I looked down at my hands. They shimmered gold as my skin transformed from pale and freckled into to a beautiful tan.

I looked back at the others and they gazed at me in awe. I could see pride in my father's eyes. In the reflection of Carter's glasses, I could see the symbol of Ra's eye – the Egyptian symbol for protection – glowing around my right eye, just underneath my skin. The glowing stopped, but my eyes remained a subtle golden color.

Carter pointed at my hair. I tugged on my ponytail and saw that my hair was pitch black instead of my natural dark chocolate color.

It was like I had gotten an extreme makeover just by walking into this place.

A long, dark gray stone passageway stretched ahead of us as far as our eyes could see. The only light in the passage was from Dad's flashlight. The passage was a lot cleaner than the rest of the pyramid – there were no cobwebs or dust anywhere.

"Let's go," my father insisted. We followed inside.

"Hey, dad?" I spoke up after minutes of silence.

"Yeah, Mags?" he replied.

"So... how did you even meet Isis? " I asked curiously.

R.J. chuckled.

My dad blushed a little through his worried expression. "Well, it all started when R.J. and I stumbled upon that Realm entrance back there. Once we were in, the doors sealed behind us, and we were stuck inside. We wandered around for a long time—until Isis' guards found us and dragged us into her throne room. Isis was mad, at first, but she was impressed that we had survived the Realm."

"Survived?" Carter blurted out.

"This place is not exactly a walk in the park." R.J. said bluntly. Carter gulped.

"Anyway, Isis ended up having a banquet with us, because she hadn't seen humans since the Seven-Year War; she wanted to get to know us."

"What he really means is – she wanted to get to know him," R.J. corrected, smiling.

My father laughed to himself. "That may have been true. Isis and I talked for hours. That is where our friendship started."

"What I don't get is how mortals are even able to walk into the Realm," Carter spoke up.

"You're right. You would think that they wouldn't be

able to, but the three of us are walking in it right now," my father answered.

"Three?" I said, puzzled. *Uhh, there are clearly four of us.*

My father stopped walking. Everyone did the same. He turned around and looked me straight in the eyes. "Magi, do you really think you are human?"

"I don't know. I thought I was like half mortal. A demigod. Like a real-life Percy Jackson or something."

My father laughed a little. "You are definitely not a demigod, Mags."

"Okay, so what am I?" I pressed further, confused. *If my dad was a human and Isis was a god, how could I not be like a demigod?*

My father sighed. "I think it's best you ask your mother that question." He turned back around and kept walking. The others followed him, and I stood rooted to the spot – even more curious than I was before.

CHAPTER 12

"Whoa." My father raised his hand in front of us. We had come up to a long stone bridge with no handles, covered in dark hieroglyphics. The bridge hung over two large pools with massive crocodiles swimming about. The walls of the chamber were covered with fresh dark green, gold, and black hieroglyphics – and most of them were of crocodiles.

"We are going to cross this bridge very carefully," my father warned us. "Whatever you do, do NOT step on the sun—"

"Sun-shaped stone," my father and I spoke in unison.

"How did you know?" he asked me.

I shrugged. "It's a visual puzzle—an Illusion. The sun is painted in a reddish color. Red usually represents danger, and in this case, it looks like it could be something bad."

"You are exactly right. If you step on a sun stone, the bridge will fall about twenty feet and land right above the water down there. When that happens, large spikes with blades will shoot up from underneath the bridge. Not to mention the pools on either side of the bridge are filled with crocodiles."

"Oh." Carter swallowed.

"Let's walk slowly—and match my movements perfectly," Dad ordered.

Carter and R.J. followed right behind him, stepping right where he had. I took my first step following Carter. As soon as I put my weight down on a tan colored stone, a green puff of smoke coughed up from the bridge.

"Huh?" I stopped moving, waving the smoke out of my face, gagging. It smelled like rotten eggs. The others turned around.

"Don't move." My father yelled, pointing at the bridge. "That's not supposed to happen."

"Oh, great!" I loved hearing that.

Awful, loud scratching noises echoed throughout the chamber.

"What is that?" Carter looked around, searching for the source of the haunting noise.

"The bridge has been tampered with!" R.J. exclaimed.

"Everyone, hug your backpacks," ordered my dad. In that same moment, the bridge dropped beneath our feet.

The four of us were falling through the air as the

bridge crashed into the pools—water splashed everywhere as we landed roughly.

"Everyone, on your feet!" my father screamed.

"Move, move, move!" R.J. yelled.

Everyone sprung up and sprinted.

A large spike almost struck Carter between the legs— panicked, he ran even faster. The spikes were shooting up all around us. One sliced into R.J.'s left arm. Another sliced into my father's shirt, and another one slashed me in the leg, ripping a trail of fire through muscle and skin. I glanced down for a split second, and saw my thigh spilling blood. Every few seconds, someone yelled in pain. We were getting cut open – and there was maybe fifty feet more of this insanity.

My instincts kicked in. I delayed a silver spike that sliced inches away from my face. I released everything back to normal speed, but I didn't realize that there was nowhere for me to move. I was between a sharp spike and crocodile-infested water. Then, to my horror, I began to lose my balance. Without thinking, I grabbed the spike to stop me from falling. It sliced both of my hands open. I cried out in pain, accidentally releasing time.

As soon as I let go of the spike, I was falling face first into the murky crocodile-infested water.

I screamed.

Several seconds went by, and I opened my eyes. I laid on a golden glow that felt like glass but was a strong as stone. Underneath the glow, a crocodile snapped at me, but he couldn't touch me. It was like the golden shield was preventing it from attacking me—like I was standing on a glass floor in a skyscraper, seeing everything below my feet.

Wait. I'm doing this! This is my power! When I looked down, I saw my hands were glowing. I carefully stood up on it.

Your power is also growing. As you grow, you will discover new abilities, I remembered Isis saying. *I think walking on air qualifies as a new ability!*

I then realized that my father, R.J., and Carter were still running for their lives. I panicked and delayed everything. The spikes stopped moving, the crocodiles stopped swimming, and everyone stopped running. Delaying all of this made my head ache.

Wait a second. What if I could delay just the spikes? I left out a nervous sigh and closed my eyes, concentrating as hard as I could. I ordered my powers to create a walkway for the others. If it worked, they would be able to jump up onto it and walk above the spikes to safety. I released my father, R.J., and Carter. I almost accidentally released the spikes, but they stayed delayed.

It's working. "Guys!" I yelled.

They all turned around to see me standing on my powers. They stared at me like I was on fire. "Step onto the path above you! Walk on it carefully to get to the other side!"

Without hesitation, they all climbed up on the golden pathway floating above them. Oh my god, they were heavy! Having them on top of my powers felt like I was lifting weights that were too heavy for me. I released the spikes and the crocodiles so I could fully concentrate on the pathway, in hopes that the piercing pain in my head would go away. We were all walking safely as we watched the spikes below our feet shoot up from the ground, but they failed to reach us.

"Magi! How are you doing this?" Carter beamed.

"I don't know!" I honestly didn't. But saying so broke my concentration, and the pathway began to crack like glass below our feet.

"Magi?" My father's tone was uneasy.

"Run!" I yelled. "I don't think I can do this much longer!"

The boys started sprinting. Under their feet, my power continued to shatter, and pieces began to fall to the ground. They all made it to the other side and jumped off the pathway. R.J. and my dad landed first. Carter landed and fell to the ground after impact. My pathway was giving way underneath my feet. I couldn't stop thinking about falling through and getting impaled.

"Mags, hurry!" my dad yelled.

"You got this, Magi!" R.J. tried to encourage me.

I started running. I only had maybe twenty yards. I was making progress when one of my feet fell through. I screamed.

"Dad!" I yelled with tears in my eyes.

"You're so close. Keep going!" he cried.

"You can do this, Magi!" R.J. called out once more.

"Hurry!" Carter added.

I climbed back up and made a break for it, sprinting as fast as I could. The pathway was shattering to pieces—I had ten feet left to go.

"JUMP!" Dad cried.

I leaped into the air as my pathway completely shattered to the ground. R.J. and my dad caught me. We all fell to the ground roughly.

"You okay?" My dad held me in his arms.

"I think so." I tried to catch my breath.

"Hey, that was pretty impressive, though." R.J. patted my back.

"Yeah, it was," Carter said as he squatted down next to me.

"We will work on the not-panicking part, but good job Mags." My father gave me a reassuring look.

I nodded my head and grinned a little.

"All right," said Dad. "Let's catch our breath and bandage up, and then we need to keep moving. No doubt Apophis had something to do with rigging that bridge to drop as soon as Magi touched it."

I lay down on the stone floor, trying to relax before we continued further into the Realm of the Gods.

∾

"WOW! THIS PLACE IS HUGE," I said, gaping at our surroundings.

The four of us had traveled into the largest chamber we had seen so far. It was more like an enormous cavern that, from the bottom to the stalactite-covered top, seemed to stretch for a mile. The stalactites dimly illuminated the ceiling like slow-burning candles. On the ground level were hundreds of towering columns, covered in bright hieroglyphics that stretched over five stories tall.

I glanced at Carter, who was also starstruck. R.J. crossed his arms and showed off a gritty smile as he looked down. *Oh, you have got to be joking...*

Stretching down for what looked like forever were thousands of stairs that went all the way to the ground level of the chamber.

"What is this place?" Carter asked.

"The original Karnak Temple," my father replied.

"Original?"

"Sometimes, when the ancient Egyptians were preparing to build a temple of worship for the gods, the gods themselves would send the architects visions of how they wanted their temples built. The gods must have sent visions of this place and then they created Karnak Temple."

"Seems about right," R.J. agreed.

"So, where to, now?" I asked.

"There," my father said. "That's where we need to go."

He pointed to a tall, climbing set of stairs that zig-zagged through jagged rocks on the opposite end of the chamber. From where we were standing to the opposite side was an easy three football fields.

"Well ... who wants to go down the freakishly long set of stairs first?" R.J. asked with a grin.

No one answered. "All right, then." He shook his head, laughing. Carter and I shared a giggle.

A few minutes later, we were already making progress down the stone steps. The steps went down in a zigzag fashion, and then spiraled around a gigantic obelisk. As we walked by, the hieroglyphics on the obelisk began to glow golden orange. The glow floated away from the obelisk like a 3D movie. The hieroglyphics floated all around us; it was magical.

Carter and I tried to catch the mystical glow in our hands. If we touched it, it would dissemble into tiny glowing particles, and then disappear.

I tried to translate some of the hieroglyphs in my head. My dad told me that, one day, when my power grew strong and I did enough good ol' fashioned studying, I would be able to read hieroglyphics like a first language.

We finally reached the bottom, and the four of us began to stroll through the towering maze of columns. The hieroglyphics on them were so beautifully detailed. I walked over to one of the columns to take a closer look.

They were like moving pictures, displaying ancient Egyptians playing music and dancing together, as the children ran around chasing their dogs and cats into crop fields. Their parents drank precious wines, ate delightful foods, and laughed and sang together. I could hear the music they were playing. A few were blowing into sweet-sounding wooden flutes, plucking harps. Others were beating on drums.

Carter and I caught each other's eyes. He grinned at me and kept walking.

Wow...he really has the most beautiful eyes.

Out of nowhere, a blistering shriek rang out through the whole chamber. All four of us hunched over in pain and covered our ears. The noise ceased. We all looked around, perplexed, trying to find the source of that awful sound.

I covered my ears again when another screech rang through the entire chamber. *What the heck is that?*

I turned to my father for answers. His eyes were fixed on something behind me, his hands clutching his sword. R.J. drew his two blades. Even Carter drew his sword, his hand shaking. I clutched my necklace nervously.

Together, the four of us faced the entrance of Karnak. A dark, eerie green smoke was entering the chamber. It snaked towards the gigantic obelisk, its movement as fluid and effortless as a dancer's.

The hypnotizing orange glow from the obelisk was consumed by the dark smoke. Once it wound its way to the top of the obelisk, the smoke darkened from dark green to pitch black.

The smoke twisted and writhed, taking shape. It looked almost alive. My breath rushed out of me. The smoke had transformed itself into a giant falcon the size of a school bus. Its feathers were black with hints of shiny brown. One of its eyes was light green, and the other was glowing a dark, smoky green, like the demon bandits. It flapped its wings and screeched. Then, the falcon launched itself off the obelisk, stretched its wings, and flew directly at us.

"We've got a problem." My father grabbed my shoulder.

"You know what you do when you have a problem?" I asked.

"What?" my father replied.

"You run away from it!" I yelled.

With that being said, everyone sprinted as fast as they could.

The falcon screeched as it flew towards us. The exit to the chamber was still far away, and we'd have to climb up a heck of a number of stairs to get to it.

The falcon screeched once more as it flew over our heads and landed in our path. We halted. The bird slowly turned around, its talons clanking like chains against the stone floor. It raised its wings and screamed.

"Spread out!" my father yelled.

The four of us split. My father and I took cover behind the pillars to the left of us, while Carter and R.J. took cover behind the ones to the right. The falcon marched over to my father's pillar and snapped at him, but my dad repelled it away with his sword.

The falcon then turned and descended upon R.J.'s pillar. It snapped at R.J., and he fought back. The falcon flapped one of his wings towards him.

R.J. let out a scream in pain—from my vantage point, I could see that the falcon had somehow slashed him in the chest. The falcon screeched and flew towards Carter. From what I could see, R.J. had three large cuts.

"Don't let the feathers touch you," R.J. warned. "They'll cut you!"

My eyes widened. We were fighting a bird with knifes for feathers? This just kept getting better.

Carter remained calm and quiet as the falcon attempted to attack him; he ducked and rolled out of the way, dashing to R.J.

The falcon swooped towards my column, and I pressed my back up against the pillar. The clanking talons stopped. Seconds later, the falcon peeled itself around the pillar and repositioned its head directly in front of me.

"Well, you're really close to me, aren't you?" I said.

The falcon nodded its head like it understood. Out of nowhere, one of its talons wrapped around my waist.

"No!" my father screamed.

Before I knew it, I was in the air, its talons gripping my stomach so tight, I could barely breathe. Only my right arm was free—but it was enough.

As quickly and carefully as I could, I yanked my necklace off and turned it into a sword. I delayed the falcon as I swung into its leg. I released time, and it screeched out in pain, dropping me.

I screamed out in terror. I was free-falling, and my landing zone was rough stone. With quick thinking, I created a golden platform to land on. Instead of landing, I body slammed into it, then rolled off, hitting the ground— my entire body ached. *I've got to learn how to control my power better.* I slowly struggled to get back on my feet.

When I turned, I discovered the falcon inches away from my face, staring right into my eyes. *You really like to get close to me, don't you?* It raised its great wing and smacked me, sending me flying across the chamber. I crashed into the ground and rolled into a pillar, losing my necklace in the process. Dark red blood seeped out of my side, courtesy of the razor feathers. I tried to stand back up, but the pain shot through me, stealing my breath. I could barely prop myself up on my elbows, but I still inched my way towards my necklace.

The falcon thumped towards me, shaking the ground with each step. My heart thumped with it—I was too injured to use my powers, and the boys were too far away to save me.

I finally managed to grab my necklace and, with one thought, turn it into a sword.

The Falcon loomed over me, hoisting its wing up for one final strike. *Death by bird...wonderful.*

"MAGI!" screamed my father.

With an ear splitting shrill, the falcon swung, and I gasped for my last breath. I shielded myself for the piercing blow just as someone tackled me and rolled me away from the creature.

I crashed to the ground, and the falcon screamed in frustration. I laid face down, trying to figure out what just happened. *Who just pushed me? It couldn't have possibly been my father, R.J., or Carter. They were on other side of the chamber.*

A blinding light shot into the cavern like lightning, but it disappeared almost immediately. As soon as it was dark again, an unnerving growl echoed through the space. I slowly turned over my shoulder to find a silky, black, hound-like creature standing directly over me. It was the largest dog-like creature I had ever seen in my life. While it was closer to a Great Dane in size, it looked like a hybrid of a wolf and a jackal. Its ears pointed up sharply, and its eyes were glowing a deep red.

The falcon shrieked once again. The hound snarled a nasty, vicious growl, showing its dazzling, white teeth. The falcon flapped its wings, generating a fierce wind, and charged me and the hound. The hound took a strong stance over me.

Out of nowhere, a large black panther leaped into the air towards the falcon. The falcon raised its wing to attack, but it was too late. The panther roared savagely, driving its long, sharp claws into the falcon's chest. The falcon let out a scream as the panther ripped its body open and the bird fell to the ground—the fight was over. The Falcon desperately escaped the panther and flew away before dissolving into thin air.

The hound quit snarling and turned its attention towards me. I watched its every move, clutching my necklace. An intense bright light consumed the hound. I squinted my eyes and tried to see what was happening, but the light was too bright for my eyes to handle.

The light vanished. The hound had transformed into one of the most attractive men I had ever seen in my life. He had caramel skin with short black curly hair, and dark eyes. He seemed only slightly older than me and wore a white and gold Egyptian shendyt that exposed his perfectly defined chest. Golden cuffs wrapped his wrists, accentuating his masculine arms. For a moment, I was sure I was dreaming.

He reached out his hand, offering to help me stand up. I was about to grab his hand, but I hesitated.

"Who are you?" I asked suspiciously.

"Anubis," he stated. "Embalmer and judge of the dead."

I was so taken aback that I was in the presence of a god —an insanely hot god—that I didn't realize that I was staring at him like a complete idiot.

"I remember studying about you in school, but you are nothing like I imagined you to be," I said, looking from his face to his abs, then back to his face.

"Well, the Egyptians weren't the most skilled artists."

"No, they were not," I grinned then winced in pain. My large gashes were still bleeding.

Anubis examined the wound. "Looks pretty deep—I'm sorry, what's your name?"

"Yeah...uh, my name is—"

"Magi!" My father ran up and hugged me so tight, it felt like he was squeezing the living daylights out of me.

"Ow, ow, ow." I gritted my teeth.

"Ahh, I'm sorry! Are you okay?" he asked.

"I'm fine, Dad. I promise."

I looked deeper into my father's eyes and reassured him that I was all right, despite the aching pain. He nodded his head, but he was still shaking.

I felt someone place their hand on my shoulder. I turned around to see R.J. looking down at me, making sure I was okay. I gave him a gentle hug, soft enough that I wouldn't hurt the large gashes on his chest.

Carter stood behind R.J., waiting patiently for me to acknowledge him. He carefully wrapped his arms around me, grateful that I was all right. It surprised me how much comfort I found there, in his arms. I never wanted to let go.

Anubis snapped his head. He eyed the panther as it approached us. Everyone was on edge as the panther just stared at all of us with its bright yellow eyes. All of a sudden, it was consumed in a magnificent light and transformed into a girl.

This girl looked about my age and wore a black Egyptian-inspired dress that cut above her knees – complete with a golden belt wrapped around her waist. Her wrists sported black cuffs and her feet were clad in black sandals. Both set of nails were painted pitch black, and thick eyeliner was coated on the lids of her brown eyes. She appeared Asian-American to me. She had dyed dark-red hair with bangs across the forehead – most pieces in front were longer than the rest of the hair. She strutted towards us with an attitude like she could kick all of our asses. But the strangest thing about her was that she had a deep scar down her left eye that had a faint dark orange glow. *That looks really familiar...*

She joined the five of us and scooted up next to Anubis.

"Was that weird to you?" she asked Anubis as she pointed to where the Falcon had dissolved.

"Yep." Anubis was deep in thought, still suspicious.

"Hmm." The girl shook her head then faced the rest of us. She examined us as we examined her. She then glanced at me and gave me a smirk—the smirk that I usually give to people when I'm confident.

"Nice to see you again, Bastet. You look well." my father spoke up, smiling at the girl. I turned to my dad, surprised. He knew her?

"Thank you Mr. Davis, " the girl replied with a slight grin.

"Magi, Carter, this is Bastet," my father announced to me and Carter. "The daughter of Ra. Bastet"— my father turned to her—"this is Magi and Car—"

"Oh, you don't need to introduce them to me, I already know them," Bastet spoke up.

Carter and I narrowed our eyes, confused.

"I know you know Magi, but how do you know Carter?" my father asked.

"Oh, I accidentally met them in the pyramid the other night," Bastet explained, biting her nail.

"Ohhhh!" My father nodded his head.

I stared at her, confused. I had never met this girl in my life—I would have remembered her if I had.

Carter and I gazed at Bastet. We both looked at each other like we were thinking the same thing: "We've never met you."

Bastet rolled her eyes a little. "You might recognize me like this."

After she spoke, a radiant light shined from her body. The light vanished, and Bastet was gone.

Meow.

My jaw dropped. Sitting perfectly still in front of me, staring into my soul, was the little black cat with the scar down its left eye!

The little black cat tip toed over to me and brushed up against my leg. It purred loudly as it flounced over and brushed up against Carter's legs. Then, it traveled away and sat in its signature statue position. A bright light shot out from the fur of the little black cat. A light bulb went off in my head—it all made sense.

"It's you!" I said in awe. Bastet was the little black cat!

She was the cat that we saw in the pyramid – the same one that sat on my balcony every day.

Back in her human form, Bastet nodded. Carter's mouth dropped. All she did was grin, as if she were enjoying watching us freak out.

"Bastet," began R.J., "is the goddess of cats and protection."

"Oh, and by the way?" Bastet pointed to Carter and I. "I really didn't appreciate you two chasing me around the pyramid. Do you realize how tired I was?"

"We didn't know," Carter tried to explain.

"We didn't," I said, following Carter.

"You almost got them killed?" Anubis crossed his arms.

Bastet stopped herself. "Okay yeah, I shouldn't complain about that, then. I was just trying get back in the Realm. I was so excited to go home and, each time, they kept showing up. But *you*." She pointed at me. "I also didn't appreciate all the times you yelled at me to get off your balcony."

"I didn't know!" I defended myself. "Why were you there in the first place?"

"Let's just say my dad grounded me, and my punishment was to remain a cat and guard your house until you grew up and could defend yourself. By the way, you talk in your sleep."

The others giggled. *Thanks a lot, you little fur ball.*

"Can we go now?" Bastet said. Anubis eyeballed her, slightly annoyed.

"Yes, we need to speak with Ra immediately, and get Magi to safety," my father's harsh tone cut off the annoying small talk.

"Follow us." Anubis reassured us with his reserved, gentlemanly way.

CHAPTER 13

The four of us followed Anubis and Bastet through a series of chambers – all in varying shapes and sizes – until we reached a small wooden door. When Anubis opened it, bright light beamed through from the other side.

"Welcome to the kingdom of Ra," Anubis announced.

On the other side of the door was the most spectacular scenery. To the right of us rested a beautiful ocean. An orange sun hung in the deep blue sky. To the left of us, magnificent mountains stood covered in fluffy white snow. The snow sparkled from the moon, which dominated that part of the sky. Half the sky was day, and the other half the sky was night. The ocean was the only thing both landscapes had in common.

"This is unbelievable," Carter whispered.

We trotted along a stone path, through a vineyard with thousands of grapevines. We weaved down until we reached a grand palace with orange flags blowing from the ocean breeze. The palace itself looked like a modern Spanish mansion, but ten times bigger with guards poking their heads out of many turrets. I half expected a Rolls Royce to be parked out front.

As it all came into view, I saw an ancient Egyptian sailboat hovering in the starry night sky. It slowly descended until the wooden planks grazed the water, and then floated on top of the blue waves.

"Father's home." Bastet grimaced. Her scar began to glow a deep blood orange. She shook her head and kept walking.

The boat sailed towards two tunnels carved into the cliff atop which Ra's palace stood. One tunnel faced the mountains, and the other tunnel faced the orange sun. The boat sailed its way into the tunnel closest to the snow.

Bastet and Anubis led us to a towering, brown iron gate with a large symbol of a sun. There were many guards patrolling the perimeters of the castle, donning shendyts and gripping the hilts of the swords resting in their hostlers. Two guards opened the gate for us, and we followed Bastet and Anubis inside the palace.

The interior showcased extravagant cylinder pillars with, of course, hieroglyphics – and a bronze chandelier hanging over the entrance with tiny orange orbs emanating light. *Are those miniature suns?*

A servant with a shaved head approached us.

"Take us to my father's wharf. We must speak to him immediately," Bastet ordered the servant.

"His majesty has just returned from the journey of Solar Rebirth, and must prepare for his journey again tomorrow. He does not speak to anyone until his duties are complete." His face was blank, obviously stuck in routine.

"He's going to have to make an exception this time. Take us to the wharf. That's an order," Bastet said.

The servant nodded, almost flinching. He did as she requested, and led us down a long hallway until we reached a manually operated lift. The six of us stepped on. As soon as our feet touched, six chiseled men used a rope to lower us down into darkness. Sounds of clanking and pounding echoed through the stone shaft. The moisture in the air increased dramatically, almost like a smack to the face, and the smell of salt and fish became prominent. Orange light from the bottom grew brighter and brighter, highlighting the angles of our faces.

"Woah!" Carter gasped.

He took the words right out of my mouth.

We were lowered into a massive cavern that was an underground shipyard. Everywhere we looked, men pounded nails into new war ships, sawed heavy timbers, and repaired the existing docks. Seagulls screamed obnoxiously as they soared over rows of ships swaying the waves. But the most impressive ship was the one currently being docked.

The mighty sun on the white sail rippled in the wind

as a team of rowers – ten on each side of the boat – pushed and pulled the yacht-sized ship. Ropes flew over the sides, caught by men below to secure the boat to metal horn cleats. Wooden planks were lowered, and the rowers and guards quickly stepped onto land in a routine fashion.

I narrowed my eyes; my stomach churned with nerves.

Swiftly rising from the golden throne on the ship, with his dark orange cape blowing behind him, was Ra. In his hand, he held a miniature ship. He tossed it into the air, and the tiny ship soared over the shipyard until it reached the other side of the cavern and landed in an empty slot.

Carter and I exchanged looks of disbelief as we watched the miniature ship grow in size until it was as big as the ship Ra was standing on. The only difference was that sail had a moon and stars emblazoned on it.

His guards made way for him as Ra marched down the wooden planks onto the docks. His ancient golden and leather battle armor clanked against his tan, masculine body has he walked. All he was doing was walking, yet I shivered from the pull of his power. My chest also tightened from excitement, and my hands felt warm and sweaty.

Ra made his way to another golden throne where servants swarmed him, offering him options of clothes to change into after his journey.

"Father!" Bastet yelled as she made her way towards him. The rest of us followed.

"Bastet, you know the procedure. I am not to be interrupted." Ra's commanding voice echoed in the cavern.

"We can explain the interruption," my father spoke up.

Ra shook his head in shock. "Steven!" He waved his servants away and approached my father, shaking his hand. Dad lowered his head in respect. "What are you doing here?"

My father turned to face me. Ra froze. "I have to keep her safe. This is the safest place I know."

"Is that... *her*?" he whispered. My father nodded.

Ra gazed at me like I was a lost friend who had come home from war. He inched towards me until his brown-orange eyes were locked on mine. His face was strong and sweet-looking –Bastet definitely resembled him. He scanned me up and down, and then placed his hands on my head as if he were making sure I was real. The excitement in my chest intensified as my body temperature rose.

"Margaret." Ra cracked a grin as he brushed my sweaty hair out of my face. "Welcome home." He shook his head as if he were taking himself out of a daydream. "Wait, you said you brought her here to keep her safe?" He turned back to my father.

"Yes." My dad exhaled.

"From what? From whom?"

"Apophis," I spoke up.

There was a sound of metal tools falling to ground. I jumped, startled, and bumped into Carter. The whole cavern silenced, and the only thing we could hear was the water crashing against the docks. All the workers around us stared at me with horrified faces. I wanted to crawl into my boots and hide.

All the blood had drained from Ra's face. "Apophis?" His eyes flickered orange, like fire surrounded his pupils. I took this as not a good thing. "How do you know this?" Ra interrogated me.

"I had a dream." I shifted in my stance, suddenly realizing how stupid I sounded.

"A dream?" Ra said.

"Apophis is trying to kill her," my father explained.

The three gods all looked at each other darkly.

"What else did you see in your dream?" Anubis asked.

"I-I saw Apophis stab Isis, poisoning her... and then her palace was attacked. That's it."

"She's right!" a voice yelled from behind all us. Running into the wharf was Nesu, along with a bunch of wounded guards from Isis' palace. Ra's servants moved to help them. "Isis's palace was attacked. Now Isis is gone. Apophis has her." Nesu reported. "Only a few of us are left."

"What?!" My father exclaimed.

"Horus went to assess the situation, but has not returned," Nesu continued.

"Anubis!" Bastet gasped, with terror in her eyes.

His eyes widened. "Do you think that was—"

"Mind control? It's possible," Bastet said, rubbing her head.

"Where's Isis, then?" my dad questioned.

"*The Mire.*" Ra turned away from all of us.

"The Mire?" I tested the word on my tongue.

"The most undesirable place in the Realm," Ra explained.

"We can still save her." Hope burned in Bastet's eyes.

"How?" my father asked.

"My blood," Bastet revealed. "Apophis is a snake, and he'll use his poison on special victims. My blood counteracts the effects."

Carter leaned into my ear and whispered, "Egyptians used cats to protect their homes and families from snakes and other pests."

"But...wait. I thought gods couldn't die." I said.

Anubis overheard. "If a god kills another god, they can."

"That's why this is so serious." Bastet stared at the ground, deep in thought.

Ra's eyes flickered orange again. "Take Nesu and his men to the infirmary, and get them well," Ra ordered several of his servants, who began to escort Isis's men out. He then began to order his men in another language – I wondered if it was the same language the ancient Egyptians had spoken. Several strapping soldiers stood at attention in front of Ra. "Osahar."

The soldier with most decorated broad collar stepped forward.

"Go to the Mire, find out if he has taken Isis, and bring

her back. If Apophis is behind all of this... she won't be the only one who ends up dead... *Em Heset!*"

"Em Heset!" Osahar repeated, as if this were a way of saluting.

The soldiers bowed. Osahar bowed his head to me, grinning, giving me a sweet look of reassurance as he led the soldiers towards the docks.

"Osahar is my best warrior; he's fought along my side for thousands of years. If Apophis has Isis, he will find her." Ra spoke to us with confidence.

"So, now what?" R.J. asked as he comforted my father, who was obviously anxious as he watched the soldiers sail out of the wharf.

"Now, we wait." Ra sighed. "Not ideal, I know, but while we wait, let's get you all cleaned up and fed."

RA'S SERVANTS escorted us to the palace guest bedrooms. A servant showed me to a room with a stunning bronze and crystal chandelier hanging over a king-sized bed with a shiny dark turquoise comforter on top. The walls were tan stone, and the ceiling was painted the same dark turquoise. To the left of me was a crescent-shaped balcony that overlooked the split sky.

I immediately threw my backpack off my shoulders and lowered myself on the bed. Out of the corner of my eye, I spotted a tiny glass bottle filled with glowing orange liquid sitting on a vanity. A note sat next to it. "Drink this. It will rejuvenate your body." *All right, Alice in Wonderland.* I walked painfully over to the vanity, popped out the little cork, and swallowed. I felt instant peace as I watched my wounds heal rapidly before my eyes. I rubbed my side where I had been slashed by the feathers. There was no evidence left of the attack. My skin instantly shimmered gold, and the cut on my face finally vanished.

Next to the note was a change of clothes with another note. "Picked these out for you. Bastet."

I smiled. *Wow, she really knows my style.* She'd picked out white skinny jeans and a white tank top, brown lace-up boots, and authentic brown leather jacket. The coolest thing to me was a leather belt with Isis's symbol in solid gold as the buckle.

I pulled the tie out of my tangled hair, and my new jet-black locks fell perfectly straight past my shoulders. As a girl with curly hair, running my fingers through smooth hair was a fascinating experience. It only took my thirty seconds for my hair to look neat again.

I sighed and began to take my jacket off, when I heard a loud growling noise. I yanked off my necklace and turned it into a dagger. The noise was coming from the balcony. I peered my head around to look and saw a large black panther striding towards me.

I jumped, startled. The panther growled some more, and then a ball of light swallowed her.

I covered my eyes from the light and when I opened them, Bastet appeared, sitting on the edge of the balcony.

"You are such a spaz." Bastet chuckled.

"Because you appeared out of nowhere! As a panther!" I shot back.

Bastet smirked. She launched herself off the balcony and flashed into a little black cat. Bastet pounced around in a chair, plopped down, and became comfortable. Once again, Bastet flashed and turned back into her human form with her arms crossed over her chest, still smirking.

"What do you expect? I'm a cat; I sneak up on everyone." She grinned, delighted.

Bastet had a sly deviousness about her. I actually kind of liked it, when she wasn't freaking me out. She was a very interesting person ... er, god.

"Hey, um, I just wanted to say that I am really sorry about your mom." Bastet stared at the floor, twisting her ankle. "She is one of the best leaders I know. I look up to her. She stood up for me at a point in time where everyone thought I was a lost cause. And, after all this time, you deserve to meet your real mother." Bastet spoke with complete sincerity, something I could tell was hard for her.

"Thank you." I sighed, letting a grin slide. "I need to meet her," I admitted. I felt easier admitting this to a stranger than anyone else. "I need to know who I am, and she knows who I am. Everything will all become a lot clearer if I can just talk to her. I just don't want the worst to happen... first..."

"It won't. We won't let it." Bastet reassured me, but then stared at me strangely. "It's really weird…"

"What?" I shifted in my stance, avoiding eye contact.

"I have been around you for seventeen years, and have never had a conversation with you… except for when you frequently yelled at me."

I cackled, quickly covering my mouth. "Sorry about that."

"No, it was funny. You're real passionate about me not sitting on your car."

"It's kinda my baby." I smiled.

Bastet and I laughed, struggling to keep the conversation alive. "So," I began, "what do you like to do? When you're not sitting my car." It occurred to me I had no idea how to talk to a god.

"Scare people," she deadpanned.

"Of course…"

"Well, it's better than killing people," she laughed.

I froze.

"Oh, I'm so sorry!" she blurted out. "My therapist suggested that if I make jokes about my past, I would heal faster, but then I forget that I freak people out."

Therapist? I continued to hold my breath.

"I used to have a problem with killing humans," she flat out admitted. "I'm okay now, but that's why I was grounded."

"Oh," I whispered.

"Since then, I have turned to scaring people. My

favorite thing to do. Every Halloween, I try to scare as many people as I can. People are already superstitious about black cats, and it's unbelievable about how superstitious they get on Halloween. It's the most wonderful time of the year."

I chuckled to myself. "That's actually pretty funny. Halloween is my favorite too. I'm a little biased. It's my birthday."

"I know." Bastet grinned.

"Right. Of course you know." I felt strange that she knew everything about me, and I hardly anything about her.

"This year," Bastet continued, "we should go out and celebrate together. The daughter of the Queen of Illusions, with a black cat? Things could get pretty funny."

"Oh my god, you are so right."

"Yeah, we can go as Catwoman and Cleopatra."

I laughed pretty hard for the first time in a while. Bastet grinned, satisfied with herself, but her demeanor quickly changed.

"What?" I said.

"There's just something I don't get about all this..."

"What's that?'

"I don't understand why Apophis used venom."

I titled my head, still not understanding.

"Apophis hardly ever uses poison; he gets *creative*..."

A huge lump in my throat formed, and swallowing suddenly became hard.

"It just makes me wonder..." Bastet's eyes flickered bright yellow as she jumped up onto her feet. "Get dressed, find your father, and head to the banquet hall!" she ordered me.

"What's going on?" I questioned her.

"I have a bad feeling we are in danger."

Bastet flashed and completely vanished out of my room.

AFTER I FRANTICALLY THREW ON my clothes, a couple of guards escorted me out of my room. We met my father, R.J., and Carter there – and they all had on new clothes as well.

"Not bad, Ms. Davis," Carter complimented me politely – just to get on my nerves.

"Ms. Davis?" I stared at him.

"A gentleman should always address a lady properly at a special occasion." He grinned, and I could tell that he knew that he was, indeed, getting on my nerves.

"Shut up." A lip bite slipped through my state of panic. Carter grinned to himself, satisfied.

The guards led the four of us to the top of the grand, polished stone staircase that stretched all the way down to a single, long table in a magnificent banquet hall. *Whoa* ... Floating near the top of the ceiling was a miniature sun, the size of a human hamster ball. Unlike the real sun, it wasn't blinding to look at – but it produced the perfect amount of warm lighting for the venue. Millions of glowing balls the size of marbles swirled above us, producing silver light. Some of them shot across the ceiling like shooting stars. *Wait! Those* are *tiny stars. So, that's what stars look like...*

Servants swarmed the table, putting down bread, grapes, strawberries, turkeys, salmon, steamed vegetables, cheese, wine, and much, much more. Ra and Anubis hovered over the table, deep in conversation.

"Any news?" my father asked Ra.

Nothing yet." Ra shook his head.

My father sighed as everyone began to pick at the food. He lowered his head, placing it in his hands.

All of a sudden, Bastet flashed into the banquet hall next to all of us.

"LOCK DOWN THE PALACE!" she screamed. "LOCK IT DOWN!"

"Bastet!" Ra yelled. "What's going on?"

Something launched itself from the table towards Bastet. I gasped and delayed whatever was flying towards her. Everyone in the banquet hall held their breath.

Inside the glowing, transparent sphere that I had created with my mind was a baby cobra. Poison dripped from its fangs as it kept trying to attack her from inside its glowing cage.

"Are you all right?" Ra placed his hand on his daughter's shoulder.

"We're too late!" She glared at the snake. Its eyes began to glow a smoky dark green. *Oh no...*

"Lower it?" Anubis asked me.

I placed the sphere on the ground, and Anubis got close and pulled a sword put from his belt. I made the sphere vanish, and he swiftly cut off the snake's head.

Suddenly, all of the doors to the banquet room swung shut. Ra's guards dashed over to all of the entrances on the ground level and up the stairs, and they discovered the same thing: the doors were all locked shut.

"What's going on here?" Ra raised his voice.

A deep, menacing laugh echoed throughout the silent banquet hall. "You shouldn't have come here," the voice taunted. Chills crawled up my back.

My father grabbed my arm, pulling me close, and positioned his sword in front of my chest. I felt instantly sick to my stomach.

My legs began to shake at the sound of vicious animal growls filled the room—it was Bastet and Anubis, snarling in their human-god-like forms.

Another horrifying sound entered the banquet chamber. My eyes immediately shot to Carter—we had heard that haunting sound before. It was one of those things that you never forget. It was the same bloodcurdling screeching sound that we heard before the Egyptian warriors came out of the wall.

And all around us, the walls began to move.

The back walls crumbled and swirled around before

compacting together to form human-like stone figures. The stone figures stomped toward us. A bright glow flashed in their hands, dimming to reveal khopeshes and spears.

Ra's guards swarmed the banquet table to protect us.

The back entrance to the banquet hall opened slowly. Everyone watched in silence as an object that had been tossed into the hall rolled in between the legs of Ra's guards.

I covered my mouth—it was Osahar's head.

Ra gawked at his prized solider with watery eyes, but quickly looked up.

A tall, muscular, bald man stepped over the threshold. He moved with deliberate steps that told me he enjoyed the sound of his own footsteps haunting the hall, I choked. *Oh, my god ... he is real.* The Master from my dreams was standing in Ra's banquet hall. My nightmare: Apophis.

Apophis," Ra snarled.

"Brother." Apophis grinned.

Apophis raised his hand, and his eyes turned the same evil smoky green. Multiple pythons broke through the ground beneath Anubis, Bastet, and Ra. They wrapped around each god and tightened. Ra's serpents slammed him into a wall near Apophis.

"The more you struggle, the tighter they will squeeze," Apophis warned.

One by one, Apophis' stone warriors began taking out Ra's guards. Two warriors grabbed Carter. R.J. screamed and tried to help, but he was quickly restrained by other stone figures. My father managed to fight back a few warriors before one snuck in from behind and snatched me away from him.

"No!" Dad yelled as he was captured by warriors.

The warrior held my arms behind my back and carried me to Apophis. I tried to kick and punch my way free, but the warrior was too strong and brought me before Apophis. My whole body trembled as tears streamed down my face. The fear of death swam through my veins like eels, ready to electrocute me.

Apophis leaned in close to me, gently brushing his bumpy hand against my cheek. His slimy gaze made contact with mine—not once did his eyes ever blink. *He's gonna kill me.*

"Keep your hands off of my daughter!" my father yelled.

"You two should have stayed in hiding," Apophis hissed.

"Apophis, don't you dare touch her! You will regret this," Ra threatened, struggling to get free from the serpents around him.

"You know?" Apophis grinned. "I don't think I will."

Apophis marched away from me and headed straight for Bastet. A bronze dagger materialized into hands as he reached in the air. Bastet's yellow eyes widened.

"NOOOO!" Ra screamed.

Apophis raised his hand to slit her throat, but a flash of light consumed her. Bastet had flashed into a black kitten and escaped the entanglement of the serpents, dashing away. Apophis, already in mid-swing, sliced into his own snakes.

"FIND HER!" he yelled with rage.

Several guards chased after Bastet as she somehow snuck out of the banquet hall. Apophis, furious, turned back the us.

"Take them to the Hold!" he ordered.

His warriors dragged us out of Ra's palace, with Ra and Anubis yelling threats at him the entire way.

THE NEXT THING WE KNEW, our hands were cuffed in chains above our heads in a dungeon Apophis called the Hold. Carter and I were in one cell together, and my father and R.J. were in one to the right of us. Machines that looked like they were made to rip limbs sat in dark corners of the cells, surrounded by discarded skeletons. The cells stretched as far as I could see. I yanked on the chains that cuffed my hands in hopes of freeing myself, but it was useless, and I was bruising my wrists. "What's going to happen to us?" Carter whispered. His solemn voice broke my heart. I stared down at the wet and rotten floor of our cell.

"I don't know." I wished with all my heart that I could have said anything else to him. I wanted him to believe that there was going to be hope for us, but I feared the worst.

"Are we going to die?" Carter asked.

I looked up from the dirty floor. There were tears in his worried eyes. I couldn't stand seeing him this way. Frustrated, I yanked on my chains.

What is wrong with me? A realization hit me like a rock. The choice was ours: give up up, or fight with everything we've got.

"No," I said, making my decision. I was done being afraid.

Carter raised his head and gazed at me.

"No, we are not going to die," I spoke up.

"How can you be so sure?"

I looked to my left; my father and R.J. were listening too.

"Carter, I'm not. But what I am sure of is that I don't want to die at *his* hands. I want meet Isis and have all my questions answered. But if I am going to die, I'm gonna make it real hard for him."

I could tell my words were working their way through to him. And the more I spoke, the more I believed what I was saying.

"You need to promise me that you are going to stay strong," I said. "I need you. We all need to stay strong and fight back. We can't give up."

Carter nodded, determined. "Never give up."

That's right. "Never give up."

FOOTSTEPS ECHOED THROUGHOUT THE HOLD. Apophis was coming for us—we all knew it.

Apophis, flanked by his stone warriors, stepped in front of our cell. We were all on high alert.

"I trust your stay here has been comfortable so far," he taunted.

"The smell of a death is always refreshing to the lungs," I stated.

Apophis cracked a smile. "Aren't you a clever girl."

The guards opened our cell doors and detached us from the chains that kept our hands above our heads. They aggressively yanked us out of the cells, forcing us to walk in a single-file line. We were each accompanied by two warriors on either side of us, with Apophis as our line leader. I had the displeasure of walking right behind him. I snapped my head backwards and made eye contact with my father. He surveyed our situation and nodded his head, his unspoken approval.

I slammed my body into the guard closest to me as the others began to overpower the warriors next to them. Apophis peeled around, snatching my hair and yanking me backwards.

"Magi!" Carter screamed.

Apophis let go of me. I tried to control my breathing. He had planted something on my head; it felt heavy and secure. Whatever it was, I didn't like it. I tried to take it off, but when I touched it, it shocked me like it was charged with electricity. He shoved me backwards, and I landed in my father's arms.

My power was stirring inside me, and I realized I had a clean shot at Apophis. I let my power fly...only nothing happened.

Apophis sneered. Instead of my power surging through me, it stayed within my body, causing an extreme adrenaline rush. I felt intense palpitations in my chest and sense of terror that was as overwhelming as being caught in a riptide.

"It's not working. It's not working," I whispered to myself. My father grabbed my numb, tingling hands.

"What's wrong, Magi? I'm right here."

"Dad, I can't use my powers. I can't use my powers!"

Apophis laughed.

"I have harnessed you. That crown on your head keeps your powers contained in your body. If you try to pull it off, you'll give yourself such an intense rush of energy that it will stop your heart. Trying to use your powers with it on will cause the same effect – and fry your insides. What a shame that the only crown you will ever wear in your life will be the key to your death."

APOPHIS' guards led us through a labyrinth of giant stone

walls and columns. They marched us up to a steep wooden ramp and handed each of us a sword.

That's weird. The four of us all looked at each other with suspicion. The guards pointed their weapons at us, forcing us to walk up the mysterious plank.

As we got closer to the top, the sound of loud drums and yelling entered the ramp shaft. We walked onto the dirt floor of an enormous ancient arena. Hundreds of Apophis' warriors were spectators and were screaming at the top of their lungs. Apophis himself was seated on a bronze throne on a balcony that overlooked the stadium. Ten-foot-tall, ten-foot-wide fire pits lit up around the arena, exciting the onlookers even more.

"I'm not sure about this," Carter whispered to me.

"Don't worry. It'll be fun," I tried to act supportive, even though I was about to pee my pants. *This is it.* I was pretty sure we were about to die.

"Ladies and gentlemen!" Apophis stood up and addressed the crowd. "We are gathered here to witness the extraordinary event: these unfortunate four fighting to their deaths in a gruesome, exciting, battle. My people and guests"—he pointed to us—"welcome to the Colosseum."

"The Colosseum?" R.J. blurted out.

"This place does look almost identical to the Roman Colosseum. This is not good," my father said.

A large iron gate under Apophis' balcony began to rise, and the assembly cheered louder. Monstrous sounds echoed from inside the cage. Carter and I grabbed each other's hands for comfort. With my other hand, I handed R.J. my sword.

"That's more like it," He thanked me.

I yanked my necklace off, and turned it into a sword.

Moving deliberately inside the cage was a creature with the ferocious mouth of a crocodile, a mighty head and mane like a lion, and the body of a beefy hippopotamus. The hybrid animal growled, thumping into the arena.

"My friends!" Apophis raised his arms. "Ammit! The Devourer!"

Oh, this can't be good. The four of us all looked at each other hopelessly. The creature snarled an awful roar and charged us.

"Run!" my father shouted.

We bolted across the hilly terrain. The beast produced horrific noises as it tore through the ground. We took cover behind a fallen obelisk in the middle of the deadly playground. I could hardly catch my breath, thanks the continuous adrenaline rush of the harness.

"Everyone, back-to-back," my father yelled. "Carter, get behind us. R.J., on my command, lift him on top of the obelisk. Magi, turn your sword into a bow." Carter looked at my father, distressed. My father gripped his shoulder. "Carter, you know how to shoot...now shoot."

Carter shook his head, determined, as I handed him the bow and arrows, and he handed me his sword. My father and I guarded Carter as R.J. locked his hands and hoisted Carter on top of the fallen obelisk. The beast made its way around the corner.

"Here it comes!" I yelled.

The Devourer slid on loose sand as it rampaged towards us.

"Now!" my father yelled.

Carter fired his arrow. He hit the Devourer in its shoulder. The beast snarled and roared in pain. It turned its head, bit the arrow, and ripped it right out of its own shoulder. Carter's jaw dropped.

"Oh, this is really not good," R.J. blurted out.

"Carter, stay where you are and shoot it again! Everyone else, scatter on three to distract it!" my father ordered. The hybrid sped faster in our direction. "One..." Saliva dripped from its hungry mouth. "Two...."

Ammit roared again.

"Why aren't you saying three?" I asked my dad. It was less than forty feet from us! "Dad!" I screamed at him.

"Three!" he finally yelled.

My father, R.J., and I sprinted in different directions. Carter aimed his bow as the beast went after me. *Oh great!*

Carter fired and hit the Devourer in its hind leg. The beast bellowed with fury and tore the arrow out of its body again. He shot his head towards Carter, hatred lighting its eyes, and charged him.

"Carter!" I didn't know why, but I began to run after the beast myself. The Devourer launched itself into the air towards him.

"Carter!" I cried.

Carter hit the deck and rolled off the obelisk towards me. The beast had missed him, but managed to claw his arm open. He yelled out in pain as he hit the ground. I ran up to him. Dark blood seeped out, staining his shirt. The crowd was going insane.

The Devourer pivoted and leaped back over the obelisk. It stood directly in front of us. I took my necklace back from Carter and turned it into a sword—Carter took back his own. The monster swung at me with its large, sharp claws.

Carter and I retreated back to R.J. and my dad. R.J. quickly ripped off some of Carter's bloody shirt and helped bandage up his wound.

"I think it's time to split up again," I suggested since we were all in the same area.

"Agreed!" Carter and R.J. said in unison.

Carter and I dashed around another fallen obelisk onto higher ground as my father and R.J. stayed to fight the beast. We leaned up against the obelisk, attempting to catch our breaths. I looked down at my arms and noticed some claw marks. They weren't as bad as Carter's, but I was bleeding a good bit. I hadn't even felt him scratch me.

"I truly wish I was in Michigan," Carter said.

"Me too!" I blurted out.

"You haven't even been to Michigan." He gazed at me, confused.

"So?"

We watched as, below us, my father and R.J. did their best defense and offense – but were getting clawed alive.

"Carter, shoot it again," I ordered.

Carter was a little hesitant; I guess getting your arm ripped open did that to a person.

"Carter!" I pleaded.

He nodded. A tenacious look washed over his face as I handed him the bow and arrows. Carter carefully raised the bow and arrow into the air, aimed at the beast, and waited for the right time. My father and R.J. were now out of the line of fire.

"Now!" I yelled.

Carter released. The arrow soared through the air and struck the Devourer in its stomach. It roared wildly. Again, he ripped the arrow out.

"This is impossible," I groaned.

The beast figured out where the bow had come from and viciously darted around the fallen obelisk we hid behind. My father and R.J. tried to stop him from turning the corner, but their efforts failed as the creature knocked them both onto their backs.

The Devourer was hot on our trail. It was only a few feet from Carter.

"Carter!" I screamed.

Ammit rammed its body into Carter's, sending him flying. Carter was thrown on top of an obelisk. He rolled off, but managed to catch himself from falling with one hand.

The Devourer pursued me. The beast launched himself into the air to tackle me, and I dropped to the ground. The beast leaped over me.

"NOOO!" roared Apophis as he rose up from his throne.

When the Devourer leaped over my head, it caught the crown on my head with its sharp claws and ripped it off.

"YES!" I screamed. "My powers! I'm free! I can use my powers!"

Immediately, my power surged inside my body. I felt stronger than I had ever felt before.

"Carter, my necklace!" I yelled.

Carter threw it to me. With my powers, I guided my necklace into my hand. I transformed it into a two-edged spear, a weapon I had never used before. Immediately, I liked how it felt in my palm more than anything I had ever used before.

I rose from the ground. The Devourer shook as if it had been electrocuted and stumbled as it rotated around to face me once again. This time, when he charged, I delayed him, stepped slightly out of his way, then released and blasted him with my golden energy.

Good to be back!

The Devourer savagely scrambled past me and slid across the sand. It advanced on me, angrier than ever before, and roared. In order to fool him into thinking I wasn't paying attention, I turned my back to him. I heard him charge.

I didn't move a muscle, even though the others screamed at me to move—I stood my ground, instead, waiting. I glanced over my shoulder and waited till it was almost close enough to touch.

I jumped into the air as high as I could. Using my powers, I created a step and planted my feet, pushing my legs off of it.

With the momentum, I backflipped over the Devourer and delayed it midair. I landed on its back. Before it even realized I was on top of him, I drove my spear straight through its neck and released. It roared out weakly in pain. Its body suddenly became cold against my legs. I jumped off, and when I did, the Devourer fell. The crowd was completely silent. I glared at Apophis, power and confidence flowing through my body. He gawked in disbelief. We held the stare, and I didn't flinch. My father, R.J., and Carter united behind me, standing their ground beside me.

Sweat dropped down from Apophis' red face. "Attack!" he screamed.

Apophis' warriors jumped out of the stands and into the arena. The four of us got back to back and began taking out the warriors. But we quickly tired.

"There are so many of them!" I yelled.

A loud roar echoed throughout the arena. To the right of us, warriors fled in terror. Entering the arena was Bastet and Anubis, in their panther and canine warrior forms. They made their way, effortlessly, through the stands. No one dared go near them. They launched themselves into the pit and trotted toward us. Bastet treaded up right next to me, and Anubis came up next to Carter. I made eye contact with Bastet. Through the intensity of her glowing yellow eyes, I knew that she was ready to fight anyone who dare lay a finger on me. My eyes glowed back, thanking her. Bastet nodded.

The warriors around us began to flee. Anubis and Bastet growled to scare the last few off. Apophis kicked his throne off his observation balcony and stormed out of the arena.

Bastet and Anubis flashed into their human forms. Bastet was wearing a skintight black suit covering her body like a superhero. *Okay, yeah. She really is Catwoman.* Anubis was wearing brown boots and tan pants. He also wore a leather chest protector over his defined stomach.

"Where is he going?" I asked, nodding toward where Apophis had stalked off.

"My guess? He's retreating back to his palace," Anubis said.

"So we go after him, right? Isn't Isis there? We can rescue her!" I said.

"Whoa, whoa, whoa, we need to think this through," my father calmed me. "It's probably a trap. What better place to lure us in and kill is than his own palace?"

"With all due respect, Mr. Davis – trap or not, we might not be able to think all of this through. Isis may not have that kind of time," Anubis said.

My father dropped his head. He sighed, acknowledging the truth in those words.

"He's right. I have a bad feeling my uncle is going act quickly on whatever he has planned." Bastet said.

"Uncle?" Carter blurted out.

"Technically, we have disowned him," Bastet shrugged.

"Uncle or not," said Dad, "if we do this – we get in, find Isis, and get out. We avoid Apophis at all costs."

"Okay, so now what?" I searched everyone for answers.

"We really need to teach these people how to flash from place to place," Bastet blurted. Anubis glared at her. She just snickered.

"Anybody got a plan?" I pressed further.

"Yeah... I just might." R.J. smirked.

CHAPTER 14

A n unsettling breeze ruffled through dead trees as the six of us maneuvered through nasty swamp water in a well-crafted Egyptian rowboat. Dark storm clouds flickered across an eerie green sky off in the distance.

My father and Anubis rowed through a small clearing and entered Apophis' domain.

Oh, no no no no no...

Not too far from the swamp bank stood a palace made entirely out of black stone. It sat ominously amongst dark gray sand dunes, its highest point shaped like a pyramid. Apophis's palace looked more like a fortified prison compound – with countless watchtowers along the perimeter – than a grand palace. Fire pits were glowing with green fire that lit up disturbing statues of serpents.

We had reached the shore and Anubis and my father

jumped out to pull the rowboat onto the land. The rest of us quickly hopped out into the squishing mud.

"All right, quiet everyone," Anubis ordered.

The six of us made our way towards the palace grounds. Running became more difficult when the mud changed to deep sand. *I can never seem to escape sand, can I?* My father motioned for all of us to take cover behind a small sand dune near the exterior wall—we all followed his instruction.

"There is a small entrance in the courtyard towards the front of the palace," Anubis began. "The entrance is locked and warded by two guards."

"We would need to be a guard to get in," R.J. added. He turned to my father. "Can she do that thing you taught her?"

"Mags, I need you to do the duplication illusion," my father requested.

My father, during our training at the step pyramid, had taught me how to create an illusion to fool people into believing I was someone else.

"Okay, it shouldn't be too hard." I lifted my head over the sand pit to see if any guards were outside—I couldn't spot anyone. "Dang it!"

"What's wrong?" My father frowned.

"I can't see any of the guards."

"Why is that important?" Anubis asked.

"I have to see who or what I'm trying to duplicate, so I can correctly transfer their image onto all of us."

"So, what you're saying is...you need a guard." Bastet eyed me deviously.

I sighed. "Yeah, I need to see one."

"Well, why just see one when I could get you one." She smiled as if she were about to get me the best Christmas present ever. She flashed into a black kitten.

"Bastet!" Anubis scolded.

The kitten hissed at him, then dashed off.

Everyone watched as Bastet scurried towards the palace with her lightning-fast paws. She crept along the outer stone wall and crawled effortlessly under the iron gate of the courtyard.

Two guards dressed in shendyts, battle armor, and dark bronze capes walked past her. Bastet followed behind them.

Meow.

The guards stopped in their tracks and found Bastet sitting behind them, licking her paws. One of them snatched Bastet up by the neck.

"How did this get in here?" the guard whispered.

The other guard shrugged. The guard – with the obvious intention of killing the kitten – threw her forcefully into a water fountain filled with overgrown plants that rested in the middle of the courtyard. Bastet splashed into the water. The guards strolled over. When they found the kitten's body floating below the surface of the water, not moving, they walked away, satisfied.

The kitten flashed under the water, and Bastet lithely

slipped out of the water – in her panther form. Her glowing yellow eyes peered out like a crocodile in a bog, stalking its prey.

Bastet pounced out of the fountain, flashing into her human form and ambushing the guards. She kicked in one guard's leg and twisted his neck before he knew what hit him. The one that had thrown her in the water tried to fight back – but Bastet swiftly propelled herself off his knee and flipped over his shoulder, landing behind him.

Bastet put the guard in a headlock.

"I. Hate, *water*," she breathed in his ear.

She snapped his neck. Bastet made sure that the coast was clear before flashing into her panther form. She dragged the two guards by their feet all the way back to the pit outside the palace.

Bastet approached us with the guards. She flashed. "You're welcome." She crossed her arms.

"You killed them?" Anubis admonished.

"They're not humans!" Bastet became defensive. "They're hellions. Totally different."

"Hellions?" Carter asked.

"Hellions are essentially demons. They come in many forms, and tend to always follow the wicked," Anubis explained.

I knelt down by one of the hellions. His veins were green around his neck. "I would bet money that the bandits that attacked Carter and I were hellions."

Carter knelt down beside me. "Yeah! Their blood was green too."

I refocused on the task at hand. My hands began to glow as I created a golden mold of one of the guard's bodies. I raised the mold into the air and positioned it vertically. Then, I duplicated it six times and placed a mold in front of each of us. Once the molds touched our bodies, the golden power disappeared, and the real image of the guard's body and armor appeared on us. Everyone saw each other as the guards. I waved my hand, and everyone appeared normal again.

"Everyone see their normal selves?" I asked.

They all nodded.

"Now tilt your head. Everyone should see their guard disguise. I did this so we don't accidently kill each other."

"Good job, Magi," my father whispered. "Let's move."

One by one, we all crawled out from behind the sand dune.

I was about to go when Bastet grabbed my arm and said, "Wait!" She pulled out a small glass bottle and a knife from her belt. She cut her hand open, her dark red blood spewing onto the sand.

"Bastet! What the heck?" I backed away from her.

"It's okay! Remember when I said my blood can cure Isis? Well, here is some of my blood just in case you get to her before I do." Bastet squeezed her blood into the glass bottle, filling it up. "Just pour the blood directly on the wound, and it will heal instantly."

She fastened the bottle shut and handed it to me.

"Thank you." I nodded, and then shoved the bottle into my pocket.

Bastet ripped off a part of the guards' cape and tied it around her hand. "Let's go."

Bastet and I maneuvered our way out of the sand dunes and crept up against the external wall, joining the others. One at a time, we cautiously entered the courtyard. Once someone went through, the person at the beginning of the line would count to fifteen and then follow. We didn't want it to look like a bunch of guards popped out of nowhere. That way, our whereabouts wouldn't be questioned.

The courtyard itself was a large rectangle-shaped mess of random plants growing wherever they pleased. Dead leaves raced across the ground, chased by occasional gusts of wind.

Each of the six of us made it in safely. My disguise was fooling the guards. Carter and I made eye contact and smiled at each other; the plan was working.

"Follow our lead," my father whispered to me.

He and R.J. silently knocked out two guards. We all took note of this—silently take the guards out.

Carter and I marched in unison, passing two more guards, and then hit them from behind. Bastet and Anubis stalked a cluster that roamed near the fountain—I joined in on the hunt.

I scanned my horizon, making sure the coast was clear

before creating transparent golden steps that hovered over the fountain. I ascended the stairs and spotted five guards below. Bastet and Anubis flashed into their warrior animal forms.

Front-flipping off the highest step, I landed directly behind a guard and hit him in the head with my elbow, stunning him. I kicked him the stomach, and Anubis finished him off. The others drew their swords and, as I fought back with my two-edged spear, Bastet and Anubis promptly finished the job.

All the guards in the courtyard had been taken care of. But when we all entered Apophis' palace through a side door, we heard a yell as another guard entered the area and saw the piles of guards lying around. As he called out, swarms of other guards began to run into the courtyard. Our rescue mission had officially begun.

SERVANTS YELLED out orders to the rest of the staff, who were running like lizards without tails throughout Apophis' three-story throne room. Apophis seated himself on his bronze Cobra throne in between two green-flamed fire pits. The hieroglyphs on the walls glowed an unsettling green.

"Adom!" Apophis yelled.

Rushing into Apophis' throne room was a slinky man in a tunic—he knelt before his master.

"Yes, my lord." He bowed his head with the utmost respect.

"Secure this place! Not a soul gets in or out. And if you find her, don't fail to kill her like your predecessor."

Adom nodded his head nervously. "Yes, yes my lord." He shot up from his knee and commanded the guards, eager to please.

The six of us crept into the throne room on the second story and watched the chaos of guards preparing for the lockdown. Apophis appeared angry and deep in thought.

"There!" Anubis whispered as he pointed to a descending set of stairs on the right side of Apophis' throne. From where we were hiding, we saw a set of stairs that led underground, to a place filled bars. Hands waved between the iron, begging to be freed. "That's the dungeon. That's where we need to go."

"There is no way all of us can make it in there without someone ordering us to take a battle station." My father shook his head.

"Sounds like we need a distraction," I whispered to myself, thinking. *Lightbulb moment.*

"Well, if he wants me..." I stood up.

"Magi! What are you doing?" My father whispered harshly, pulling on my shirt.

"I have an idea so some of us can get inside and find Isis," I reassured him. I performed the duplication illusion so the others appeared to look like me. "Follow my lead."

"Magi, please." He tried to yank me back.

Gently, I held his hand in mine. "Dad, trust me," I begged him.

He nodded, not liking any of it, but let me go, understanding the plan. I trotted down the steps as fast as I could and marched towards Apophis. I sighed loudly. *Here we go.*

"Looking back on it, your best opportunity to kill me was when you pulled my hair and put that pretty crown on me," I said, as I faked a confident strut towards him.

Apophis glanced up, leaning back with surprise he quickly tried to hide.

"I mean, after all, you are powerful enough to kill me." My father, looking just like me from the illusion, walked out from behind a statue of a serpent next to Apophis.

Apophis jolted in his chair, startled.

I like these illusions. I like them a lot.

"But, the problem you're having is the actual killing part." Bastet popped out from behind Apophis' throne.

Apophis scrambled to his feet and backed away from her. He drew a dagger from his belt, holding it out in front of him as he tried to figure out if she was the real me.

"The Colosseum was a good idea, but apparently – not good enough," Carter spoke up from the third level.

"Ha! You should have seen your face when I killed your little beast!" R.J. laughed, leaning on a pillar on the second level.

"You underestimate me, Apophis," spoke Anubis from the third level.

"Don't underestimate me," I finished.

"SEIZE THEM!" Apophis ordered furiously.

His guards swarmed the room and began attacking each of us. Apophis snarled, scanning the throne room for anything that would reveal which one of us was the real me. He roared; the ground shook. Everyone lost their balance, including the guards. My head slammed into the ground, almost knocking me out, causing me to break our disguises.

I landed directly in front of Apophis.

Satisfied with himself, Apophis waved his hand – and the floor beneath me opened like a trap door.

"Magi!" the others screamed as I fell.

I yelped when I crashed into the ground, then immediately popped up on my feet. In the back of this new chamber stood another bronze throne, and, through five glowing pillars, were large iron torture machines. I looked around, realizing that there were absolutely no exits.

"It's fascinating—"

I spun around to discover Apophis glaring at me from his second throne. I rapidly transformed my necklace into a two-sided spear.

"—how you would risk everything to save someone you have never even met." He tilted his head in thought. "I don't know if that is idiocy or heroism."

Apophis gradually stood up and smirked a devilish smile. I was alone. It was just me and him.

"It's a shame to have to kill such a beauty, though... I'm

going to be generous." Apophis held up two long fingers. "I'm allowing you two options."

"Generous, huh?" I wasn't fooled.

"Option one: you voluntarily allow me to kill you."

"Why on Earth would I let you do that?"

"Why? Because if you do, no harm will come to your father or your little friends."

Apophis gestured over to the stone wall to my left. Dark green smoke floated against it to form a large rectangular shape, and similar to my second dream, the smoke rippled with color to present images.

I saw my father, Carter, R.J., Anubis, and Bastet in an enormous chamber filled with obelisks of many different heights. The group trudged through fallen statues and bones that were scattered across the dusty ground, wandering aimlessly – looking for a way out.

"Inside this chamber is my second body," Apophis divulged.

"Second?"

He waved his hand to change the smoke to a gasp-worthy image—a monstrous black cobra sleeping in peace. *That thing is the size of a building!*

"*That* is my other body. Just as easily as you can move your hand up and down, I can bring this part of me to life."

I waited to see where he was going with this.

"If you don't allow me to kill you, I will bring my other half to life, and then you and your pitiful father and friends will all die. That is option two," he finished.

"Why do you want to kill me so badly?" I seriously didn't understand his motive, and if I was going to die, I wanted to know why.

"I can't kill Isis without killing you." He revealed.

"What?" I asked, confusion coiling through my chest. What the heck is he talking about?

"They haven't told you." He laughed to himself, amused. "My dear, when you were born, Isis created a little security policy for herself. She placed a part of her soul into you so that she cannot truly die unless you perish along with her." He shook his head. "What kind of mother would do this to her child? She made you a walking target. You are simply her life insurance – albeit life insurance with a nauseating potential for power. A potential I think *they* underestimated."

I was flabbergasted.

"I have to kill you in order to eliminate the others, before you obtain your full capability and become the peacemaker."

Peacemaker?

Apophis shook his head in disbelief. "They really don't tell you anything." He leaned in close. "You are the *Mediator*. You are destined to become the overseer of both the Earth and the Realm – to become the protectress of worlds. You will be the first with human blood with direct authority over the gods. Outrageous."

Why hadn't my father told me?

Apophis inched closer to me. It was as if something

snapped inside him – like he suddenly remembered the purpose for his vendetta.

I have to do something, or he will definitely kill me.

"Once you are out of the way, my plan will be set in action, after years of patiently waiting."

"You're insane."

Apophis' mouth twisted into a furious, ugly scowl, "Your *existence* is insanity. You are the disgusting creation of an inconceivable act. Killing a human like you is going to be more satisfying than annihilating the Realm. "

"But you got one thing wrong."

"What's that?"

"I may not know exactly what I am, but I am *not* human."

I surged a concentrated blast through my hand – a golden light beam – right into Apophis' chest, sending him flying backwards. He tumbled to the ground, rolling into his throne.

Apophis, full of rage, slowly climbed back onto his feet. Blood trickled over the bulging veins on his shiny bald head.

"Oh," he said, raising his hands in the air, conjuring up his power, "you should not have done that."

I snapped my head towards the smoke screen that displayed a horrific image as the palace shook. Apophis' other body had awakened. It hissed to consciousness, slithering out of its hole towards my father and the others.

I turned back to Apophis in horror; his eyes glowed

pure white. Green smoke appeared around his right hand, forming into a bronze sword as he shifted his body into an attack position.

A blistering screech rang through the palace. I turned to look at the mirror on the wall— Apophis' other half screamed at my father and the others. It smashed its head into the ground, creating a giant crater as everyone scattered away. I snapped my head back just in time to change my necklace into a two-edged spear to defend against Apophis himself.

"EVERYONE MOVE!" ordered Mr. Davis.

Everyone spilt up, taking cover behind obelisks and fallen statues. The serpent slithered while it hissed obnoxiously, ramming itself into obelisks, hoping that someone was behind it.

"How on Earth are we going to kill this thing?" Carter yelled.

"We have to attack from all sides!" Bastet answered, waving her hand in circles.

"Not all at once! It will take us all out at the same time!" yelled Mr. Davis, focused on the snake.

"One of us will get its attention, and that person will distract it as long as possible for the rest of us to attack," yelled Anubis.

"Who wants to go first?" yelled out Mr. Davis.

There was a silence between all of them.

R.J. cupped his hands around his mouth and yelled, "One, two, three, not it!"

"Not it!" yelled Mr. Davis.

"Not it!" Bastet spit out.

"Not it!" Anubis yelled.

"Not it! Dang it! You've got to be kidding me!" Carter cried, displeased.

"Ha, ha!" Bastet laughed. "Let's see what you got, kid!" She saluted him.

Carter glared at Bastet. Anubis patted Carter on the back. "You can do it, Carter."

Carter took a deep breath. "I can do this!" He stepped out into the open and he drew his sword.

"Hey!" he screamed at the serpent.

The cobra turned its head, eyeing Carter hungrily.

"I'm right here! I'm making it easy for you!" Carter taunted.

The snake slithered full speed towards him.

"Now!" Mr. Davis ordered.

Mr. Davis led the pack. Anubis and Bastet flashed into their warrior forms and barked and growled viciously as they charged. R.J. sprinted, waving his swords manically at full speed—the attack had begun.

I SLASHED my spear at Apophis, but he effortlessly blocked

every strike. The smile grew on his face every time I became a little angrier. His blade swung to slice my arm. I delayed him but—*slice!*

What had just happened. Apophis chuckled, knowing that my trick hadn't worked.

Out of nowhere, Apophis grunted in pain. On his shoulder appeared a small cut, spilling with dark red blood—though I hadn't even come close to touching him with my blade. His combat skills were too good.

Then, again, three smaller cuts appeared on his arm. Puzzled, I shoved my spear into a position where I could examine his bleeding cuts. They appeared to have been caused by an animal's claws.

Apophis thrust forward, causing me to stumble backwards a few feet. A deep gash had appeared on his thigh. He bent over, irked, wiping the blood off his leg like he didn't care.

The image showed the others fighting the serpent heroically. As we both watched, R.J. sliced his sword into the serpent's side. A clean incision appeared on Apophis's side. Each time someone slashed the serpent, a cut appeared on Apophis himself.

Apophis charged me again. It didn't matter that he was getting sliced open; he was a fighter – and he was not going to give up until I was dead.

∼

THE SERPENT WAILED out in pain as Bastet sunk her claws into its scales. The serpent whipped its tail, swinging Bastet into the air. She flashed, turning herself into her human form, landing directly on her feet like a ninja.

Everyone stuck to the plan of attacking one by one, but Carter found himself always being the one to distract the beast.

The serpent slammed its tail into the ground, sending everyone airborne from the impact. Mr. Davis shook his head, forcing himself to recover from the fall. Bastet, in her human form, wiped away the blood that dripped from her lip.

R.J. laughed angrily at the beast. "You are going to pay for that."

Anubis dusted himself off while helping Carter to his feet. Carter gazed up at the serpent—his eyes widened.

"Look!" Carter yelled, pointing at the serpent.

Everyone stared—tension filled the chamber. The serpent was growing in size!

"Everyone, get ready!" Mr. Davis yelled. "This is about to get a whole lot harder."

Carter gripped his sword as R.J. waved around his two. Bastet and Anubis, in their warrior forms, readied to advance.

⌖

"It's useless to continue to fight me, Davis," Apophis warned.

"So, I should just surrender so you can murder me?" I sassed back.

"You would make my day."

"I'm pretty bad at making someone's day."

I dashed through two pillars towards the torture machines, leaping on wooden table resembling a medieval rack—a joint-ripping device. Apophis joined me on the table, continuing our duel as he sliced his blade into my arm, leaving a sticking gash.

I hissed in pain, blocking several cuts before getting lucky and kicking him off the rack. He landed swiftly and slashed at my feet. I jumped up, created a golden platform, side flipped over him, and landed behind him.

I thought I had a clean shot, but he elbowed me vigorously in the nose with so much force that I staggered back into the main part of the chamber, slipping onto my back.

Apophis stomped towards me. Ignoring the pain from the hit, I wiped my nose, then countered his attack.

Come on, guys!

"What are we going to do? That thing is getting stronger and more powerful!" Carter cried as he waved his hand and sword around like a madman, drawing attention to the cobra.

"Just keep fighting!" yelled Mr. Davis as he charged the cobra again, slicing his sword into the cobra's side.

"Mr. Davis, as strong as we are, we can't keep fighting forever," panted Anubis, as he got back on his feet.

Mr. Davis saw that Anubis' shoulder had slid against the rough stone, wearing off layers of his skin. Bastet dashed up to examine his wound. Anubis nodded to them both, reassuring them he was all right. Mr. Davis nodded back; he was right—they didn't have forever.

"NO!" R.J. screamed.

Everyone snapped their heads. The snake had snatched Carter in its jaws. Carter wailed for help, and then the room fell silent. It had swallowed him whole.

APOPHIS' sword sliced into my leg. I let out a cry of pain as he kicked me in the chest, knocking me to the ground. The force of it knocked the wind out of me. My spear slipped out of my hands and rolled away from me, turning back into a necklace, out of reach. Apophis laughed.

Loud screams filled the chamber. Apophis and I snapped towards the smoke screen.

"CARTER!" I screamed.

The mirror displayed Carter being swallowed whole by the cobra. I watched as my father and the others tried to rip the cobra to shreds.

"You should have surrendered while you had the chance," Apophis taunted.

No...no, this is not happening. Tears rolled down my cut-up cheeks.

"It's a terrible thing to see such a young boy die. And to think, you could have saved him. This is all *your* fault."

Apophis glared at me as the cobra screeched with pride. He then grabbed my head and yanked me towards him. He placed his other hand on the green diamond on his board collar. His eyes began to glow green as he attempted to gain control of my mind.

My head pounded as his mind tried to suppress my thoughts. I yelled out in pain.

"Just give in. You're finished."

Get out of my head!

"Maybe I will even command you to kill yourself."

GET OUT!

"Better yet, I will command you to kill your friends and your father."

I raised my hand, and tremendous power shot out and smashed into Apophis. The cobra and Apophis yelled in pain. He crawled back onto his feet. The power inside of me was so overwhelming that my entire power was shimmering gold – Egyptian symbols shined through my body. I translated the symbols—"the daughter of Isis." My feet, I realized, weren't touching the ground—I was levitating in the air. My power was so absolute that it healed all my wounds, rejuvenating me. I summoned my necklace to my hand and clinched my weapon of choice—my trusty two-edged spear.

I was invincible.

"I WILL KILL YOU, Apophis! I will kill you!" R.J. slashed the cobra's scales with his sword.

All of a sudden, the cobra started shrieking in pain. The snake flailed, its body knocking over statues and obelisks in the process.

"R.J., look!" Bastet pointed to the stomach. Sticking out of the stomach was a sharp silver sword.

"Carter?" R.J. whispered to himself. "Rip it open!"

APOPHIS FLINCHED IN PAIN. He charged me, screaming, waving his sword manically. I didn't move, not a bit. I wasn't afraid of him anymore.

"THAT'S IT!" Mr. Davis encouraged as they expanded the laceration in the stomach. The silver sword finished the job from the inside. Falling roughly on the ground, covered in snake bile and blood was—

As Apophis was charging me, a rip in his chest ruptured, spilling dark blood everywhere.

He stumbled, struggling to keep his balance, weakly thrusting his sword at my heart. I delayed him and ripped the blade from his grip with my bare hands. I placed my right hand on Apophis' bloody chest and surged power, propelling him through the air. His body collapsed right into his throne.

I threw his sword on the floor. It had created a large cut on my left hand, though I didn't feel it. My power healed it immediately.

I turned to look at the screen.

HE'S ALIVE! Tears of joy filled my eyes when I saw R.J. holding Carter in his arms! Carter was alive, though disgustingly drenched in guts, and smiling from ear to ear. He needed assistance walking out of the cobra's cavern, so everyone helped in way they could, overjoyed— he was alive!

I turned back to Apophis, who trembled in pain and trying to get back into the fight. I marched up the three steps to reach his throne, stomping onto armrest, blocking him from going anywhere with my body. I shoved my necklace-turned-dagger against his throat.

"Where's Isis?" I demanded.

My power had hit Apophis' chest so hard that it had

broken a couple of his ribs—he was having trouble breathing.

"Don't make me blast you again," I warned. He narrowed his eyes. "Where's Isis?" I repeated.

His shaking hands grabbed iron keys from his belt. "The dungeon. Below." He pointed.

A descending spiraling staircase emerged in the middle of the chamber as Apophis pointed. I snatched the blood-soaked keys away from him, then hurried away.

"Wait!" Apophis yelled with a wheeze. "Why don't you kill me?" He gazed into my eyes.

I stood rooted to the spot. "I don't know." It was true; I honestly didn't. I turned away from him to run down the staircase, and I heard feet paddling behind me.

I delayed him in just enough time to stop him from slitting my throat. With all my strength, I stabbed him straight through the heart.

As the tears rolled down my face, I released him. Apophis wailed violently. I tugged the sword out of his chest watching the blood gush.

As fast as I could, I sprinted down the spiraling staircase as the life drained from him.

"Adom!" Apophis wheezed as loud as he could. "Adom!"

"Master!" Apophis' faithful servant sprinted into his

torture chamber. Adom fell to his knees, sniffling as held his master's frail hand.

"F-find her."Apophis pleaded. Adom readied his weapon, full of spite.

"No." Apophis coughed up blood as he handed Adom a necklace made of two snakes wrapping around each other.

"Find *her,*" Apophis begged.

Adom shook his head, understanding his master's final request. As tears streamed down his face, he watched his lord die in his arms.

CHAPTER 15

I reached the bottom of the spiral staircase and entered into a cold, unsettling, dimly-lit dungeon. Prisoners ranging from strange creatures to humans stretched their hands out, begging for me to free them. A couple of them grabbed my arms and shirt.

I tugged my arms away from them as they yelled. My body was trembling from the adrenaline of ending a life—I couldn't stand it. Apophis' guards were just hypnotized, soulless creatures, so I hadn't felt any remorse in killing them. But I felt an overwhelming amount of it when it came to Apophis, even though justice had been served.

Isis?

I jogged, searching inside and out of every gray, barred cell. Finally, I froze in my tracks.

Lying motionless, chained on muddy, wet ground in a stunning white dress stained with blood, was her—Isis. Even though she was on the brink of her body dying, she was just as beautiful as she'd been in my dreams. My shaking hands nudged the keys into the keyhole, twisting as I prayed I wasn't too late.

Carefully, I knelt down beside her and propped her head into my arms. Blood seeped out of her wound as I moved her. I gritted my teeth.

Bastet's blood! I removed the wooden cork of the little bottle and poured the blood directly on the wound like Bastet had instructed.

I waited. Nothing was happening! Fearful thoughts swarmed around in my head. *Is this even the antidote? Can Bastet's blood truly heal her? Am I too late?*

Suddenly, Isis began to cough. A beam of light emitted from her wound, healing rapidly before my eyes. The blood softened and turned back into liquid, like butter melting in heat. The wound closed up without a single scratch, and her tan skin sparkled. Isis hunched over in my arms, wheezing at she regained consciousness, trying to figure out where she was. She noticed my arms and jolted up beside me. My stomach churned as she locked eyes with mine. She tilted her head, spotting my necklace. Immediately, her face softened, and the flood gates opened.

"Margaret?" Isis whispered as she examined me over and over, biting her quivering lip.

Emotion washed over me, so powerful I could barely breathe. "Mom?"

"Magi!" Isis wrapped her arms around me, crying

with joy.

We embraced, taking turns laughing and crying. This feeling of being in another mother's arms was foreign and weird – but comforting.

Isis sobbed. "I am so sorry," she blubbered, "for making you a target. It was in the agreement for you to be born. I didn't realize the repercussions—"

"Hey, it's okay." I forgave her, even though I really didn't know what for. She squeezed me tighter.

She placed her hands on my face. "Thank you. And thank you for saving me. I knew you would." Faith and pride shone in her eyes.

"Let's get out of here." Isis smiled.

WITH HER ARM over my shoulders for support, I helped Isis out of the nasty dungeon and into the throne room.

"Magi!" my dad cried as they entered the throne room from the opposite side. Joy filled his eyes as he ran to me.

Isis stepped back as my dad twirled me in his arms, kissing my head over and over.

His eyes had wandered off of me, as if he were hypnotized by the sight Isis. They embraced, tears streaming down their faces. They kissed passionately. Several times. It was a little hard to watch, if I'm being honest. But I had never seen my father so happy. *He really loves her.*

My father turned back to me, "You fell through the floor. Where did you go?"

"Apophis' torture room? I don't know – but I saw you guys battling the snake."

"You saw?"

"Yeah Apophis showed me..."

"Where is he now?" Isis leaned into my dad.

"Dead... I killed him."

"You what?" Isis whispered.

"Well *we* killed him. You killed his snake form and I killed... the other one." I stared at the ground.

Isis placed her hand on my face. "I know we just met, but I am so proud of you." She laughed from her belly.

"You did it, Mags!" My dad squeezed me shoulder.

"No – *we* did it." I smiled.

Out of the corner of my eye, I saw Carter leaning up against a pillar, soaked in snake liquid and insides. I sprinted away towards him and he grinned—though I could tell he was in pain.

"Are you all right?" I asked him.

He grinned at me. "I am now."

In a split second, my arms were around him.

"What are you doing? I'm disgusting." He tried to push me away.

"I don't care." I closed my eyes, so thankful he was alive.

He laughed, wrapped his arms around me, and squeezed. "Hey...never give up," he whispered.

I laughed as I pulled away. "Never give up." I beamed a bright smile as I looked into his ocean-blue eyes. *Those will never get old.*

"Well done, Magi." Anubis and Bastet stood behind us. Anubis nodded to me—I had gained his respect.

"Yeah, not bad at all, Davis," Bastet added, actually smiling – with teeth and everything.

"Thank *you*. Seriously, thank you." I hugged Anubis even though I was now disgusting. I went in for one with Bastet – and she put up her hands.

"I don't do hugs," she said.

I laughed. *Wow, she really is a cat.*

"There she is!" R.J. swooped in with a giant hug, laughing enthusiastically. "I'm insanely proud you, Magi."

I squeezed back, smiling.

I turned back around to see my father with his arm cradling Isis, grinning at me with pride. I nervously made my way over to them. Once I was there, they pulled me into their embrace to cry and laugh. We held each other as family for the very first time.

I sat on a balcony overlooking the large pool behind Isis's palace as her servants ran around decorating and repairing the damages Apophis had caused.

"Shouldn't you be getting ready?" a soft voice asked me.

I turned to see Isis staring at me with a smile on her face.

"Yeah, I probably should." I sighed. "I just really like the view."

"Peaceful, huh?" She gracefully sat down next to me, situating her blue and gold dress, making herself comfortable. We sat in silence for a while, enjoying each other's company, but also not knowing what to say.

"You don't have to love me," she said, finally breaking the silence. "I wouldn't be surprised if part of you hated me and your father."

"I don't hate you. I just...don't know you." I took in every detail of her beautiful face, trying to memorize it.

"Would you like to?" Her brown eyes teared. We really did have the same eyes.

I smiled. "I really would."

"Can I hug you?" she asked, adorably.

"Yes, of course." I laughed as I wrapped my arms around her.

"I love you," Isis said. "I just want you to know that I do. Even if you may not know me yet, I have loved you all your life. And I want you to take as much time as you need to discover how you feel about me."

I grinned. "I have a good feeling it won't take too long."

"Your majesty?"

We both turned. Nesu stood, smiling at the both of us, almost crying. "Magi, her majesty's servants are ready to assist you."

"All right, I will be there in a minute," I said. Nesu nodded and walked away. I turned back to Isis, not wanting to leave.

"Go. You need to get ready. I will see you at the celebration." Isis kissed my forehead. I nodded and went to leave, but stopped short.

"Wait, I have a question," I spoke up nervously. "What am I?"

"Excuse me?" Isis asked, confused.

"Like, what kind of species am I? Dad said I should ask you."

"You are... undefined," she answered honestly. "Magi, you are the only one of your kind. You are the best parts of humanity and the best parts of, well... me. I see many possibilities for your future."

"So, it sounds great, but it also sounds like no one really knows what's going to happen to me," I said, worried.

"I'm not going to lie to you. We don't know your future. I know it won't be easy, that's certain. Because there has never been someone like you, we don't know what to expect. But since it's your life, you're the one that decides if it's a good life or not."

"I want it to be good. I'm definitely stressed out, though, about this new world and my powers. My powers really scare me."

Isis giggled. "Only because you don't know how to wield them. And that's where I come in. I will teach everything you need to know, and I will be there every step of the way."

"Thank you," I said, truly grateful.

"Now, go get dressed. I am ready to celebrate."

SERVANTS CONTINUED RUNNING amuck in Isis's palace, giddy, as they fussed over my hair and face before the Egyptian mirror. Meanwhile, I was ball of nerves. Out of the corner of my eye, I spotted Carter leaning against the door frame of my preparation room. Butterflies fluttered around in my stomach.

"Carter, are you staring at me?" I turned around to face him, trying to play it cool.

"Well, um, you are really...pretty. Actually, no...you are really beautiful." He grinned.

A guy has never called me beautiful. I looked away from him, not knowing what to do or say.

"How are you feeling?" He cleared his throat, quickly changing the subject.

"Nervous, to be honest. I've never had ancient gods throw me a welcome-home party."

"Why nervous?"

"Everyone keeps asking me how it feels to finally be back, to be home... I feel guilty because I don't really have any emotions towards this place yet. Yes, there is something familiar about it, but I'm worried that I will disappoint a bunch of people, especially Isis. She amazing, but I'm just worried. Even though I really want this place to mean something special to me...I don't know, I'm just nervous it will never truly be my home."

"Magi, home should be with the people you love. And that can be anywhere. Even with a bunch of ancient gods. Your father is here; Isis is here. Bastet, Anubis, R.J...and I'm here too."

"When did you become so wise?" I gave him a slight smirk.

"After I cut my way out of a god's intestines."

"Ahh..." I cringed out of disgust, trying not to laugh.

"It changes you," Carter said.

I covered my mouth, giggling. "I'm sorry. I shouldn't be laughing."

Carter just smiled at me. "Hey, just know, I will always be there for you." He grinned sincerely as he placed his hand on my shoulder, almost romantically.

"Always?"

"Always."

LARGE WOODEN DOORS swung open to a full crowd huddled in a throne room—my throne room.

Four guards, with Nesu in the lead, escorted me down a long pathway covered with palm leaves. *I feel like I'm getting married.* They had finally talked me into wearing a dress. It was the dress my reflection wore in my dream: flowy, white, and form-fitting dress with modest leg slits and a golden belt around my waist. I also wore golden gladiator sandals, cuffs around my wrists, and bracelets around my upper arms.

I climbed three steps to reach a solid gold throne with a beautiful sycamore tree engraving. The guards parted to both sides of the throne, Nesu by my right hand. I faced the crowd. They were all dressed impressively for this event—my welcome-home celebration. Nervousness entered my body when I saw the crowd of gods and goddesses I had never met.

I grinned when I saw my father and Isis's animated faces, holding each other's hands. Isis donned a sparkling golden dress, and a simple gold crown of her symbol on her head to match. My father wore a button-up white shirt and brown pants with golden cuffs on his wrists. He looked very handsome, and stood next to an also hand-some R.J. – who wore the same exact thing, but with a bigger smile, somehow.

To the left of my parents were Anubis and Bastet. Bastet smirked proudly in a two-piece black dress, a golden crown atop her red hair that was beset with a yellow diamond. Anubis wore a traditional shendyts with a large Egyptian broad collar across his caramel chest. Ra stood next to Bastet in pretty much the same thing, plus an orange cape. He was over-smiling like crazy, and it was super contagious.

Tears instantly fell down my cheeks when I saw the person next to him: my mom, or now step mom, Mariah—the woman who raised me. She had tears in her eyes too.

I dashed away from my throne, entering the crowd, and threw myself into her arms.

"You're here?" I asked, with tears rolling down my face.

"Of course I'm here. I wouldn't miss this for anything." She sniffed and fixed my dress perfectly in place.

"You gave up everything...," I said, not even knowing where to begin.

"You were worth it," she said as she wiped away my tears.

Loud drums sounded behind me, cuing me.

"Get up there." My mom nudged me. I hugged her tight one last time before returning to my throne. She tugged on the blazer she wore over her magenta dress, pulling herself together before inching closer to R.J.

I carefully sat down on my throne for the first time. *Gold is cold on the butt!* I tried not to squirm.

Ra walked up the steps and positioned himself to the left of me. Walking up to Ra was a cute teenage boy with dirty blonde hair, bright ocean-blue eyes, and a nerdy smile. *There you are.* Carter stood next to Ra, holding an orange pillow with a modest gold crown. It had dainty purple gemstone at the center. *Who knew this little nerd would be my best friend.* Carter was the crown bearer, and I couldn't have asked for a better one.

Ra spoke with authority, "We are gathered here today

to celebrate a truly extraordinary day. The day the child of both the Realm and Earth returned home. The day where families can finally be reunited. The day a daughter will be given what is rightly hers by birth."

Ra turned to Carter and carefully picked up the small crown. Carter, finishing his job, joined R.J. in the crowd. Ra raised the crown in the air and held it over my head, gently placing it over my black hair.

My life had officially changed forever.

"Margaret Ann Davis, daughter of Isis. Welcome home."

Everyone cheered. Flower petals flew. I smiled uncontrollably. My parents and Mariah had tears of joy in their eyes. R.J. whistled, shouted, and clapped loudly as Carter, Bastet, and Anubis joined in with him.

I never would have imagined, in my wildest dreams, I would be standing in a room before gods. I never would have dared to dream that my real mother was an Egyptian goddess. Despite all of my nerves, I was so excited to discover all the secrets within me.

A dom, dressed American-casual, crossed the street in a run-down part of town in a Miami suburb. He read the outdated sign – *Exotic Pet Store* – over the store entrance in a not-very-busy stripmall. He opened the door —*ding!* He eyed the frogs, spiders and turtles uncomfortably, making his way towards the back of the store. He froze when he noticed a teenage girl with straight, bleached-blonde hair carefully placing a corn snake into an exhibit.

"Serena Tanith?" Adom said.

The girl gazed at Adom, bewildered. "How do you know my name?"

Adom opened his fist to reveal a necklace with two twisting serpents on the pendent. "I have something that belongs to you."

ACKNOWLEDGMENTS

First and for most I thank God for giving me this idea to create and share with the world. I thank my incredible family and friends for believing I could accomplish the crazy task of writing a book. A very special thank you goes out to everyone who donated to my Indiegogo campaign and helped launch this book towards publishing. I then have to thank my incredible team of editors, Kirby Bowles, Krystal M. Myers, Stephen Fritschle, Kim Chance, Kate Angelella and Katharyn Blair who helped shape this book into the story it is now. I also thank my team in Hollywood, my manager Kim Matuka for being there every step of the way. From the bottom of my heart, thank you everyone...

ABOUT THE AUTHOR

Liana Ramirez, a young girl from Austin, Texas has dedicated her entire life to the art of storytelling through various mediums. Ramirez is a well known Hollywood actress with a passion to bring joy and entertainment to people through her acting and writing. She dreams that one day her books will make to the big screen and hopes to star in them. In her down time, she enjoys spending time with friends and family, trying every ramen house in LA, and sipping on Starbucks while writing or studying scripts.

Made in the USA
Monee, IL
24 June 2020

34811773R00184